10/8

‖‖‖‖‖‖‖‖‖‖‖‖‖‖‖
D0347349

This book should be returned/renewed by the latest date shown above. Overdue items incur charges which prevent self-service renewals. Please contact the library.

Wandsworth Libraries
24 hour Renewal Hotline
01159 293388
www.wandsworth.gov.uk

Wandsworth

One Star Awake

One Star Awake

Andrew Meehan

NEW ISLAND

ONE STAR AWAKE
First published in 2017 by
New Island Books
16 Priory Hall Office Park
Stillorgan
County Dublin
Republic of Ireland

www.newisland.ie

LONDON BOROUGH OF WANDSWORTH	
9030 00006 0006 7	
Askews & Holts	14-May-2018
AF	£11.99
	WW17027595

Print ISBN: 978-1-84840-627-8
Epub ISBN: 978-1-84840-628-5
Mobi ISBN: 978-1-84840-629-2

British Library Cataloguing Data.

A CIP catalogue record for this book is available from the British Library.

Typeset by JVR Creative India
Cover design by Anna Morrison

New Island received financial assistance from The Arts Council (An Chomhairle Ealaíon), 70 Merrion Square, Dublin 2, Ireland.

New Island Books is a member of Publishing Ireland.

This is a work of fiction. The characters in this book are fictitious and any resemblance with any real person is coincidental and unintended.

For Áine Prendergast

'And then she turned homeward with one star awake,
Like the swan in the evening moves over the lake'

—Padraic Colum

Map of Paris

It began with my sweet tooth—although it wasn't my idea to walk all the way across town for an éclair. There were hundreds of places closer to home but I had been asked by my boyfriend to meet him at Bertrand Rose and that's what I was going to do. For as long as I could remember I had valued the opinions of others more than my own. The walk from my place beside Buttes Chaumont in the nineteenth to the pâtisserie in the eleventh would take an hour. After that there would be another half an hour on foot before I got to my job at the restaurant. A walk of ninety minutes on an April morning should not have been considered a hardship but Parisians, so I was told, were not so intrepid. But I was not a Parisian and my life, then, did not consist of very much.

It was a good job that I liked to walk, since I was unable for the hubbub of the métro and would not have dreamed of paying for a taxi even if I was able to find one at this hour of the morning. Rue Paul Bert, where I was headed, was not in my neighbourhood but since I couldn't claim to have a neighbourhood—not yet—I had no qualms about where I went and what I did when I got there.

The walk to Bertrand Rose took me along Avenue Parmentier. The streets had been rinsed by an oily rain and there were starchy gusts from the China Star dry-cleaners. The young man smoking from the window looked so forlorn. Only very early in the mornings did I feel that way too, although it was impossible to avoid—in Paris, you lived in an infinity of sadness. Moping princes writhed on Avenue Montaigne, dinner ladies flung four-course lunches at bawling children. If anyone was going there expecting cloaks to be thrown over puddles, if they were seeking old-fashioned rapture—well, I hope they found it.

I reached Paul Bert with half an hour to spare. Immediately I was amazed, upwind from the pâtisserie on the corner, by more sweet aromas. At that time in my life I was always hungry, simply because I never ate enough and because I moved around a lot. Away from work, I never bothered with anything other than sweets and the cheap stuff usually suited me just fine. Different foods appealed to me now and again—waffles from the truck at Jaurès métro—but never for long. A new bag of fizzy cola bottles was a big event in my life but, since this was Paris and I worked in a restaurant, I had to make an effort when it came to food. I struggled with most of it, the lingo especially.

I was amazed, too, by a note pinned to a doorway accusing someone of taking a shit in the stairwell and that the note featured a P.S. with a doctor's phone number heavily underlined. I was amazed—no, hypnotized—by the conquering hero in a tuxedo exiting a taxi alongside the barefoot girl who was pulling her skirt down to cover her knees as she followed him to the doorway with the note pinned on it.

I was amazed more than anything that Daniel had already joined the long queue making its way out of Bertrand Rose.

—You must really like éclairs, I said.

—Only one way to find out, he said. Chantilly? Chocolate? Hazelnut?

My answer included all my stored-up feelings for him at that point in time.

—Dunno.

Daniel was from somewhere near New York and was white yet he had dreadlocks that reached all the way down his back. The dreads resembled a rope you might use to tie up an old fishing boat in Connemara or wherever. You didn't need to have just arrived on the planet to find this peculiar, but I tolerated it like so much else because I found him funny. I found him funny even when he called me his little autistic, which was definitely not my problem. He moonlighted as a sommelier in Gravy and because of the dreadlocks and his feline eyes—which gave many women, myself included, the shivers—he also modeled from time to time. They were the colour of the hashish he bought daily at Pyrénées métro. A close-up of them, speckled brown like a suntan, had once been magnified and suspended above Hôtel de Ville in an advert for contact lenses.

I was tall—and thinner than I am now—with the long feet and slender hips of a Masai. I was as white as the average dinner plate. My lips and my cheeks and bum were almost non-existent and my biceps were beefier than my breasts. I was to look at about as substantial as a ribbon but I was much, much tougher than I looked.

It was also said that I would have made a handsome man. And Daniel was intrigued by my accidentally punk-rock hairdo, washed the night before with Fairy liquid.

—What happens now? I asked, motioning towards the shop's door.

—We wait, he said. You know what this city needs? Chairs in the street. I spend on average ten hours a week waiting. Fucking standing.

—Not practical.

—Why does anything have to be practical? Look at that shit in the window. Next year we buy our Easter eggs at the Monoprix.

I didn't want to admonish myself in front of Daniel for not knowing this was Good Friday. I had vague notions of days of the week—it was either a work day or a day off. Of course there would be people waiting at the pâtisserie.

The shop opened and we all shuffled forwards. The black smocks and the granite countertops gave Bertrand Rose the feel of a pharmacy in a nightclub. I was baffled by it all, this small sweet citadel, and I did a run-through of all the incurably Parisian things I saw most mornings—the great human surge from Bastille métro, prammed babies trouncing each other, maliciously, with cuteness. Perhaps it was all Parisian, even the things—being coughed on, death-stares at traffic lights—you weren't supposed to think of as Parisian.

It was then that I saw the young man heading the queue. First of all, he seemed out of place in a room perfumed with such self-regard. He stood apart and looked like the kind of man to stand apart in happy rooms. The kind of man I saw impeccably alone at Enfants Rouges on Saturday mornings or alone in queues for Christmas trees.

He had just taken a croissant and was eating it so greedily that he did not notice the pastry flakes floating in slow motion onto the sun-bleached hair on his arm. I was watching his back—there was an illustration of eagle on his T-shirt—when I noticed the blaze of psoriasis at his hairline. He had dusty blonde hair and a coarse copper beard so deluxe as to seem artificial. The hair on his arms was as thick as reeds. His eyes were of the watery, wary variety and the skin on his cheeks above the beard was blemished—a person who'd been set on fire but the fire had been quickly put out.

I fixated on his conversation with the female assistant. The woman, who had facial hair to rival his, produced a dark chocolate orb he had specially ordered. They were discussing whether this

4

kind of bitter chocolate would be suitable for children. My French was limited but I heard the woman—whom I named Bristles—wondering what kind of chocolate wasn't suitable for children. The orb was not an Easter egg by any means. Without tasting it I guessed it would have been too bitter for a child, and most adults for that matter. If he was buying this for a child he was bound for trouble.

The negotiation continued. His accented French was creamy and round. He was English, I guessed, from the way he pronounced vous as view.

—I recognise him, I said.

I knew him as you would your family's former postman or someone off the TV—but, remembering from where was as impossible as sending a boat over a mountain with your mind.

Eagleback, that's what I'd call him—even though I wasn't one for names. Everyone called me La Plongeuse, anyway.

The dishwasher.

—It suits you, Daniel used to say. Until we find you another one.

Imagine Wanting To Touch the Fire and You Can Touch the Fire Without Getting Hurt

Eagleback was getting so angry with Bristles that his head was almost rotating. I was dizzy, too, but that was down to the hunger surely. I was enchanted by the crumbs still resting on the hairs on his arm, and that I would have liked to pick them off and eat them, when I felt it—a sense of certainty and fearlessness only found in suicide bombers and the insane.

Daniel, meanwhile, was singing a stupid song about cakes and pastries.

—Tarte Citron. Macaron macaron.

Eagleback paid for his chocolate orb and was coming towards me and—this was no choreographed scene—I was being raised up by a warm wind, I was certain of it. I had to take Daniel's arm to steady myself. I tilted my chin, finding the light with my face in expectation of a moment of recognition.

I was sure Eagleback looked at me, but a customer had entered the shop and I was jostled from behind and rocked towards him. Eagleback was cradling his cake box and did not see me until I was right there, less than an arm's length away, closer for being pushed together. I would like to be able to report a flare of recognition between us but Eagleback was scanning the space over my shoulder in order to squeeze his way out of the shop. His toing and froing about the orb had increased the sense of impatience in the room and the waiting customers mutinously groaned as one. My forehead, too, had a particular feeling that I recognized and could mean only one thing—another arbitrary migraine, thick enough to fell me on any other day of the week.

Eagleback left the shop and, with no good reason to follow, I imagined myself past the crowds and out the door.

Directions, even the distinction between left and right, still baffle me. Whether it was the headache or even the hunger or probably just confusion over which street Eagleback had taken, I didn't know which way to go. Paul Bert is at the intersection of three busy streets and my mind was making a maze of them—peeled eyes useless for anything other than expressing alarm.

The area had woken up in the time we had been waiting at the shop but Rue Jules Vallès was empty apart from a man in overalls staring at the steaming bonnet of a white van and an old lady scolding a constipated dog. I shielded my eyes and looked up Rue Chanzy where a car pulled out and drove towards Boulevard Voltaire, which would surely be choked at this time of the morning.

The headache had not gone away. I knew that from my watering eyes and the urge to vomit right there on the pavement. There was a call as I began to run. I recognized Daniel's voice as I ignored it. Other sounds rushed to fill my head—the normal ambience you get in the city as well as a muffled echo I compared to a violent form of tinnitus.

Chanzy was free from cars apart from the one I was pursuing, but I ran on the street to avoid a young mother with a stroller. Usually when I ran I felt airy—even in kitchen clogs—but here I was lumbering like an injured insect. The street felt spongy underneath me. A cyclist passed in the opposite direction and he shouted something to me. When I think about it now all I see is a crazy woman running along a city street.

His car was pulling up to the junction with Voltaire and I was within shouting range at the very least. Having missed my chance when Eagleback had exited the shop, this was going to be a moment I would control. Then the headache went off, a ship's siren in fog—that was the first thing. The metal on the car's bonnet appeared to melt from the heat of the engine. The entire car was disassembling and the rivets and bolts that weren't floating away were transformed into balls of burning liquid. In my mind the roof was being soldered to stop it coming away. I was the only one who seemed to notice the smell of encrusted metal but it attacked my throat and brought these hot tears bubbling through my nose.

I drew level with the front doors but the driver—a woman in her twenties at the most—was Indian. She had not heard any of my shouting. I thought of kicking her door but my legs were shaking too much. She barely noticed that I was miming a 'don't worry' motion at her window before she pulled away.

Wherever Eagleback had gone, he had not driven down this street in that car.

You could call it relief—I don't know what you'd call it— but I could not resist falling to my knees. There I remained for a moment or two, apologising to the air in front of me. I took my time walking back to Bertrand Rose, carrying myself proudly—as if every morning I could be found falling to my knees right on the intersection with Voltaire. And no wonder people were keeping away. Another neighbourhood malingerer. Going by the note on the doorway on Paul Bert, they saw their fair share.

I was unimpressed with the éclairs in the end—Daniel had remained in the queue—but things may have been different on another day.

—Who was that? he said.

My techniques of evasion were well practiced but any cunning had not survived the sprint along Chanzy. The best I could do was glaze over.

—You turned grey when you saw him.

—He was in the restaurant last week. Took the wrong umbrella. I wanted to see if he had it.

—Did he?

—I was too slow, I said.

—He also went the other way, Daniel said.

I couldn't tell from his darting eyes if he was going to prolong the questioning. I had been wearing a fixed smile all this time.

—You okay? he said. That was kind of impetuous.

Daniel's yawn—he was known for them—was a godsend.

I made my way through the éclairs as I ran along the street. The deliveries arriving at the cafés along Voltaire were a reminder that I would be late. I needed to be at Gravy by eight and there was no way I could be late and jeopardise another day's pay. I got meals every day I worked and I worked every day that I could.

The day before had been spent on my living room floor, which also served as my bedroom and kitchen floor. As soon as I had felt the headache smothering me I lay down—a coward expecting a beating. The signals the pain sent to the rest of me amounted to: lie down, don't move until it's over, wet yourself and cry, even though no one is listening. I was there for the whole day.

I used to run as much as I walked. There had been days when I ran myself into the filth, incommunicado with tiredness, heroic, miles from home in the nineteenth. I was never straining for recognition or training for a race—I had no desire to compete at all. Running was mechanical, bone-throbbingly fulfilling and I could have run for days sometimes, along the Seine, in the parks, along the canal, even on lovely Champ de Mars where, if you so desired, you could run laps around the base of the Eiffel Tower. Today I made do with running the length of Voltaire and eating while I ran. By the time I got to the restaurant I had finished everything in the box and the headache had been replaced by an invigorating sugar rush. Apart from stepping into the direct path of the 56 bus, it might have been one of those rare days in Paris when you could feel the city singling you out and throwing you clues.

Young Girl, Go Slowly

Once upon a time I read a book that said, 'Young girl, go slowly. The love of your life, whoever he is, will love you for who you are.'

What if it was my favourite book and I couldn't remember it? What if it said, 'I watch your movements, as though you are performing in a play I don't understand, where I have arrived at the interval and have tried to keep up. I try to anticipate the rhythm, the serious intent behind each awkward movement of your hips, the rising colour in your chest, and I come to realise that the underlying meaning in the distant, pained look in your eyes may not be distance or pain at all.'

Forgotten City

My life as I was able to describe it had begun six months previously. I had come to in the kitchen at Gravy, slicing onions like a total pro. Apart from that there was very little to say because there was nothing else I remembered. The morning like the one I was spending at Bertrand Rose affirmed one thing—wherever my life may have begun I had not been reared in a city like Paris. I knew this was France because I was told it was France but I had a good idea that I was not from there.

My teeth were the colour of parchment paper so it was unlikely I was American at all—that was one thing. Headaches were often involved and sometimes I wet myself. I guessed I was in my early twenties although sometimes I felt older and often I acted younger—my pockets were usually full of slobbered-over sweets.

I could speak, passable French as well as English, although more often than not I chose not to. People told me I mumbled anyway. I had begun to say I was Irish because that was the way I sounded— pronouncing oil as aisle. But I was very much not for chatting. For this and other reasons I knew I was difficult person to warm to and that you could not have counted on me for a dance at a party—I was dependably incapable in any social situation—or a reassuring word if you were feeling under the weather.

I was crying when I came to, for no other reason than I was peeling those onions. A stewy breeze had coated the skin on my face and anything further than a few feet away appeared smudged, as though the air around me was greasy. I was standing at a window which gave onto a murky alley and I was happy to be there although I didn't know that I was happy.

I wasn't, as perhaps I should have been, immediately looking for the local paper to see where I had ended up, because I was then—as I am now—incapable of asking the right kind of questions. If I was there tranquilly chopping onions then I supposed that's where I was meant to be—just as, if you had dropped me into the cockpit of an A380 I would have coolly attempted to rumble it off down the runway.

I was wearing the chef's clothing that seemed to be my uniform, but I was more startled by my candy-coloured plastic gloves. Had my skin been vacuum-packed? When I removed the gloves my hands were an unsettling cheese texture, the implication being that I had been wearing the gloves for some time. The dirt deep under my fingernails was astonishing. The state of the nails themselves—they seemed rusty—suggested I had been deprived of essential nutrients or had been using them to scrape cement. The nails were so soft that they made no sound when I drummed them on the aluminium work top.

There were reflective surfaces everywhere. It would have been straightforward to have a peep at myself and size this person up, whoever she was, but I was distracted by the figure moving in and out of focus. I felt the hovering someone looking at me.

This, I would learn, was Amadou. For the time being he was peeling potatoes in the sink beside me.

—Potato, I said.

Then I tittered. Well, you would.

When I spoke there were no vibrations in my ribs and no feeling in my throat. The sound was being generated from somewhere behind my ears. And my first word—I should have tried to say something more momentous than potato.

Amadou did not reply so I was not certain he had heard me. There was music playing from the kitchen's food spattered radio, although it took me a while to realise that it was music. The singer sounded so mournful that I took it for a confession. He sounded frantic and insincere and, as far as I was concerned, he needed to be silenced. It still amazes me that I walked over and pulled the plug from the wall.

A few seconds of this new existence and already I was behaving out of character.

Amadou began to mimic my walk, the way I was prowling like a panther.

—Tu es animal, he said.

There was an incident. Poor man, but I lost it.

If anything Amadou seemed quite concerned that I didn't get any more upset than I already was, that I didn't—'faire un honte' were the words he used. But I didn't care about disgrace. I was an animal and animals couldn't be disgraced.

I went to the bathroom and saw my face in the mirror.

—Quite nice. That'll do, I said.

And I went back to what I was supposed to be doing next, which was picking whatever meat I could from the fish necks and making stock from their bones. I was clearing up my fish-bones when someone leaned over my shoulder. Her fragrance was oniony, too, but sweeter. She spoke to me in English even though all the other voices I could hear in the kitchen were French.

14

—Looks like you're feeling better, she said. You were much quicker towards the end. Let's take a look at the rest of the vegetables. Or do you like pastry?

Ségo often worked ten hours day, in a space no bigger than a domestic kitchen, wearing a back brace under her whites. And she is still the only chef I have ever seen lie flat on the floor during a busy service. Her hair was as black as the enamel on our pans, and around her eyes there were little lines—tiny scores—from her worries about the world. She was in her twenties, too, I thought. I say too, but I knew as much about Ségo's age as my own. She was French and Canadian—rather than French-Canadian—counting Ottowa as a former home after a plush, troubled childhood in Nice.

Her face sank whenever you mentioned her parents.

—To give them their due, she would say, they were very committed to despising one another. Stayed up late just to hate each other for longer. Then Mom got upset when I went to Dad's funeral. Can you imagine? She was offended but she wanted to know what everyone was wearing. Black, I said. Drab, she said. Now she's alone in fucking Raleigh. Muttering to herself all day.

And Ségo's attitude to Paris was similarly cursory, particular and brutal. The only people who liked it didn't know it properly. She always said the Paris air and the water left her skin feeling sandy and dried-out and old and tired. There wasn't much wrong with her skin as far as I could tell. It was as smooth as a television screen and into it she spread moisturizer with a malevolent, sexualized intensity.

Ségo worked the dough quickly but carefully. She must have made choux pastry thousands of times but her eyes brightened once the flour incorporated itself and the mixture left the sides of the pan.

—And stop, she said. Don't overwork it. You beat harder once you've added the eggs.

15

We waited for a little while before she added the eggs and found herself with a glossy hill of dough that met with her satisfaction. In went some cheese she called Gruyère, and some chives and black pepper, before Ségo piped walnut sized buns onto some parchment paper with a subtle flourish.

—Your turn, she said.

—What do you mean?

—Do what I did. It's a rigmarole but you'll get the hang of it.

And I did—chuckling as the little bronze skulls rose in the oven, startled by something so simple as the combination of flour and water and egg yolks.

—Peter Piper picked a peck of pickled peppers, she said.

—What?

—Peter Piper picked a peck of pickled peppers. Keep saying it over and over. Practice makes perfect. Peter Piper picked a peck of pickled peppers.

I knew what I was doing, for the most part—I just didn't know what everything was called. Until I heard everyone else I had my own names for things. I had the handwriting of a slow child but I would do my best to write down the names Ségo gave me— vejetubbels, vezjtobells, vgtbls—and the characteristics. Obberjean is purple and shiny. Inside Obberjean is bitter. Obberjean like salt.

Soon, I got to know all the vegitidibbles.

Passive-Aggressive

The facts of my life could have been described as a mystery but that is not how I viewed them. It was more a matter of distinguishing what I had forgotten from what I had never known. Maybe you are supposed to feel haunted without your memory but I felt as if there had been a reprieve.

I was passive-aggressive, people said. Mordant, too. Astringent. Dictionary, please.

I cooked rice and drank the water. I masturbated in front of my window. I dropped a pea and spent an hour trying to find it. I said 'fuck this' so much that I was asked to stop. I was confused by the concept of peanut butter. I was entertained by staring at the lice in my mattress. I lent money to the gypsies outside Voltaire métro, twice. I believed people when they said 'I'll get back to you'. I bragged about my shits. I thought that when someone said 'it's okay' that everything was okay.

Everything you did in Paris involved a great pageant of paper-work but, in return for some of Ségo's blanquette de veau, her good friend Hippolyte Pinoteau was happy to usher us into his chaotic rooms in Ménilmontant with very little recourse to admin.

Ségo took charge when Hippolyte asked me to attempt the new-patient registration form. All she wrote was 'à l'attention de Ségolène Carena'.

Care of.

Without any paperwork, I was conditional. On a par with the feral cats of Belleville, although some of them had to have police records.

Hippolyte gave me the run of the uncomfortable chairs—shaped like bent spoons—before offering me some purple jelly beans from a jar.

—Tell me whatever you want to tell me, he said, massaging his fingers. I will ask lots of questions. You'll become accustomed to that.

My mouth was packed full of sweets and Hippolyte made it plain that I could empty the jar if I wanted. He started off as excitedly as a dog following a familiar scent. Had I forgotten everything? How did I function? How far back could I remember? What would be my first memory? My last memory before I stopped remembering?

—Do you want to explore your past? There are ways of doing that. We can help you. I haven't seen your papers, but I deal with people like you every day. Your memory could come back spontaneously, even suddenly, or it may never come back at all. You have no long-term memory, except little flashes. It's retrograde amnesia. It's a brain disorder, that is all. Or a hormone imbalance. If we can name it we are unafraid of it.

Hippolyte had set the proper tone, which I tried to imitate. I asked him what would happen if my memory was to return, whether I would be able to cope with the weight of information. Would there be a sign? Did your body inform you in advance? A headache, perhaps. Would the new me survive? Would the two personalities be compatible?

—Anything is possible, Hippolyte said.

He said I might regain 25 percent of her memory. Or 50 percent. Or none. Basically he had no idea.

The hospital was a worn-out building which seemed to be cut off from its surroundings—as separate from the rest of Paris as my apartment or Gravy itself. The door of the emergency room thumped me in the back and I had to pin myself to the wall to avoid the ambulance crew—two men between them controlling four trolleys bearing some injured construction workers who looked more confused than in pain.

One of the men on the trolleys was asking where he was. Were they there yet? When would this stop?

The only answer the nurse could give was, —Hôpital Saint-Louis. Onzième.

The various afflicted—all of whom seemed surprisingly relaxed for being in an emergency room—were spread out all over the seats. So many of them were staring at the ceiling that I assumed there was something to see up there—a screen or a scrolling news feed. Two men in neck-braces shared a piquant breakfast of cooked meat from a can. I didn't want to think about what had happened to the man with the hole in the side of his head where one of his ears should have been.

Ségo was pleased that they could squeeze me in for the MRI. And I could only feel self-consciousness at the thought of my brain being photographed. After a wait we were led to a temporary settlement in the hospital grounds. I must have smelled like an old battery and the searingly clean portacabin would have pronounced my pungency. The smell might have been from my plastic work clogs, which were also my running clogs. Amadou had given me an orange windbreaker bearing the logo of one of the Parisian soccer teams and I wore that everywhere. My chef's trousers were patched at the knees and I was wearing one of the two new T-shirts Ségo had bought me at the thrift store on Rue de Rivoli.

The radiographer looked quizzically at his screen.

—Pas de nom? he said.

—Portakabin, I replied.

Ségo interrupted with, —À l'attention de Ségolène Carena.

I was soon in the tube, lying as still as requested. But I didn't understand MRIs any more than I understood toasters or traffic lights. There had been a warning about claustrophobia—and to stay where I was if I felt claustrophobic—but I was more worried about disappointing the doctors. What if my brain was empty? What if it wasn't as photogenic as the other brains?

I got paid a bit—minimum wage, I think—but my visits to Hippolyte and the hospital had been reminders that I was living the life of a successful stowaway. My apartment was another sign. After my incident with Amadou and the onions, I had settled into life at Gravy more or less uneventfully—but, after four nights of sleeping in the restaurant's vegetable store and three incidents involving two different policemen and one official caution, Ségo had decided I needed my own place to live. She located the apartment—tucked away in a plain block on the stretch of Avenue Mathurin Moreau that buttressed Buttes Chaumont—and made the arrangements and she planned, too, to pay the rent. I was just happy not to be sleeping in the store room. On the lease where I had been supposed to sign my name, again she wrote 'à l'attention de Ségolène Carena'.

Apart from Ségo's friendship and dating Daniel—if that's what we were doing—I didn't have much going for me. The goings-on of the world were arbitrary but Ségo wasn't. At that time in my life I assumed everyone was as kind as her. I took it for granted because the alternative was what?

#11,158 of 13,124
restaurants in Paris

Gravy was housed in a converted garage on a lane not far from Saint Ambroise métro. Looming tenements protected us from such invasions as sunlight and what could be glimpsed of the sky was more often than not indigo with impending rain. A concentrated ambience of mop-bucket and syringe—a picture-perfect resemblance to an alleyway awaiting a movie car chase, except no one other than bin lorries ever saw fit to drive down there. Most tourists stepped out of their cabs believing themselves to be hallucinating. Several times a day people stopped to see if we sold petrol.

If Gravy did not resemble a restaurant from the outside, it hardly looked the part inside either. The dining room, even in its finery, looked unfit for paying guests. Salty dust everywhere, certified twentieth century, this was no affectation. Nor were the curry-coloured walls and tutti-frutti—as in cracked—tiles from the hand of any artisan. Although there was a very handsome zinc bar in one corner—this had, according to Ségo, come from the highest bar in the Alps—it took up space that could have accommodated more diners. I liked to sit there anyway, to eat my daily meal—a waffle flooded with cheap chocolate paste.

It was my job to keep the kitchen clean and prepare it for the proper chefs who would appear a couple of hours after me. Ségo lived nearby but Amadou lived in a faraway land with no arrondissements.

Nearly Belgium, Daniel liked to say.

Amadou had six or possibly sixteen children and, like most parents I met, he came to work for a rest. Amadou dressed the way he did because he was into hip hop—but he reminded me of a child who was about to be put to bed.

—Night-night, I would say whenever I saw him.

Night-night Amadou.

By the time I got to work my hair was stuck to my forehead with sweat and my new T-shirt was soaking. I drenched my head under the cold tap, wondering if the T-shirt would do another day. It was from Ségo that I had inherited a regard for the chef's clothing I wore all day, even to bed. No doubt that I resembled something out of a cartoon in those clogs and patched trousers, but there was no finer uniform so far as I knew. Everything else felt so drab, especially the kind of things I could afford.

I was pulling my T-shirt away from my armpits when Ségo arrived. She smiled when she saw it was the one with the Pink Floyd album cover. She had also bought me a shirt with a picture of woman in a bikini climbing a martini glass.

—Who is Pink Floyd? I said.

—It's not a person, she said. Want to hear them?

Ségo put her little gizmo into the speaker to allow me to make up my own mind. I wanted to please her but the best I could come up with was the music sounded a bit spacey and the singer sounded out of breath.

We were there for so long that I began to inspect the morning's deliveries. The herbs splashed me with dew as I picked them and I was pleased to see so many artichokes. These would take hours to prepare and I preferred time-consuming jobs.

—You hate it don't you?

—Suppose.

—What's wrong?

—Nothing, I said.

I had been hoping Ségo would let me deal with the fish this morning but she was already lining up the rigor-mortised bass at her station.

—We must get you back to the doctor, she said. If the headaches are getting worse then perhaps something serious is the matter.

Ségo made a lap of the kitchen, from her bench to mine, to look me in the eye as she said this.

—There mightn't be another headache for weeks, I said.

Of course I was going to make no mention of the scene I had created outside Bertrand Rose. I hadn't made sense of Eagleback and if I hadn't made sense of him I couldn't begin to describe him to anyone. Nor did it make sense to mention the flurry that was still occupying my forehead—the worst of it had passed for the time being.

I brought the matter to a close by volunteering to scale the fish. In seeking out the jobs the others abhorred I had made myself indispensable in this kitchen and I was pleased when Ségo curtsied and stepped out of my way. Getting down to it, I could only laugh when so many of the scraped scales ended up in my hair and in my mouth. After badly bruising several of the fish I worked through the still life as methodically as I could, taking great enjoyment in slicing open their bellies so the guts spilled into my hands.

—This is a lot of fish, I said, counting nearly a hundred for a thirty cover restaurant. Isn't this what they call demand and supply?

When it came to gems like that, I was either repeating something I had heard or it was a fluke, as it was in this instance. 'International bowel syndrome' was another one.

—I think you mean supply and demand, but it makes more sense your way, said Ségo. Anyway, we have a surprise for you.

—Everything is a surprise for me.

—You're having a birthday party.

—Why? I said

—It was Daniel's idea. He has the tone of voice that people do what he says. He really likes you, you know. Lucky girl.

But Daniel knew that I didn't have a date of birth—no evidence to show that I officially existed at all—so I couldn't have a birthday party. Besides.

—It's today, she said. We decided. He did. We'll take some wine from here when were done. It's not as if we'll be stuck for fish.

—I've never been to a party, I said.

—Now I've seen it all. Someone who doesn't want a birthday party.

Ségo looked like she felt sorry for me when I didn't seem more excited and began to scold me for taking everything, even the work I did in her restaurant, too seriously.

This birthday was news to me—Mademoiselle, I'm afraid we had to switch from turbot to John Dory. Mademoiselle, we regret to inform you that chef replaced the chocolate fondant with pistachio. News about fish and about fondants was my kind of news, but this party was an awful idea and I couldn't say so. At least I had one of those faces that didn't let on what I was thinking.

Fish blood ran down from my arm and collected in drips on the tip of my elbow. I was beginning to wish we were still listening to the music. Reluctant to be any ruder than I had been already, I took extra care with the last few fish, thus buying myself a little more silence. Soon the kitchen became eerie once more, just how I liked it.

During service Daniel would clear a table and before he had turned away I'd have the dishes sluiced and squeaking on the rack. No one knew why La Plongeuse was such a champ at dishwashing, she just was—the best they'd ever seen. First of all, my system involved doing everything at speed. I ate fast, too, spoke fast, walked fast—ran fast with my heart going fast, the blood moving through me. My sound effect would have been a plummeting firework. There was a reason I moved so fast in the kitchen—I liked to wash the plates and get them back to Amadou and Ségo without their noticing, so that there were dishes on the bottom of their piles that never got used. They just got to do their own thing.

It wasn't just dishes. My system involved doing everything fast and imagining all the time I was saving, imagining all the time I'd save by not doing anything other than the essentials. Sometimes I would speak while I was eating while walking, thus saving even more time. It got to the point where I began to breathe fast. I was a panter—not the honest-to-goodness panting of a dog or a mountaineer, but short, flustered mouth-breaths. Of course, doing everything at such high speed allowed me to think slowly. But my slow thinking rarely went further than clean plates so everything I did formed a pleasing circle. Nothing wasted only energy.

This lunchtime there was Hippolyte and other Hippolytes with their gay or not gay way of holding a fork—even if I guessed it was more complicated than forks. Daniel was slapping shoulders and doling out the bisous. He was good at knowing who did and didn't want the personal touch. Once or twice a day, for my amusement, he would pretend not to speak English to the tourists who'd found Gravy in one of the blogs. Most of our customers were very busy being in Paris—it was a full-time job. One girl, an Ellen from Illinois, asked for a picture with the kitchen crew. I'd never seen myself in a photo before—I looked about twelve and I looked about forty.

—You're all so cool in your outfits, Ellen squeaked. Can I get an apron?

From the hatch I would survey the dining room. All before me, in cargo-pants and flip-flops, in varsity shirts and flimsy sarongs, tourists were having the times of their lives. Coucouing, cavorting, pretending, avoiding the truth—surrendering themselves to the times of their lives, only, as far as I was concerned, to avoid the slow-moving disappointment of summer in Paris.

This Is Great, I Hate It

There was so much to be afraid of in this new word. Pap smears, sport, God and the like. Now I was about to add parties to the list.

Ségo's house—on a cobbled lane off Rue Saint Maur—was not at all as I had imagined, but the garden was as beautiful as I'd expected it to be. I didn't know the names of plants—I had to be told what a pergola was—but the small space was arranged to create the illusion of being in wild country. The spring breeze was bending the taller plants and insects were swarming around the blooms.

The interior resembled a tidy office with noisy art that I thought had to be bad—sculptures of question marks and posters saying POW! The hallway was bright with so many candles that I had to keep on checking the sleeves of my windbreaker. I was keeping it on to avoid conversations about Pink Floyd. But the story had gotten out and I was made to listen to a spooky piece of nonsense called 'Wish You Were Here'. It was better than the droning I had experienced earlier but not by much.

I knew I was making the wrong face but the pounding in my head was more insistent than the music. A smoky number of some sort, another one—the sound of a keyboard being dragged through mayonnaise, something to listen to as acid rain falls from the sky. The song building so gently and dourly until the melody burst with exhaustion.

—Do you like the music? I was asked.

—If this is music, then no.

One perfect, amazing moment after another. Finally I was learning to love parties. Not really—I was acting weird. I could feel it off the people around me.

I had to go the bathroom. I had to go to the bathroom in a big rush—I had no idea I had been constipated all along. Afterwards I was pleased to find Ségo's toothbrush and I used it as I combed through her cabinets. On the shelf above the bath was enough skin-gunk, in bottles and little tubes, to form a museum exhibit. A dainty finger of cream made my cheeks feel as fresh as a raw chop. I read the labels on her skincare: Avène. Uriage.

But all I saw was the word avenge.

Avène. Uriage. Avenge.

AvèneuriageavengeAvèneuriageavengeAvèneuriageavenge
AvèneuriageavengeAvèneuriageavengeAvèneuriageavenge
AvèneuriageavengeAvèneuriageavengeAvèneuriageavenge
AvèneuriageavengeAvèneuriageavengeAvèneuriageavenge
AvèneuriageavengeAvèneuriageavengeAvèneuriageavenge
AvèneuriageavengeAvèneuriageavengeAvèneuriageavenge
AvèneuriageavengeAvèneuriageavengeAvèneuriageavenge
AvèneuriageavengeAvèneuriageavengeAvèneuriageavenge
AvèneuriageavengeAvèneuriageavengeAvèneuriageavenge
AvèneuriageavengeAvèneuriageavengeAvèneuriageavenge
AvèneuriageavengeAvèneuriageavengeAvèneuriageavenge
AvèneuriageavengeAvèneuriageavengeAvèneuriageavenge
AvèneuriageavengeAvèneuriageavengeAvèneuriageavenge

Avèneuriageavenge Avèneuriageavenge Avèneuriageavenge Avèneuriageavenge Avèneuriageavenge.

The cabinet under the sink was crammed with antiquarian forms of contraception and powders that had gone too far and become cakey. I breathed too heavily into a jar and a flurry of sweet powder filled the room. When the powder cleared I found it—a pocket notebook filled with a strange script that seemed all at once uptight and wayward and belonging to me.

Unstory

January 2nd 2011, Rose Bakery. I want to meet someone. But I am not going to meet anyone here. Here, where you could fall through the door with a park railing sticking out of you and people would check their tote bags for splashes of blood. I dare you to care. I dare you to smile. And that's just the other customers. The waiters treat you like a shoplifter even when there is nothing worthwhile to steal. I took one of the sacks of garam flour anyway. Gluten-free thievery.

January 30th 2011, Rose Bakery. Interviewed P__ D__ here just now. Talk about cool. Talk about cold. Talk about frozen. Talk about being dead for a thousand years and still expecting people to care. Don't think I can even post the article. It was a series of pauses punctuated by wet, sorry sighs. The sighs were mine. P__ D__ was too thin to speak. He nearly collapsed under the weight of all that lettuce. Here, let me get that for you.

February 20th 2011, Café la Perle. I met someone. Not just anyone. We did meet somewhere, that much I know, but I can't remember where. For the first time in my life I was somewhere at the right time, even if I don't know where it was. It's a strange new feeling.

February 21st 2011, Rue de Bac. Goodbye who I am.

February 25th 2011, Rue de Bac. The second date was a little more awkward. For one thing, I had to ask Jerome what happened on the first date. We made love, that much I do know. When we fucked he seemed to move. Not just his body but his skin. His skin moved in a mist and his lips changed colour so that they resembled apple skins. We met at Oberkampf métro and walked all the way up to Belleville. Me in those new Marant boots. Not only do your peripheries expand when you have a lover, but the city obliges and opens up. We paused to look in shop windows, to demonstrate that we were in fact curious people. Funny how you start to notice things that are no use to you when you're alone. The city acquires the sheen it reserves for lovers. That is to say, us. But the reason we were walking all the way up past Belleville is because Jerome has a wife. I don't remember much about the other day but I certainly don't remember him mentioning this. What else did I need to know? That Schiste has to be the worst restaurant I have ever been to. The food was expensive school dinners and the staff resembled the kind of people you'd see on the pavement outside Busáras. Jerome made out in advance that he was friends with the owner but they didn't act like friends to me. The food I didn't want floated away from the table. The smooth plaster of Jerome's hands reaching across the table for mine. We held hands for a moment until his bobbing knees urged caution. We have to be careful, he said. That's one thing you should never say to me. It's the kind of thing that makes me brave. You need to listen to me, he said. As if listening will change anything.

February 26th 2011, Rue de Bac. Jerome just called me and we—I wish we were we—spoke for hours. We talked about Melbourne some more, Melbs he calls it. We talked about his wife again, whom he doesn't love, and we talked about his job as a schoolteacher. Teaching is something he does love. Too much talk about schools that went over my head. Where we are from and what we have done is beside the point. We talked about everything except the thing I wanted to talk about. That I want to make love with him all the time. I want to make love with him whilst I am making love with him. It's the kind of thing I want to share with the world. But I can't share it with the world or with anyone. But even when I think of him, even when I imagine what it is like to be with Jerome, imagination is not enough. I need him here. When will the mess of us become something more than feeling lost in him, being lost in him? Dumb things like the cowpat of his pants on my floor. His beautiful choo-choo. I want to take his whole ear in my mouth. I want rub my eyeball into his elbow. Weird to read that back. Not weird, not weird at all to be part of love.

February 27th 2011, Rue de Bac. Jerome has stolen my dreams. He has become my dreams.

March 1st 2011, Rue de Bac. (Dinner, awful.) Out with him in public again, though. For the second time. Let's call that progress. But I don't want to go back to Schiste ever again. I don't want to stand inches apart on the métro because that's all we can do. And his wife? He portrays her as this ethereal, devout creature. I would love to meet her, if only to see what he sees in her. So I can see what he sees in me. Which is to say, I don't know.

March 11th 2011, Rue de Bac. He was here for three nights. I wish it was a million nights. What do I have to remember the weekend by? A jar of Jerome's sweet morning breath would be good now. We stayed indoors all of Saturday. On Sunday morning, we went for a walk. I don't know how we ended up at the Aligre market, since it's so far from the seventh and Jerome said it was too close to his apartment for comfort. But that's where we went. Some things I will never forget. The gapped-teeth of the man pouring the wine in Le Baron Rouge. His bare toenails as unique as oyster shells. The smile he had for us when we kissed standing up at his bar. The amazing things we failed to see because we were too busy with each other. We managed in two hours to buy one lonely cauliflower. The market was full of delicious things and we bought a cauliflower that I didn't eat, that I'm looking at now. What do cauliflowers have to do with love? It's quite simple. I do not eat them (no offence) and have never had one in the house before. Nor am I the kind of woman who goes shopping for groceries with someone. The first stall we looked at—it took us an hour to admire the oranges, it didn't matter that they were like oranges you'd see in Spar. Best thing was the potatoes from Amiens, Jerome couldn't shut me up about them. I made them talk to each other, but the dirty little potatoes from Amiens had nothing much to say to the parsnips, which didn't seem to come from anywhere. Jerome threatened to tape my mouth shut before kissing me. I can't get over the fact that little things like shopping, and shopping for stupid vegetables, come so naturally to us. It's the hope, that big blast of health holding the promise of more weekends like this one. More mornings. This is what I think about when I look at this cauliflower. We have vegetables. We bought them together.

March 19th 2011, Rue de Bac. Didn't go to work today. Since I don't have a job that doesn't matter. I'd like to have phoned in sick anyway.

March 20th 2011, Rue de Bac. Painkillers rule. One for every day Jerome hasn't called. No, that would be too much. I woke up with my head in the fireplace again. I suppose what I'd really like to do is burn myself down. Not the most efficient way to go but I don't have that many options.

March 21st 2011, Rue de Bac. I had to dump the cauliflower in the end.

April 8th 2011, Rue de Bac. Burning myself down can wait. There must have been work stuff or stuff at home or just stuff to deal with, but Jerome reappeared. He came over one morning and we hung out all day and it was normal and lovely. I don't know what else to say. Normal beats amazing. Normal is love. Normal should be normal. We went to the café near here. La Rénaissance or La Révolution or La Répulsion. Dusk closed in around lunchtime. We spent hours there and I remember every detail, even though we spoke of nothing much. Smoking was forbidden, so said the sign. Yet people were lighting up as though they were in a remake of *Casablanca*. We sat in the grey haze that protected us from the outside world. Kissing for hours with staleish city breath. No one seemed to notice us yet we could see everything. The man with the voice box, who insisted on interrupting anyone who uttered a word. The woman who brought her own shot glass—so she could control the measures of brandy—stayed there long after the other morning drunks had gone off to find a bed. I wanted to take up smoking and brandying just to fit in. Jerome felt the same, although he was worried about going home smelling of cigarettes. Going home smelling of me. I have no idea why I love him so much and why he does not love me.

April 9th 2011, Rue de Bac. The closest I've been to love.

Mine to Take

I knew Ségo's handwriting from the whiteboard in the restaurant. The wonky e's and g's had to be mine. I suppose that I should have had it out with her—and let her have it out with me—but I did not feel it was my place to question why she had my diary. Loyalty didn't even come into it. It was wrong to go digging around in someone else's bathroom. Was it stealing when I stuck the notebook into the pocket of my chef's trousers?

The kitchen smelled of dope-smoke and was festooned with every kind of oyster available between there and Arcachon. The room was sparkling with such good intent. Ice bounced into a jug and joints were assembled and distributed more rapidly than life vests at a shipwreck. Daniel had told me there would be no more than a handful of people at the party— when I returned to the kitchen I counted many handfuls. One of his friends was for some reason dressed for mountain climbing, right down to the alpine hat. Someone else was dressed diversely as a stockbroker and a skateboarder, another one in a kilt. Everyone was cool here but all the really cool ones were dressed as bin men.

I went with a question out to the hall, in search of Ségo. I was not a party person, she needed to know that.

—Can we talk outside? I said.

—It's nice in here.

Ségo was swaying a little too close to the candles and I waited until she was steady before I spoke. The reasons I found parties so excruciating were hard to determine but had to do with being the centre of attention.

I didn't mention the notebook, but I wanted to know what they knew. Her friends.

—They're your friends too.

—But what do they know about me?

—This is Paris. Nobody cares who you are or what you are. And hey, you haven't had a drink. It's important to have a drink at a party. If it's your birthday.

I asked her for an orange juice, an order that appeared to amuse the man who had been hovering at my shoulder. It was my doctor. Off-duty Hippolyte wore skinny trousers that dangled above his ankles and a short jacket with barely-there lapels—all of it in black so that he resembled a child undertaker.

For Hippolyte's benefit—and to hear the words myself—I volunteered the information that I had a boyfriend. And Daniel, everywhere at once, had parties cracked. The secret was exchanges averaging ten seconds or less. When I considered what I would manage to say in that time I felt like not bothering.

—Bloody parties, I said.

Hippolyte laughed and I felt proud of myself for doing chit-chat. He placed a glass of something dark under my nose with a solemn nod, only removing it when I went to exhale. Whatever it was I wasn't going to have any. My mind wasn't on wine nor the juice Ségo had forgotten about. I wanted to know if he knew Eagleback.

—Ask a question, I said. Do you know a man with a T-shirt with an eagle on it?

I described Eagleback as best I could. The beard, the blotches, the arm hair—I went into some detail there. I did not want to say that I had chased him fruitlessly along Chanzy, so I made out we were old friends.

—What's his name? said Hippolyte.

—That's kind of private.

—You know where he lives? Where does he work?

—Don't know.

—What else do you know about him?

—What do you want to know?

—What do you know? he said.

—That depends.

—How do you know him?

A crowd had gathered and I had to face in too many directions. I couldn't concentrate—my brain was always a smoothie for a day or two after a migraine, anyway. An old fridge, a loud one, would hum in my head all that time. I found myself regretting that I had asked the question about Eagleback.

When the room fell quiet, and all I could see was Hippolyte's peering face, I knew I had been expected to speak.

—Why do you want to find him? he said.

Neither of us said anything else—he was mistaken if he thought I would speak first—until Daniel simultaneously darkened the kitchen and illuminated it with a cake aflame with more candles.

—How many? said Hippolyte.

My answer was drowned out by the singing, harsh at first. Accepting that the song and the cake were for my benefit was the first thing. I smiled in all directions. They were singing a song called 'Happy Birthday' and there was confusion over the line which was supposed to contain my name. Most people sang the words La Plongeuse Irlandaise. Everyone being stoned meant they found this highly amusing.

At the song's crescendo I focused my eyes on the candles—I couldn't bear to look at the adoring faces singing waywardly for me.

—Let's see you, Ségo said.

Daniel's palm on my back encouraged me towards the cake.

—Blow, he whispered. Blow, blow.

—Why?

—The candles. Look, they're going out.

Phone Home

I left the party, walking fast, attempting to outpace myself—there is that strange word again. Being on Saint Maur was relief, my legs picking themselves up into a run, the way running regulated my breathing and emptied my mind, air rushing towards me and away from me at the same time, loosening the soft, smoky sound of the city at night.

Other questions I could have asked Hippolyte or one of his real doctor friends: my shins are sore—am I running too much? Am I running enough? Why do I smell of bananas? Where have my headaches gone? What if they come back? What if they come back stronger? This mole on my neck, what's it doing there? I had my period. Will I have another one? What age do you think I am? Am I in good shape for my age? Was I a virgin before I met Daniel?

I ran all the way home—a bad idea, of course, to be in Buttes Chaumont at this time of night. There were all sorts of stories of people being dragged into bushes. But it was my park to run in if I wanted to. I had walked there so much so that, following Daniel's advice, I once tried out for a job walking dogs, but French animals seemed to dislike me as much as I feared them. I once spent a day with a cocker spaniel who expected to be carried across the road, an hour—a terrifying hour—with a young bloodhound who wanted to hump me. Poor thing, I should have let him.

When I got to my place, Daniel was cycling in loopy circles by the front door. Some kind of magician, he had left the party after I did but got to my place before me.

—As if a girl like you doesn't enjoy birthdays.

—Didn't ask for any parties, I said.

—Who is Eagleback?

—Someone.

Daniel was smirking.

—He's that guy from the pâtisserie, right? The guy you chased after?

—Fully aware of what happened, I said.

Daniel galloped through question after question. His way of flooding you with questions followed by little huffs that made it easier to say nothing at all.

—Haven't we been over this? I said. He's some guy.

—Does that mean I'm some guy too?

Somewhere in all of this I must have seemed ungrateful when that wasn't the case—I was just confused and there we were failing to clear it up.

I headed inside. There was nothing in my apartment to suggest that anyone lived there. Nor was there much space to work with and I found myself making my own laps around Daniel, who was standing directly on a spot where I had wet myself the day before. My relationship with my body was very don't ask don't tell. My vagina—in the hand-held mirror—was always perfect but the colour of my teeth was progressing from parchment to wood.

If Daniel had a problem with my stinky feet he kept them to himself. But my hairy legs and pits, he did pass comment there.

—It's like fucking a wolf, he would say.

Okay, I would think.

Under the carpet lay bare cement and the scorned mattress looked fit for burning and was probably cursed. In winter, the place warmed up when you opened a window. Other things I attempted to ignore were the exploded oven and the smeared glass giving on to the squalid gardens which had been described so breathlessly by the landlord, another regular at the restaurant. There was an old bath with worn-through ceramic as well as a wheel-less bicycle that had been on the property longer than any of the residents. What foliage remained out there—a balding pine tree—looked forsaken rather than verdant as had been promised. Verdant!

—Maybe it's time to move from here, I said. Everyone knows.

—Knows what?

As far as I had been concerned, no more than three people, Ségo and Daniel and Amadou, knew my story, what there was of it.

—Ségo's friends. Your friends. They were all looking at me.

—Because it was your party. You should have worn a sign. Given them something to look at. I was looking at you, anyway.

Daniel was already undressing. His presence here usually signalled one thing. Funny how we could make love without a single troubling thought crossing my mind.

For the same reason as Daniel always initiated our lovemaking, my desires developed more or less in proportion with his. I guffawed at his cock the first time I saw it—but I wasn't slow to catch up. Imagine you liked someone and they aroused you so much that you wanted to be near them and you put yourself on top of them—as though you were trying to protect them or hide them from someone else—and you lay there at the risk of them suffocating. Sex was the act of making someone else invisible. I never thought of it as desire. We never did it like the dogs I'd seen in Buttes Chaumont but I would think of the dogs anyway and make dog noises. No barking—just a yowl so that Daniel would know I was having fun and, before I knew it, the burning between my legs would turn to something else and I would be enjoying myself. One time he got excited and I went headfirst into the wall. He thought I was concussed but I wasn't even though I couldn't quite see straight. I didn't care what we did, anyway, as long as there was kissing. Tongues going so hard they could clean a bathroom.

Tonight I trembled in his arms, his buttocks as cold and white as a sink, his breath on my face—the sourness of wine on it—and the exposed-elements glow in his eyes I hadn't noticed before. This aroused me, the very thought that something had brought on an unexpected surge in him as it had it in me.

The one time Daniel suggested we research my past I froze him out so badly that, in the end, I felt pity for him. When he said that he was going to post my picture online, I wouldn't acknowledge anything else he said for more than forty-eight hours. As he seemed to hate silence more than anything else—Daniel actually looked lonely when he was not talking—this did the trick better than I could have expected.

To make it up to him, I agreed to visit Galignani, the smart bookshop in the arcade on Rue de Rivoli. There I felt uneasy surrounded by all these names and titles other people took for granted. I made a smooth circuit of the room without once feeling curious enough to pick up a book.

Daniel glanced my way. Seamus Heaney? Nope. He laughed when I said I hadn't heard of James Joyce.

—Do I need to?

—What about cookery? he said.

I stared at the shelves as though I was a donkey that had been dropped off in the reception of a grand hotel.

A few more minutes pretending to browse and then we'd be outside again. From where I was standing, by the books dedicated to Paris—I shoplifted one, for reference purposes—I could see the arcades outside the shop and the grey sky above the Tuilieries, which is where I would rather have been. At my insistence, we walked around the corner to Faubourg St Honoré for a waffle.

Daniel compiled a list of the things I was better off not knowing about and better off not having. 1) No need to read the great books. 2) No need to lie about reading the great books. 3) No need to vote. 4) No need to pay tax. 5) No phone. 6) No data. 7) No emojis. 8) No identity meant no identity theft. 9) No PIN numbers. 10) No passwords.

—What's a password? I said.

—You don't need to know.

—What if I need one?

—You don't have a bank account. Or an email address.

—When can I get one?

—You can't.

—Why not?

—Because you don't exist. You totally exist, but not in the eyes of the state. So let me ask you, sometimes it's like you don't want to know about yourself?

—I don't.

Daniel sighed roughly then disappeared into a shop selling vintage walking sticks. I was holding my waffle on a paper plate. I wasn't going to eat any more but the food meant I couldn't cross the threshold. Inside, the salesman—a small Japanese man with bandy legs—was cooing at Daniel as you would to a child emperor.

The skin on my palms was chapped and trying to keep one hand behind my back while balancing the paper plate gave me a scolded look. I dumped the waffle and began to read the book I had shoplifted. *Just Do What We Do* offered exactly the kind of advice I had no use for. I had been doing okay without mediation by Parisians who took a special pleasure in being graceful while vomiting up their two mouthfuls of calves' liver. To put it another way, I didn't understand any of it.

Daniel liked to educate me. He couldn't believe that I had never seen a movie. He wanted to watch me watching *E. T.* on his iPad, but I was dozing after what had been quite an adamant orgasm.

—I don't want to watch, I said. Can't you just tell me what happens? Describe it to me.

—Watch.

The film came upon me slowly. This walnuty creature appeared and there was something so touching about the delicate way he rotated his head. Not knowing much about them, it was clear to me that *E. T.* was a good film—a sedative and stimulant all in one. I don't know how many times I told Daniel I was enjoying it.

—I heard you, he said.

Films allowed you the space to think about yourself. If once I lived on Rue de Bac, as the notebook said, if I had frequented places like Schiste, then it would be little more than following the signs. I could retrace my steps—recognition would replace discovery—and the scenes in my mind would sharpen.

But *E. T.* made no sense without Eagleback in it. I wanted to see him onscreen along with the little boy, Elliot, and the alien. I wanted him to be walking into Elliot's school and down the corridors. Elliot seemed drunk except it was the alien who drank the beer. Elliot kissed a girl when the alien watched John Wayne doing the same. Did that mean Eagleback was experiencing what I was experiencing now? Wasn't he somewhere nearby? Hadn't I seen him only that morning? What if I got up and began roaming the streets now? What were the chances that I would bump into Eagleback again? If I needed to, I would climb to the top of Sacré Coeur to find him—and this time he would know me when he saw me.

We watched the rest of the film in silence. Daniel had some chocolate-covered raisins and I ate handfuls without looking at them. Elliot was cycling in the air—I was so worried he might fall. It was a just matter of believing he wouldn't. It was the best worst feeling, with beautiful Daniel dozing on my spoiled mattress.

I placed my hand flat to the screen when the film ended. By then it wasn't a film anymore, and I knew that in time the alien would get where he needed to go. I thought of his journey home, what it would be like, and mine.

Daniel #1

It made sense that he should tell her to avoid sticking her fingers into the blades of the blender. He warned her to avoid raw chicken, overcooking certain vegetables (since she was Irish), getting jam in the butter, and vice versa. He warned her to avoid imbibing Red Bull after lunch, to avoid the word imbibe, to avoid the gherkin in her burger, any foods prefixed with soy—, mixing her ketchup with mayonnaise. He warned her to avoid being greedy, to avoid eating too much food, or no food at all. Once they got to know each other better, he encouraged her to avoid the wobbly stools at the bar, tables by the bathroom or in open sun. He warned her to avoid the news, it wasn't relevant, and to avoid people who said 'that's so punk rock' when they weren't referring to music of the late seventies. To avoid people who used lunch as a verb. Party, too. He warned her to avoid yawning in people's faces, to avoid expressions like 'inner peace' and 'the system'. He warned her to avoid fear, to take it and fold it and sail it down the Seine, and to avoid anyone who said different. He warned her to avoid people who asked for her number, since she had no number, and people who asked her to show them Her Paris. He warned her to avoid strangers and, most of all, not to trust them.

Her birthday was October 13th. It was months away. And it wasn't as if he got off on blowing up balloons. Daniel threw the birthday party for Eva in case it might trigger something, knowing very well that it wouldn't. Would she be ill at the thought or would she describe it as the best ever? However, you are either a birthday person or you are not, and the Eva he knew was not and never would be a birthday person.

At the party, she came across so forthrightly and so outwardly comfortable with her own innocence that he could only assume she was hiding something, and that she was not only deep in crisis but was moving from the end of one to the beginning of another. But Daniel never judged Eva for any of this since he too knew the power of concealment. His real name was Conrad Weston and he came from a dangerously wealthy American family, in that his older brother had died of a heroin overdose and his older sister lived in a Sufi community in Washington State after overcoming her own problems with ketamine and artisanal rum.

Daniel was for that reason the sole heir to a mining and technology legacy that would one day grant him, once he returned to being Conrad, bought-and-paid-for houses in Manhattan, Connecticut, Gstaad, Bermuda, and Île de Ré as well as assets and cash enough to cause a fairground flutter in your stomach. His parents lived in as modest a way as being billionaires allowed, although Daniel was ten until he met someone without a swimming pool on their roof. As soon as he realised that's what he was, being rich (or being born rich) deranged him. The more unimaginative the expression of his parents' wealth (his and hers Cessnas, jewel-encrusted Mont Blancs) the better to enchant. Daniel's stance was fully pro-luxury until an old-fashioned humiliation (falling in love with a Panamanian girl who laughed at his tassled loafers) saw him switch teams overnight. Daniel began to pine for tender nights under canvas; would entertain nothing but Woodie Guthrie songs. When he grew his dreads and changed his accent it could have been an inoculation.

Daniel was one of the lucky ones. He could be whoever he wanted to be. His only problem, then and now, was that he had never known what to do with all the love in his heart. He was born with, in his friend Walt's words, a talent for euphoria; a conversation which took place in the kitchen of Daniel's parents' house in Connecticut that was identical to their kitchens in the city and the other ones, one astounding countertop after another.

—What are we doing this weekend? Walt said.

—I am having lunch with Karen then we're going to the beach.

—What's her cute little attribute that'll have you proposing by Tuesday?

—Her shit smells like air freshener.

—Have you told this poor girl that you love her yet?

—Probably. Yeah. Probably. I have.

—They'll still fuck you if you don't say you love them.

Karen was a server in the place where he sommed and on their breaks Daniel took her for drives in his tooth-coloured Prius. That evening they drove to the Shake Shack in Westport where, as they were conferring on the subject of crinkle-cut fries, Daniel told Karen that he loved her and he wanted to marry her. Bullet trains had more subtlety. Maybe it wasn't the best location; there was a ketchupy waft and everywhere the gargle of teenage voices. No, Daniel thought, you made the right decision; and how could she resist? He counted it was the third proposal he'd made that year, give or take.

—I won't think less of you if you need to take a minute, Daniel said. You know what you are to me.

—Do I?

His cheeks warmed as he listened to Karen's response, which was that in another place and at a different time she may have wanted to marry him, too, but not here and not now. Then she told him they were taking a break. Daniel stared at his mute phone, himself as dumb as a Wolcott cabbage.

—Why are we calling it taking a break?

—That's pretty much what we're doing.

—How long are we taking a break for?

—A long time.

Daniel was too much, Karen said. She had been planning to break up with him for a while. Almost since the start, she said. He perched, cat-like, while she covered the basics: them, over as of now. There was no persuading her. In fact, persuasion had the opposite effect. Say what you like about heartbreak, it creates adrenalin. Daniel threw his phone across the room then ahoyed a passing busboy to retrieve it. He stomped and roared, he scraped a wound in his arm, he ran around the parking lot grasping at the air. And the next day he got on a plane to France.

Old habits die hard. Once he had settled in Paris, Daniel began once more to interest himself in love as a profession. Are you supposed to renounce the thing you crave because there is not enough of it?

No. If you do not love you do not exist.

In the space of six royal months, Daniel ended one engagement, started another and, in the assumption that in time it would be required, laid the groundwork for one more. In particular he shared three and a half weeks of highly intoxicating bliss with a certain Miriam, which he decided was sufficient bliss to warrant making things permanent, a point about which they had agreed to disagree. In all of these new relationships, with Miriam and whoever, he asked the girls, all of whom he'd been seeing for less than a month, to accompany him to an appropriately ecclesiastical restaurant in the seventh. There Daniel gorged them with enough truffles to close down their systems before requesting outstretched palms and finding them shaking. The ingredients of farce were universal and eternal but the bum notes were all his.

None of these young women wanted to marry him, no way; even though he knew that with a little old-fashioned persistence he could have persuaded them, one or two anyway. Would Daniel take any of the proposals back now? Possibly, although he couldn't tell you which ones. He hardly had the stomach to admit, least of all to himself, that he had only proposed to Miriam because the vegetables at L'Arpège hadn't turned out to be the best vegetables of their lives. (Miriam later revealed that she would have preferred a good ham sandwich, and he agreed.)

Walt always said he was good at making too much of nothing.

Daniel's parents dined with Bloomberg when he was mayor and were the third largest donors to the American Republican Party. As long as he stayed off the horse tranquilizers he was destined to be number-one son and heir. They also dined with Eva's parents (where, he didn't know; in the kinds of places rich people eat) and it was on Tony and Maeve's behalf that he was asked to intervene.

He had just one conversation with her parents. Even on Skype, he could tell her dad was a piece of work. Maeve did Tony's bidding, much like Daniel's own folks who were the ones he was trying to please in the first place. His father thought he was just bumming around Paris anyway, and there was no good answer to that. He knew his son needed a project. And Daniel couldn't deny it, Eva was a project. It was not as if he had anything else to do. His life had not been what you'd call full lately.

Her parents described her with a combination of awe, wariness and regret. Eva might smile at you while accusing you of the most terrible thing. No further details were forthcoming, but Daniel needed to be aware of one thing: she had a vivid imagination, or, more accurately, a dangerous imagination. Thanks to being an only child, she was a dreamer, they said. Always in a hurry and quick to shift positions, they said. If he did find her he would have to keep up with her, the chaos, the booze, the noise.

There had been a boyfriend, a certain Australian. When they spoke to Jerome he said he hadn't heard from her in a year, maybe longer. They themselves hadn't heard from her in more than two years. Not a completely unreasonable length of time, they said, given their relationship and all that had gone on.

—Lookit, Tony said. I've had this thing: Tony Blair. It's my cancer. Goes where he's not wanted.

—Where?

—Invading Iraq.

—Your cancer invaded Iraq?

—Tony Blair invaded Iraq and destroyed the Middle East, which—

—Shouldn't that be George W. Bush?

—But my name's Tony.

—And I've made you explain your joke, I'm sorry. Where is your cancer?

—Was lung. He's been and gone and been and gone but this is the last I'll see of him. So there's a reason why we feel we should be … a family again.

It wasn't as if they expected her to be spattered at the foot of the Eiffel Tower, they just wanted to know how she was.

—It might be better if you don't tell her anything about speaking to us, Tony said. Just tell us she's okay, or well. Tell us what you see.

Paris isn't that big and Daniel was told Eva would stand out. His job was to find her and befriend her.

Ségo Carena he had come across at wine tastings at La Cave des Papilles and sometimes Daniel would stop into Gravy for a late drink that turned into an early drink. She had no idea who he was. Daniel supposed she had him down as a dabbler; another excitable American toying with being French for an extended semester or two.

He hadn't considered taking another job (he didn't need the ones he already had) but then he saw who was washing the dishes and asked to help. As soon as he met Eva, he sent the mail that Tony and Maeve had been hoping for: she's here, she's fine, all is well.

He didn't mention her memory. They would have asked questions he couldn't have answered. Amadou's theory, a watery one, was that Eva had been bitten by an insect and in time would not only lose her mind but her reason and her ability to function in a working environment. Other days he thought she was an undercover journalist. According to the meat guy she was an Irish terrorist on the run and he advised Daniel against tackling her. The fish guy just thought she was gorgeous and wanted to ask her out.

Daniel didn't tell Eva's parents that everyone called her La Plongeuse. To call her that was to mythologise her. It was so strange to think he knew Eva's name and they didn't. She didn't. There was of course the small matter of her mind but they'd soon get to the bottom of all that.

Daniel had a picture in his head of his perfect lover and, although Eva wasn't quite it, she was it. She was the type of woman around whom he was a piece of boiled meat with a mouth. And she was not at all the dreamy creature Tony and Maeve had described. There was something submerged about her. A solemnity of a very persistent kind; some kind of space cadet, her chin tight with dried egg. There had to be reasons why she did everything so quickly. She got lost in the tying and rapid retying of a lace. Sometimes she accompanied her actions with a light sigh and sometimes not—it was all in a private code and that's what made it so rousing.

At staff-meal, she would gum an apple or a waffle then study it faintly, whereupon she would disregard the food in the manner of someone who had just been reminded of something unpleasant. At first Daniel thought it was a formulation, created precisely so that you would wonder and lean forward.

Some act, he thought. Brava. Good show.

Then Daniel was the one leaning.

Since her scorn seemed to be reserved for his benefit, it was something that he grew to crave. Her at the sink and him in the dining room delivering scalded coffee and patronising wine advice. Nevertheless, at lunch, Daniel imagined Gravy belonged to him and they were welcoming people into their home and once they had closed the doors after service and swept the floors Daniel and Eva would be resuming their lives together.

Sometimes he felt sad to leave after work and he couldn't help but wonder if Eva felt the same. Ségo, having eyes in her head, noticed all this.

—You think she's hot, right?

—Is it that obvious?

—You know she's kind of tuned into a private station.

—You warning me off?

—A little.

—What's the harm if we feel like a relaxing drink after a long day at work?

—I'm just saying be careful. But, I suppose she could do with someone to stare at over the top of her Orangina. Just remember she's fragile.

—Taking it slow, he said. I like that idea.

Mostly Eva hid away in the kitchen, transcribing recipes and avoiding Amadou and cleaning things she had already cleaned.

The moment she drifted into Daniel's airspace, he didn't hesitate, making the case that someone washing pots for a living might appreciate a little looking after.

—Want to get a taco? he said.

Her gaze lowered but she didn't reply. There was all of a sudden a deserted feeling in the room.

—No, was the eventual answer.

—Why don't you watch me eat a taco? he said.

—Okay, she said.

They went to some place on Rue Santoinge. Inside, morale had hit an all-time high. In spite of all Daniel's offers of cash to the manager she would not allow anyone to skip to the top of the line. After a long and silent wait, they were allowed to proceed to a bar where, before taking her seat, Eva asked for tap water. Room temperature.

—I don't know what it is, Daniel said. I never have it anywhere else, but when I have tacos I have to drink beer.

—I asked for water, she said.

—Do yourself a favour, he said. Order a beer. It's on me.

—Why do you want to pay for everything?

—I have money. I'm telling you that up front. So you won't have to worry about it.

—I don't need your help, she said. And you talk about money more than you talk about anything else.

—I won't talk about it anymore, he said. But can I take that as a yes for a beer? I'd really like to buy you a beer. I hope that's not a problem.

Eva sipped her water.

This being Paris, there was a wait for the tacos and an argument about the wait. When the food arrived, she took a knife and fork and addressed her taco so studiously that Daniel felt he was listening to a recording of an epic and anxious silence. Off came the sour cream and so too the avocado, although the onions received the official pardon. She cut the taco like it was a cake, arranging everything on the plate until she seemed satisfied there would be four identical bites.

They ate in silence, her lips and cheeks devilish with grease. If wiping Eva's chin was the culmination of his life so far, then good. He took a sheaf of napkins and she lowered her eyes so that they did not have to share any sense of recognition.

If he had been waiting for something to happen, it just had.

—Can I kiss you?

There was still pork in her mouth when she kissed him. And she bit his lip, although that made it no less significant.

Bristles and Cheeks

In case anything ever occurred to me, I slept with a notebook by the bed. Nothing occurred to me apart from refinements to my systems and the comings and goings at the storeroom in Gravy. It seemed crucial that I should draw pictures of a corn on the cob—kernel after kernel. And I didn't stop there. I drew all the in-season vegetables.

I found myself at Bertrand Rose before dawn on Easter Sunday. The light was gone in my bathroom so—when I didn't even need to—I brushed my teeth with my finger in the dark before heading off.

I always slept in my kitchen clothes so I went from asleep to awake and outside and hoofing it along Mathurin Moreau in less than three minutes—this would allow me plenty of time to explore the streets between there and Bertrand Rose in good time before they opened.

I could not expect to bump into Eagleback as randomly as I had before so I decided to assemble on that junction at Paul Bert every day until such time as he would return. Daniel said I was a fool for going back to Bertrand Rose. I wasn't a backpacker, he said. I didn't have to live on chocolate bread. But I had stolen enough from the till at Gravy to buy something small every day for a month if need be.

Insofar as I could tell, no one ever took much notice of me around Paul Bert, and I felt wearing my chef's clothing offered me some cover.

As I waited for the shop to open, I imagined our perfect day together. Our perfect Sunday would have begun early. Breakfast in bed, or out of bed, I'm not fussy. Then we'd go out, so people could see us. We'd flit in and out of different Sephoras, layering the scents. If it was hot we'd take shelter in a Monoprix by the fish counter's mist—a kind monger might give us a bag of ice. I could get an hour out of staring at the cut ham. Strange desires for yoghurt. At night we wouldn't do much because we'd both be tired from all the fresh air and I'd have to get up early the next day anyway. It didn't matter that my perfect day with Eagleback was a little like every Sunday with Daniel.

Bertrand Rose opened. Delivery vans swept in and were gone. I stepped inside then delivered my rehearsed question. Did anyone know a man with impressive arm hair who had been in the shop at this time on Good Friday?

—Non was sung in unison.

Bristles—the woman with whom Eagleback had negotiated over the chocolate orb—was as evasive and perplexed as before. I pressed on. It was his face that you couldn't mistake—prowling eyes, a top-class beard, skin with one or two marks. In fact I continued to have concerns about Eagleback's skin condition. Why would he have gone around with psoriasis like that? I hoped he was getting someone to look at it.

I couldn't get Bristles to tell me where Eagleback was. I tried every trick in the book, couldn't have tried harder—even though my French was drying up under pressure.

I might have said, —Comme ci comme ça.

I might have said, —Où est la gare?

I supposed I cared and didn't care what Bristles thought of me—as in I altogether didn't. Or most of me didn't. I felt useless in the face of her apathy. I used all the French I had, writing down some of the hard-to-explain stuff—the eagle on his back for one thing. Bristles would not acknowledge that she remembered a thing—even as I recounted their exchange verbatim. The bitter chocolate, the child for whom it was intended.

She sighed and called over my shoulder for the next customer. I took my mille-feuille—quite good, better than the éclair—and she glared at me. The little hairs shooting out of her at all kinds of angles. Her cheeks blazed with tiny, fibrous veins. The patterns of a broken leaf.

The thought of returning to the pâtisserie kept me awake all night—imagining I was on the look-out for Big Foot or the Loch Ness Monster. I wanted to leave home at 2 a.m., 3 a.m., 4 a.m. but I fell asleep and woke again not long before I was due at Gravy. Outraged, I had to go straight to work.

I didn't make the same mistake the next morning, turning onto Paul Bert just as it hit seven o'clock. My new plan depended on Bristle's absence. From the corner opposite, I strained to watch her, faraway in her own incidental universe—a talented multi-tasker of sorrow and aggression.

Home again to wait.

The next day I patrolled the street, wondering how I might explain myself to one of her colleagues should the opportunity arise—best to appear meek and confused to disguise my ignorance of Eagleback's real name.

On Thursday, Bristles was gone. Where I could only guess. Nor was there anyone queuing and before I had a chance to talk myself out of it I was talking to lovely young woman—with cheeks of pink chamois leather—who honoured my questions with great curiosity. Within seconds I had made more progress than I had in days. Cheeks had a cold and I offered commiserations. I stuttered in French and she smiled, helping me along as she moved around the shop slowly—as you would do if you were in pain or you were lazy.

I told her I was buying a gift for someone, a special surprise, with an emphasis on the special. I hadn't managed to prepare a story to divert her from asking Eagleback's name. In the end an airy tone and the language barrier overcame that obstacle. Cheeks remembered the cake—she usually worked in the kitchen—as well as the man's conversation with Bristles. He had seemed so disappointed as he left the shop.

Cheeks even pitied me enough to speak English and to look at me with shared disappointment when it was revealed that, yes—yes of course, they could make another orb just like the last one, but it would not be ready for a few days.

—I myself remember him, she said. He do not seem happy but I am so happy that it work for the best.

—Can you deliver? It's better that way, don't you think? For a surprise.

—As you wish.

—You should have the address.

—Let me look for the place. Jerome Cooper? she said.

—Jerome, I said.

I had to stop myself from shouting it out loud. If I knew his name then I knew everything—that he was Jerome from the notebook, for one thing. It was already a happy ending, or that's how it seemed to me.

Cheeks' little fat fingers fluttered as she looked for the address in the order book. I asked her if she had enjoyed a good Easter.

—Mais yes, she said.

—And if I change my mind and decide to take the cake myself, will that be possible?

—As you wish.

I had not planned to be so chatty but Cheeks' good humour permitted me to appear so casual. I can't remember what else she said when she searched through the old orders—but then she had it. It was so very hard to believe that she was holding Eagleback's address in her hands. Without giving the slightest warning, I reached across and attempted to hug her.

Cheeks didn't pull away, I'll give her that much. Her eyes were open in astonishment. She made a sound like laughter, which I mimicked, before she handed me a strawberry tart

—I offer this, she said.

Taking a guess that Bristles was regular with her days off, I proposed the same day the following week for delivery. If Cheeks could arrange for it to be sent to the same address, the one she was holding in her hands, I would gladly pay for it right now. I kept away from any more intimacies but from the way she processed the rest of the order it was irrefutable that Cheeks thought this was all a lovely idea.

Someone's request for bread brought our conversation to a close. I got out of there as quickly as possible, calling goodbye with a mouthful of the strawberry tart—not bad, either.

I ran as if I was being chased—this time my sprint along Chanzy brought on a feeling of joy, as if I had passed a test of initiation.

Unstory

June 28th 2011, Rue de Bac. It's easier to have an affair in the summer. So long as you're smart about it you can conduct your impetuous business out of doors and not feel seedier than you do already, which is not at all. I can't remember whose idea it was to go to Buttes Chaumont, whose idea it was to make love in the bathroom of Rosa Bonheur. Last night was so humid and I don't think we were the only couple in the park with that idea. The bathrooms there had caught my eye before so I suppose it was my idea, since I led us straight there. We were hardly furtive about it either. A mocking smile from the waitress who knew exactly what we were up to. 10-9-8-7-6-5-4-3-2-1-2-3-4-5-6-7-8-9-10. Timber! All our troubles left us as we lapsed into noisiness. An actress's gasp. Oh my and so on. I remember Jerome was making monstrous faces. So was I, I suppose. Growling. Howling. His knees went in the end, the little lamb. Afterwards we bought mercifully cold beers, tipped the waitress, and sprawled on the grass. It was quite some time before we were able to lumber down the hill and home.

Of Course There's Something
Wrong with Her

—Guess what? Daniel said. Ségo has some news.

—What is it? I said, feeling agitated by some arrythmic drumming from Amadou's radio.

Daniel was taking the pins out of a brand-new work shirt— they arrived weekly wrapped in beautiful white tissue—while Ségo was removing the cheeks from a gallery of monkfish heads. She delivered the news in a kind of ecstasy.

—A__ B__ is coming for lunch next week.

—Is that good?

Cooks, especially cooks like us, were supposed to be disciples of this man. Confident that Ségo and Daniel were excited enough for everyone, I tried my best to play along. It was perfectly normal for me to zone out during certain conversations. A__ B__, whoever he was, was the least of it. Ségo produced a picture on her phone—there he was in snug jeans and new cowboy boots and despite pretending otherwise I found him attractive. He had a look of elsewhere which I related to.

Ségo's next move was to list the menu for A__ B__'s visit. We would be cooking the same menu—odd offal, suckling pig—every day in preparation for his arrival, but I was more concerned that she was using up today's valuable prep time. The monkfish, cross-eyed some of them, were staring at me in the way of gargoyles.

—I want you to cook something for A__ B__.

That was Ségo for you. She wanted everyone to be a part of it, whatever it was.

Daniel gave me a beseeching look that said, be happier and, —How long have you worked here?

—All week, I said. My brain tended towards such slippage.

—Let's say five, six months, Ségo said. Since November. It's time to step up.

It was a tempting offer. Never having experienced the real thing, washing pots every day felt like jetlag incurred from staying in one place for so long—finding potato peelings in my pockets, tending to the creeping rash on my crotch as though it was a love letter. Imagine cooking and not just cooking but cooking for—I had forgotten his name again.

Tongues, lungs, tendons and what have you—I was getting a start on the menu for A__ B__ by skewering chicken hearts onto sharpened sticks of rosemary. Upon finishing the job I lined up the hearts so that they resembled ruby necklaces. Never having tasted offal, I decided to have some for myself. I was standing over a pan of frying hearts when I heard Ségo and Daniel talking. One of them was pushing, the other pulling.

The topic—me.

—She's fixating on things. People. Random shit.

Ségo's reply was fierce. —It's quite factual. She lost her mind. And she's here.

—I know why people reinvent themselves. I am, as you know, an asshole American in Paris.

I banged a few pans to alert them of my presence but they continued talking.

—You need to stop this, Ségo said. She is what she is.

—She belongs at home.

—Do you live at home? Do you belong there?

—But I'm not fucking sick in the head. And if I was, I would hope my family would come for me.

—Want me to call your parents? Have them come pick you up? Ségo said, to end the conversation.

It was so hot at the stove that I spared myself an immediate answer to the questions. I tipped out the hearts without any appetite for them. What remained of the offal needed to be packed away. A few minutes tidying the walk-in fridge focused my mind. There the suckling pigs lay, side by side, as if in a morgue.

My analysis of what I had just overheard from Ségo and Daniel was a level or two above panic. Daniel was (a) announcing himself of being tired of me—this was alarming, even though I would have been tired of me, too—and if I (b) wasn't about to seem more excited about roasting a pig for an American celebrity I had never heard of, Ségo might (c) come around to his way of thinking and hand me over, nameless and everythingless, to the authorities.

Daniel found me hanging around in the kitchen. Tidying the fridges and admiring my handiwork had become something of a hobby and I had stuffed the refuse bags so full—they were fat little bears. From an amassed memory of close to nothing, I knew one thing—I loved it here. The kitchen at Gravy wasn't slick, it wasn't clean, nor was it especially safe, but it was my home and I was happier there than anywhere else.

Daniel would not hear of my plans to go to my apartment. I was beginning to confuse his attentions with intrusion. Not only had he begun to ask harsh questions, he would not tolerate any in return. Putting myself in his shoes, I tried to wonder why he devoted so much time to me, since there was always something else to demand his attention.

—My place, he said.

—I thought the only way to get into your building was to deliver pizza.

Most of us lived near the restaurant, or further out, but Daniel lived on the marzipan-scented Left Bank. I assumed I was being invited there out of concern and pity. Not only that, it was also unlikely that I would run into Eagleback in the Luxembourg Gardens.

He wondered why I asked to detour via Rue de Bac—but stalk this old street and, as sure as Daniel was Daniel, one thing would lead to another. I took a few minutes to search for Café Répulsion, or whatever it was called, but the long stretch of antique shops and cafés was just like any other street.

—Do you know where you are? he said.

—Not really.

—Just exploring?

I liked the sound of the word so I repeated it.

—Exploring.

—Such a pity, Daniel said. The seventh has become an American colony.

I had hoped to see a familiar face, but no. The street's indifference was startling. Rue de Bac held me in its gaze—as unimpressed with me as I was with it—and I concluded that, since the street hadn't made much of an impression on me, it couldn't have been home for very long.

I was in any case much more interested in seeing where Daniel lived. The lobby of his building, near the church on Saint Sulpice, resembled a sleek hotel bathroom. If ever I lived somewhere with a lobby I'd want it to be like that lobby. He would not accept this was in any way out of the ordinary or a million light years from my concrete bunker across town.

The apartment's hallway managed to accommodate several insolently closed doors—no indication as to what went on behind them as we rolled into the kitchen, which repeated many of the motifs of the lobby downstairs. The gleam on the tiles, for one thing, was no simple matter—I could only speculate at the upkeep. I was a cleaner by profession and couldn't have delivered such a shine. You would always have been guaranteed a thumb print or two.

Daniel described the army of staff who maintained the place.

—The comic twist is that they earn more than I do, he said. Even the help has help.

There was some shammy memorabilia—a collection of lacquered cigarette cases, including one that was supposed to have belonged to Marlene Dietrich. On a dining table lay a number of surgical looking wine gadgets and several encyclopaedias, wine again I assumed.

A line of glasses—fastidiously arranged by type—were poured, filling the room with refracted diamond light. It may have been one of those ceremonies where you get a tune out of a procession of vessels filled to differing volumes. There was apparent skill in Daniel's uniform meagre pours—the titillation on offer merely from the shine on the glasses.

—What do you expect me to do with that?

—Taste, he said. Unless you don't want to?

I held the glass reverently aloft in two hands—a votive candle. When I sipped the wine I said it tasted like grapes.

—Hardly anyone mentions grapes, he said.

Before I knew it there was more of it sloshing around and I was, for Daniel's amusement, developing the nose of a wine writer—noticing cinnamon, star anise, furniture polish, tar, bursts of sap and the rare stench of canal mud.

—Let's quit being sommeliers, he said. I kind of thought tonight we could talk. What's the story? Why Eagleback? Why Rue de Bac?

—What story? I said.

—Shall I ask you another way?

—How do you mean? In a different voice?

Daniel laughed. I was still good at evasion. I can't remember what else he said or did not say, or what I said or failed to understand. I kept drinking whatever he poured, feeling progressively warm, dizzy, lazy, but never as content as I thought I would feel. All that wine did its work in me—little did I know the unpicking of a single thread had undone the entire seam. The next thing I knew I was hitting the floor with a sore bump. Daniel's face refused to settle on one position, his Adam's apple scurrying around his throat and the vein in his temple pulsing. I remember waving away an outstretched hand.

Waking the following morning to a scatter of change on the kitchen floor is about all that comes back to me. Now Daniel was there, pacing and panting and gesticulating—it was hard to tell where his grunts ended and words began. The polished room had become murky and my chalky mouth was thick with a sour film. I had the skin of a pterodactyl and my hand was bleeding and, if truth was to be told, I felt horny. I hauled myself up and sat cross-legged. Even that was difficult and could have been an error.

Ségo would love this one—the girl with no memory who couldn't remember a thing.

Daniel #2

If you wanted to you could have called anything entertainment. Dogs fighting, midgets fucking, Daniel would have been all yours, but a beautiful woman whom he felt he loved flaying the wall with insults was not his idea of a fun evening. They did have their good moments; it was all shoo-be-do-lang-lang around about the two glass mark then the night descended into a brawl. Eva's parents had been right about the booze. The bags under her eyes grew and she began to pace back and forth, spouting random numbers, an excited bookie. She was possessed, drinking from the bottle and from the tap.

Daniel watched her, her eyes searching for someone. She began calling for this Jerome guy, sweetly, as if he was in the next room.

—Come back, she said. Come here. Come on.

Daniel tried to smooth things over and get her to bed and onto the next phase of the evening but she wasn't having any of it. She would barely allow him to wipe the spittle from her face. Oh, and she dumped him, mid-sentence and without even drawing breath. Then it was the next morning and she was standing in the doorway, clenching and unclenching her jaw with the air of a hungry gull, her red eyes impassive.

Daniel walked her home.

—Did I say anything bad last night?

—Not really.

—Then please let me enjoy a few more seconds of blissful ignorance.

At that point, it would've been so straightforward to reveal all, who she was, what Daniel knew, what he had been told. But every time he tried to tell Eva about herself his throat refused; swallowing and swallowing, his mouth as dry as velvet. The moment for that was passing, it had passed. He couldn't tell her, because her parents asked him not to. And Daniel couldn't tell her, because he liked Eva the way she was. He couldn't tell her because he knew he might lose her if she knew.

Her hell hole on Mathurin Moreau. From time to time there was a waggling hand at a window, not a sill without an overflowing ashtray. That was it as far as humanity was concerned.

Daniel felt so guilty for leaving Eva there alone that he called Ségo. She had company, a good thing as far as he was concerned. Daniel hadn't met them all, but he had seen enough to know that Ségo moved from one soulful sociopath to another. A parade of the unlikeliest assholes.

When they first met, Ségo informed Daniel that she used to be one of those people who, when bored, would up and move to a new country. Now that she had employees and back taxes and this that and the other to worry about, moving house with hand luggage was no longer part of the plan. She woke up one morning, found she was the boss and that she liked it. She had also found herself one of the best little houses in the eleventh and all that remained was to find someone with whom to share it.

It was Sunday, Gravy was closed, and there was a slow sarcasm in her voice when she answered. He got as far as asking Ségo if she had known anything about Jerome Cooper and there he got nothing. She didn't know a thing. She asked him if he was stoned when he mentioned Eagleback. He'd researched Jerome and found he was the guy from Bertrand Rose, a thirty-year-old Australian who through family connections had lucked into a settled job teaching primary school. Fair to middling in the looks department. Sporty, once. A poet, too.

—How was last night? she said.

—Pro-tip: don't waste Clos Rougeard on an amnesiac alcoholic.

—I bet she didn't care.

—It was a 2003, a hot year. Mind you, those guys don't have off-vintages.

—I don't give two fucks about the wine.

—I'll be straight with you. She looks cute when she freaks out. At first, but then she doesn't. Oh, and she dumped me from a great height.

Ségo thought this was funny.

—If she was so drunk maybe she'll forget that she dumped you.

—Good point.

—So she'll take you back if you ask nicely.

He knew Ségo wanted to get off the phone, but he didn't want to let her go.

—You know what I think? I think her life is a shitty hot dog that someone has spat in.

—Why do you say that?

—She has nothing.

—She did have nothing. We are her safety net. Do you understand?

—You should have seen what I saw last night. She needs proper help.

Ségo was being very calm but Daniel had to assume that when it came to Eva she was somehow dishonest. That's all he could say upfront. She didn't know what he knew. And she was acting as if Eva was all hers when he knew Eva was all his.

—She's spoken to Hippolyte, Ségo said. And I've taken care of it that she can talk to him whenever she wants.

—Why did you hire her in in the first place?

Ségo's laugh sounded like a bridled horse.

—Good fucking question. But she wasn't for hire. She turned up and she needed a soft landing. I just took her in.

—Just like that?

—Comme ça. I gave her a job later on. I got her somewhere to live to get her out of the fucking vegetable store. Anyone would have done it. Remember what I said to you at the start. She needs a friend. Be her friend. Daniel, love is stupid, people are stupid for falling in love, you're stupid, I'm stupid. And I'm gonna go, it's a day of fucking rest.

An Open Door, Go Into It

Thursday was A__ B__ day so Gravy was best avoided. I had more or less given up on Daniel, too, since the night at his place. There hadn't been a headache for days, not since the hangover, but the rest of me was in bad shape—lumps in my phlegm and a mucky mattress from a particularly heavy period. My hair was fine though.

Eagleback was real—I was on my way to Bertrand Rose to find his address—but he would not be real if I had said anything about him to Daniel and he had repeated it to anyone else. But I knew what I was getting in to as soon as I turned onto Paul Bert.

If Bristles was there, I would have to wait things out.

I no longer thought of Bertrand Rose as a pâtisserie and hadn't been much for cakes, or eating at all, lately. A man came out of the back shop to work the counter—for all the world an incurably beautiful count from an old novel about handsome royalty. This was Bertrand Rose himself. Dark, bouncy hair with eyebrows darker still. Everything had to be set out, the many tarts one by one, before he would speak to me. Between his meticulousness and my uncertainty I found myself becoming muddled. I'd been told that once upon a time cakes and bread were made in different places. A cake-maker was different from a bread-maker just as one person was different from another. Once upon a time but not any more. Now all the sweet and savoury got mixed in together. One thing I noticed—the baguettes were fat in the middle and pinched at one end. Bertrand Rose seemed to be dextrous when it came to sweet things but a galoot when it came to bread. These were the baguettes of an anxious man.

Nor was it easy to get through a conversation with someone who was looking at himself in a mirror behind you as you spoke a language you could barely understand. I did my best to explain that I was there to meet his colleague Cheeks and that I wanted, on the spur of the moment, to pick up an order that was due for delivery. It took everything I had to get my point across. He was looking at me as though I was a bald man asking for a haircut. When, to emphasise my point, I made the shape of the chocolate orb with my hands he squirmed with displeasure.

Usually, it was a matter of attitude—it was easier to be belligerent about speaking English. Just as some people avoided eating tuna or dodged housework, I got through life in Paris with minimal French, happily withstanding the devastating winces and sighs. Not so with M. Rose. Unable to make myself properly understood in French, I substituted it with the poor English as had become my habit when I was nervous.

—You have destabilised my morning. This cake is something like a treasure for me. Is it possible that you have retained the particular information pertaining to the cake's final destination?

—Quoi?

I thought I had made it plain.

Logic sent me out of the shop so I could enter one more time. Satisfied that I was properly humiliated, M. Rose gave me a knockout smile as I shepherded myself to the end of the queue. When it came to my turn I failed to make myself clear in either language. M. Rose would not answer any more questions. I kept on asking about Eagleback's cake and where it had gone until he clapped his hands to silence me.

Cheeks was sick and the order had been sent already, he said. His eyes were roving back to the mirror behind me. The cake was in the van in the street outside.

—Howt. Seed, he said.

Before the words had hit the air I was ducking under the arms of a baker carrying aloft a tray of bread. I felt the warm waft as I left the shop. A white van was all I saw—and I took to the road again, thumping a car's bonnet as I passed.

The traffic was so heavy that I was able to outstretch the van and run to the intersection where I caught my breath and waited for it to make its turn onto Voltaire, left towards République or right towards Nation. I could polish this street corner with my feet all I wanted—the van could turn either way and just slip off into the city.

The grumble of moving traffic and the van swept past me, heading right when most of the traffic that was entering Voltaire was going left. I took off in the knowledge that he would surely lose me in a matter of seconds.

The van rolled past and there was no more time to think when I saw that it had indicated to make a sharp turn left against oncoming traffic. Another street forked sharply off Voltaire and I got myself across the road just as the van was turning and slowing, presumably so the driver could read the numbers on doorways. The van was floating along at such an agreeable pace that I was able to walk alongside. I stopped to linger behind a strutting pigeon. Had you caught sight of me you would not have thought I was following the van at all.

There was an empty travel agency and a recruitment bureau, but the driver was positioning the van right before the entrance to an apartment block. Number 25—I stood across the street as the van door opened and the driver tossed his cigarette before removing a familiar-looking black box. Another man—small and dark and spry in lurid blue overalls tied at one shoulder—waited with a trolley loaded with cardboard packages.

There were plenty of rumbling cars to cover me and I dared to cross the road and study an old lady entering the building with her shopping. I memorised the code—4963—as she typed it with the care of a monk over a manuscript. Through the glass doors was a deserted courtyard where kitchen smells vied with the scent of neglected soil.

The man in the blue overalls was the building's caretaker and after dipping his nose into the box he said that the cake would hardly survive his morning coffee. His bottom lip was heavy and protruding and it slapped as he spoke—I could picture him spitefully choking it down in two or three bites. He placed the cake box on his trolley and made his way into the apartment complex, at which point something got a hold of me—I wouldn't call it courage.

I negotiated my way through the door behind him and was strolling through Eagleback's courtyard without a thought as to how I got there or what I was about to do.

The caretaker had a nook tucked away in a corner of the courtyard. I watched him undo his laces and step out of his boots before unwrapping a cling-filmed chicken leg. He was consuming it as if in a trance when a lady appeared at his door with two groomed dogs whose leashes had become tangled like kite strings. On went his boots and he left to help the woman.

I should have been in work. I should have been basting pork for a famous chef. Now I was snooping around a room that looked like it was still in shock after an earthquake. There was a shelf of detective novels and a picture of a young girl and, due to the removal of his boots perhaps, a retch-inducing gaseous smell—that of a pet shop or life itself escaping.

It looked as though the caretaker had been reusing cotton buds and exploring non-specific uses for the toilet plunger. The walls were fire-blackened and the ceiling was ornate with splattered food. The toilet paper and rusty shears resting on top of the warped filing cabinet needed no further commentary. Floating in a bucket I saw a streaked facecloth and a brick of soap in army green. There was an open wallet, too, but I ignored the urge to slip it into my pocket.

The caretaker had done nothing with the packages. They just lay on his trolley. He wouldn't be long untangling the dogs' leads so I took the box and read the label.

Ghislaine Cooper, 25 Rue Léon Frot, 75011 Paris. How could a single name imply so much? I wanted to scratch off the label.

Again I looked at the wallet and started counting to ten— Ségo's tactic for whenever things were getting too much for me. I got as far as three before I was brought back to earth by a shadow— and a meaty hand on my shoulder. The caretaker's hot breath was pouring into my face. There were deep violet pools under his eyes and his nose had cauliflowered dramatically. A couple of black hairs grew straight out of it. His hair, which obeyed no worldly logic I was aware of, was sandy—as in, there was sand in it. But there was something else, eagerness in his eyes, as if he was peering at me from behind a veil. When I tried to scream he went to restrain me. He wasn't quick enough to grab my wrists because I swung up my hand—harder than I meant to—and then he was holding his eye.

I was not so sassy that I would strike up a conversation with a stranger—but I told him I was sorry. And, do you know what, he listened to my apology and accepted it. He didn't seem angry, just embarrassed. When I tried to move around him he startled me by announcing his name.

Hospitality was a priority chez Elias. He made it clear that, no matter how many times I clouted him one, I was to think of myself as his guest. The foam on the bar stool in his room had exploded through the vinyl and, as if it was a winter evening in some dimly lit tavern, he motioned for me to make myself comfortable.

The meat I was being offered from a foil tray had been bought at the halal place on Charonne. Elias boiled it up in a five-gallon pot in the basement, flavouring the soup with herbs that appeared— forlorn and wild—in the courtyard. Elias pecked at his chicken leg with the decisive moves of a kestrel. His proudly stained overalls— his stomach stuffed into them like a sack of rice—were another of the giveaways that he lived alone. Now I recognised it—he smelled like the stock pot back at the restaurant.

Whenever I came unstuck with my pidgin French, Elias, unable to offer assistance, folded his arms and looked away. He sat up as tall as he could on his seat and closed his eyes whenever I resorted to English. He spoke in a pungent accent and we made quite the din, talking in languages the other one couldn't understand.

I thought he was saying, —Roohi.

Over and over.

Roohi.

I heard all about the work he did at home in Tunisia or about the work he used to do or would have liked to have done given the chance. He was either a bus driver in Tunisia or he took a bus to the work he did or might have done. Or there were no buses at all and he couldn't get to work—that was the problem, he had to walk. Did he? It wasn't easy to make him out at all. Roohi. Roohi. I knew that he had something to do with buses, perhaps driving a bus or being on one—although it was also possible he had nothing to do with buses. I imagined his hairy hands on a foreign steering wheel, anyway, holding it tight.

The pictures in his room were of his daughter. Yasmine was in Tunisia with her mother, living in a house Elias had paid for but was barred from entering. The reason I was sitting on this stool and eating his chicken—and not down at the commissariat de police—was my resemblance to his daughter, or how he imagined she might look, since the picture on the wall had been taken over ten years ago. I didn't want to know why he had been banished from his own home. Sooner or later we might want to reveal ourselves to one another but not yet.

I needed help in the solving of a mystery—that's how I put it to Elias, that casually.

In French I asked him if a man in his position saw many comings and goings.

In French he told me he saw a thing or two.

In French I asked him if he knew anything about a man called Jerome Cooper

His eyes opened—a fist-strike into his palm.

—Le gâteau. Le gâteau.

He took a fresh chicken leg, raising it high in the air and started to pace as if addressing a political gathering. The Coopers lived in Block D, on the eighth floor, the one facing the street. Elias had left the cake with their neighbour because they were both schoolteachers and at work. Often they went for an apéro when they were finished for the day, but today they had gone to the Grand Palais to see an exhibition about Augustus the Emperor of Rome. Ghislaine had bought the tickets online and they had arrived by special delivery. Elias made the motion of a signature to show that he had signed for the tickets himself—this was all delivered in dialect and in an excited half-whisper.

He began wrapping up the chicken bones in old newspaper, wiping his hands and face with its pages. He was certain the Coopers were carrying the weight of recent tragic events. One day Jerome and Ghislaine were beside themselves with the joys of life and, almost overnight, it was as if some bad news had been broken. They had, when they first moved in, been the type of couple to kiss in the rain but all that seeeemed over and done with. The young woman carried herself fearfully and the man, himself out of sorts, would be gone for weeks at time, even during term time.

Et alors—there was a call to say that someone had thrown a cat off a balcony in a Block B. Elias was finished with me for the day.

The lobby of Block D housed an empty pool and marble tiles in many shades that were not orange and not pink. It was a ten-storey building so I could have imagined traffic jams at certain hours of the day by the single golden-doored lift. I was not familiar enough with myself to know if I was the type to snoop through letter boxes—no harm from peering in one or two—but that was my inclination when I got inside. The building was silent but not serene. Even from the lobby there was the aura of an old asylum. There was another door with another keypad—4963 was no use—and on either side of the letter boxes was a stickle-board list of residents' names. As I examined the names—Beauger, Grappe, Labet—I thought of Eagleback living here and what he might be doing. One o'clock—perhaps he had come home for lunch. I would have to get to know his routines.

Young Girl, Go Slowly

What if, once upon a time, I read a book that said, 'What we had is gone, what we are is no more. I have never thought it was my place to say these things. That one's love for another is never something to be truly sure of. Sadness is not a permanent state. There is no such thing as security without captivity. You must help yourself to what it is you think you want from life. I would like to help you realise all this, and something else too. That it is possible, when it comes to love, to use the same language but in different ways. And it is also impossible for someone to describe something they can't see.'

Unstory

October 13th 2011, Café la Perle. Mum and Dad want to visit. They're coming to see what's become of me. They say. They want to see Paris. They say they'll get a hotel. They'd want to get a bloody hotel. I can't have them seeing where I live.

October 27th 2011, Café la Perle. They're coming by ferry. Who gets the ferry nowadays? It makes me sad just to think of it.

October 30th 2011, La Pure Café. They want to know about parking. Is there good parking in Paris? No, Dad, there is very bad parking in Paris. Paris is full.

November 3rd 2011, Rose Bakery. I don't know what brought me to Paris (bonbons, music, boys) but I do know what sent me out of Ireland. My attitude to my body is one thing. It's the sag in my mattress, the sweat on my pillow. My splintered nails, my matted hair, my sweaty pits. Dad's is—another thing. The way he talks about it—Tony Blair yes, yes—his cancer is a dinky little thing. But I've seen it wash right through him, bleaching him from the inside. Your body is your life story he says, but I'd rather he stayed perfect. I'd rather he went bang. A bullet in the head, fine. He says it doesn't matter how many times you beat cancer as long as you beat it. But I don't think he's beaten anything. It's down an alley waiting to fuck him over. It'll leave him chopped up in a bin bag. And Dad chooses to ignore this scenario with God, God, God. The day I left he adopted the tone of a TV priest—soft and persuasive and pervy. It was June 3rd, the feast day of St Kevin. As I packed I listened to Dad's stories about this hermit monk of Glendalough. He's told me these stories before, but I've a mind like a sieve for anything God, God, God. I got stood up on my first date and Dad said it was God's will. I failed the Leaving and that was God's punishment. What did God have to say about Tony Blair? St Kevin was a hundred and fucking twenty when he died. A man so noble and pure that when he was born his mother felt no labour pains, none at all, and the snow that fell on the day of his birth melted as it hit the ground. At the age of seven, Kevin's parents sent him to a monastery in Cornwall or Glendalough or somewhere. One day, Kevin was kneeling with his arms outstretched in prayer, when a bloody blackbird landed in his palm and proceeded to construct a nest. Kevin remained perfectly still so as not to disturb the bird. For the full forty days of Lent. The bird fed him with berries and nuts and licorice allsorts. By the end of Lent, the last hatchlings had flown from the nest and Kevin returned to the monastery to celebrate Easter. Was this supposed to keep me in Ireland? I don't think Dad knew what he was saying except that he was saying what he thought had to be said. Later in life, Kevin considered an invitation to Rome to gather relics for his monastery. There was still a bounce in his step but he resisted the urge to travel in order to focus on life in the monastery. Birds don't hatch their eggs while they're flying, he said. Righto, Dad. I told him I loved him to shut him up. He needs to hear that more often. We sat in the car and he squeezed my knee and said, God bless. I put it down to shyness. And the news blaring. Let him listen to it if he wants. He needs to hear what's going on in the world.

I Tried To Forget Eagleback, Truly I Did

I tried to develop feelings for Amadou who told me I needed a husband, at least one. I tried to develop feelings for the fish man and the veg man and the meat man. I tried to fall for Hippolyte who would fall for anyone, anything—a bird, a little lamb—apart from me. I didn't think it would be possible but I tried to develop real feelings for Daniel.

Ségo and I were carrying carcasses out of the walk-in fridge. I was listening, insofar as I was taking it in, to her story of A__ B__'s visit.

—How did he enjoy the pork?

—Loved the pig. Too much if you ask me. Anyway, how about you? Were you in the neighborhood and just decided to drop by?

It's not as though I didn't like talking to Ségo but I'd never met and didn't want to meet the girl who didn't want to avoid her friends from time to time.

—Headache? she said.

—No. I just wasn't here.

—You know something, I value your honesty. I wish other people were so straightforward. It's just your timing I didn't appreciate.

Even if I had been rehearsing it all night I couldn't have come up with a good reason for my absence. Withholding my visit to Léon Frot from Ségo was a concern—as when I had forgotten to wash the salad properly, say—but I put that out of my mind because there was work to be getting on with.

—So you still work here?

—Hope so, I said.

—Because I kind of got mixed messages. From you. Just that one time, yesterday, when you didn't show up for the most important day in our restaurant's history.

—Sorry?

—Are you? Because I'm worried that you're becoming a disruptive influence, she said.

—How can I be a disruptive influence if I'm not here?

Ségo laughed and kissed me on the forehead and said ohdearohdear and whispered something lovely to welcome me back.

—It's a strange path that's led you here, I'll grant you that. You're a funny one, I'll grant you that too.

We sailed along for a while, wordlessly moving onto the preparation of the lamb. Butchering had, in the months I had worked there, become my favourite form of relaxation. A whole animal was too much work for me on my own. I had tried it once or twice and made a mess of it.

The head, skin and feet of this beast had already been removed and the first job was to deal with the innards. Hooks, a saw and a cleaver. The equipment was clean and standing by. Whether she was doing pastry or finding a lamb's pelvic bone, or counting off the ribs with her eyes closed, Ségo operated by touch—it always seemed as if she could work blindfolded had it been required. And when she sawed through the top of the spine, this was a thrill. Sometimes I was allowed to remove the neck but usually I wasn't allowed to do anything more than scrape the membrane from the ribs. It went without saying that the trimmings became mince for the staff meal.

—The smart thing to do would be for me to leave here, I said.

Ségo craned her neck for a moment then returned to removing the animal's shoulder blade.

—If any of us was really smart we wouldn't be here at all. You working today or not?

—Dunno.

—It's your decision.

—I don't want to let you down again.

—There, you've made a decision.

—I didn't say that.

Now that I was somehow getting closer to Eagleback, I failed to see how I could stay at Gravy. Would I survive without Ségo? It would certainly take nerve to live without her—but she was just a socket, and sockets allowed other things to work. Pots boiled that way. But you didn't think about sockets if you didn't need to use one.

—Did you pause there because you wanted me to contradict you? she said.

Normally I'd have been itching to get the lamb's shoulder braising as soon as she was finished with it, but I was skulking around it without actually doing anything useful.

—I'll be straight with you, Ségo said. You can't leave here. It's not advisable, anyway.

—Why not?

—You and Amadou are going to cook lunch and then we're going to have a talk. You and me and Daniel.

—What about?

—Work. Life. You. Normal stuff.

—What's normal stuff?

—Stuff we should have spoken about a long time ago.

I ran. I had to. Besides.

I would have preferred to imagine a world where people ran away from me—as things stood, I ran away from people and things and situations and, above all, information that could have led me somewhere other than Eagleback. Perhaps I should have stayed to listen, but it was too frightening to think of what Ségo might say to me. It wasn't my intention to be so ungrateful. I only wished I could have said so instead of running along Saint Maur while counting one, two, three, fifteen, hundreds, none.

I went to my apartment but it was impossible to settle. I had no idea if Elias would let me stay with him, so I made the most of the bathroom, standing under the cold shower for as long as I could bear. There was some Fairy liquid left and I washed my hair and found myself wishing I took better care of myself.

I did my best to make the place presentable but there wasn't much I could do other than flip the mattress. Rather than pace the floor any more, I packed what I could into a supermarket bag and counted out my money—eighty euro plus change. I was about to go out the door when I heard Daniel outside. The door was so flimsy that the rattling was no more than someone shaking a box of crackers. I didn't wait—I dragged the mattress towards the window and dumped it outside to cushion my fall. My legs were already over the side of the windowsill of their own accord. I fidgeted myself sideways and pushed myself off just as I heard Daniel call out. I couldn't see anything when I landed—and I didn't feel much beside elation and a stinging wrist. It didn't matter that I had bitten my tongue and my mouth was bleeding. I ricocheted to my feet and ran through the courtyard, past the rotten pine towards a spooky passageway and out to the street.

I ran past Daniel's parked bike uphill towards Buttes Chaumont. At first it felt as if I was running underwater—but once through the gates of the park I started to feel better, accelerating up the hill past big breathing sequoias and a simple blue sky from a runner's tilting perspective. There was the smell of ripening summer as well as drying earth and the sweetness of frying waffles. It had been some days since I had run anywhere—I had been so preoccupied—so the firm strike of my clogs on the path and the stretch of my legs under me made me feel plainly alive, as if I had taken fuel onboard and would have a full day of easy running ahead of me. The heat of exertion under my ribs faded as I gathered speed, the undertow of guilt and adrenalin from evading Daniel propelling me through the eastern exit of the park and towards Place Des Fêtes. Puzzled looks met the young woman running in the chef's gear and, as was my habit, I was careful to avoid anyone's eye.

Unstory

November 15th 2011, Le Bal Café. I wonder what it would happen if Jerome met Mum and Dad. I mentioned it to him and he quickly said, What's the point in meeting them if this isn't going to last? Then he apologised almost as quickly. Whatever was wrong with meeting my parents, we could talk about it another time. At least Jerome is Australian. It's too long ago to get worked up about now, but no doubt that introducing them to Caesar was a bad idea. It wasn't Caesar's fault to be from Ghana and my boyfriend at the same time. It could have been his colour, it could have been his charm—he was very charming—or it could have been his religion, which wasn't theirs. Or it could have been something else. They hated the way Caesar spoke—so slowly—as well as most of what he said. The gold tooth that could have been a shiny raisin. They hated his eyes because they seemed yellow. Yellow eyes, I heard them whispering. At least Mum kept her distance, fascinated by Caesar and scared of him. And it's uncanny the way Dad decides on his subjects when talking to people he doesn't know. Uncanny his gift for distorting a perfectly ordinary

89

moment. He could startle a murder victim's parents by inquiring if their child hadn't been asking for it. Dad chose to talk to Caesar about African debt cancellation, as if they were cancelling his debts. Caesar was in his final year of dentistry. His only debts were student loans. At least none of that will happen when they meet Jerome.

$$\text{Love} = 8 + .5Y - .2P + .9Hm + .3Mf + J - .3G$$
$$- .5(Sm - Sf)2 + I + 1.5C$$

My strength faded as soon as I entered Elias' room and saw him asleep with his mouth open. A smell unlike anything other than I had experienced—rancid milk stirred into seaweed—and I thought he was dead.

My dumb luck.

When he awoke and saw me there, Elias stood to greet me and kicked the contents of a brimming bowl all over our feet. We began to quarrel unintelligibly for a moment, our feet sticky with broth, until I was moved by the pathetic sight of him mopping it up.

I tried to explain myself enthusiastically. The day before had been so much fun that I wanted to be his friend, I said. And, since we were friends, was there any way he could help me out with a roof over my head for a few nights? Either Elias refused to believe me or he couldn't understand. When I told him I wanted to help him reconnect with his daughter, Elias brought a particular sense of tenderness to the words 'pas possible'.

He produced another thumbed photo of Yasmine—folded unfortunately at the eyeline—from the front pocket of his overalls.

—Habibi Albi, he said.

I was lost in Yasmine's sad face when I saw them through the mesh of Elias' window—Eagleback and his wife in the courtyard.

The room went dark. Elias himself and all our talk of his daughter and their shared future retreated into the shadows.

I had not set eyes on Eagleback since the pâtisserie and the jolt was more intense this time, as though a match head was scratching against the courtyard wall; and the air was filling with the bite of sulphur and the burst of pale flame. And I understood what I didn't before, what I should have before, that love was assessable, as in an experiment. What I needed to happen, and what wasn't going to happen, was a pale scientist to walk in and on a blackboard write an equation for love.

—Là, là! Elias said.

I stared hard at Ghislaine, a slight woman who was nearly toppled by a condor's nose. Her colouring was obviously dark but her face was an unfortunate mess of khaki freckles. Her jogging gear aged her at the same time as lending her youth. The bouncy hairdo did nothing for her either, but that wasn't the point—she was not supposed to exist, not here. Besides.

At the window Eagleback and wife were leaning forwards. Their jaws were rotating and their mouths gaping in disbelief, as if they were pantomiming the closing of a deal in a street bazaar. Eagleback was raising his arms and letting them fall by his side. They were exhausted-looking, each of them—I was building a blooming picture of a relationship in deterioration when he disappeared from view. I stepped out into the courtyard just as they reached the street, kissing briskly before he stepped into a car—a Smart car—and drove off.

Until I followed his wife along the street and into a supermarket and closely along the aisles, finding Eagleback had been a simple matter of necessity—but this was a first, just as today had been my first time jobless, homeless, first time fugitive, of sorts. It may have been an attractive idea, at one point, when I didn't exist—and didn't understand—but now I couldn't have feared anything more than being homeless. I was used to living with very little, but now that I understood what it meant to be in the world—the small world that I knew—it felt strange to have nothing.

Ghislaine was not making an orderly circuit of the aisles. I had to zigzag in order to keep up with her. Here it became difficult because she stopped in front of the crisp-breads to take a call. I shrunk into my chef's clothing. By checking my breathing and creeping sideways, I was able to listen—important to make it seem as though I was fascinated by biscuits. There was nothing in her trolley apart from a single grapefruit. My own basket contained sponge fingers and set of plastic cutlery.

She was getting pretty hot at someone on the phone—I had to assume it was him. Yes, she was calling him Jerome. It shocked me to hear him being called that.

She was saying something about the car and the call ended abruptly. She looked sorry and sore at the world and I was beginning to regret my initial impression of her. Now Ghislaine had returned to the shop's entrance where, without much intent, she was examining apples. There was a security guard around somewhere—a sleepy looking African—and I wondered if he was watching me watching her. I got rid of my shopping and I walked to the door, where it would be easier to mind my own business. It wasn't difficult to adopt my absent demeanour—practiced in my hours on patrol at Bertrand Rose—as I kept an eye on Ghislaine as she waited to pay.

The electronic doors parted and Ghislaine exited, none the wiser to my existence. She held herself more gracefully, more poised than I had first decided—thick in the waist but as light up top as I was. Such was the dismay on her face as she tossed the fruit in her hand that I wanted to offer her some supermarket tulips.

Seeing her pass the entrance to their building and turn left onto Charonne caught me unawares. She had nearly reached the café on the corner at Voltaire by the time I had caught up with her.

Le Rouge Limé was the same as any other café in the area—one of those places that resembled movie sets. I had to urge myself to follow her inside, taking a seat as she acknowledged me with an absent smile. Saying hello didn't feel like recklessness, more that Ghislaine would rumble me if I didn't strike up a conversation soon.

I asked for a glass of hot milk from the waiter who had just delivered her coffee. In the event that I would be nursing it for some time, I stressed that the milk should be frothed and piping hot.

In the end, it was Ghislaine who spoke to me. She had heard my odd French when I addressed the waiter.

—Do we meet again? she said.

—Sorry?

—Your face is something I know. May I ask which is it you're from?

—Ireland, I said.

The first time I had given a straight answer to the question.

—You live on the potato mashings, yes? And the Irish are somewhere addicted to milk.

—I like froth.

Ghislaine laughed then removed a book from her handbag, a science textbook of some kind.

—Do you run? I said.

She panted to suggest fatigue then continued.

—Paris is so permanently very grey. If you are American I have ask to you to make a description of the smog.

The milk arrived and I drank it too fast, burning the roof of my mouth.

—Are you occupied in your life? I imagine already you are brigand in Ireland. I have been there almost one time.

—It's so beautiful, I said.

—Your family. They are in Paris with you?

—No, I said.

—You are not a chocolate pizza.

—What?

—You can't make everyone happy. And you are staying at?

—Buttes Chaumont, I said. The hills are good for your thighs. If ever you need a running partner.

—Why not? Why not? Why not?

The vulgar lighting made Ghislaine's freckles dance as she repeated these words. Her nose, moving in and out of the light, was certainly striking. Apart from the slick curls, it was as if she has been sculpted in a hurry.

We talked some more and before I knew it we were making an arrangement to meet on that corner the following evening. I was staring at my empty glass when she asked my name. I considered the question, my muscle tone vaporising and my joints constricting—tiny spiders in my veins.

Staring at the contents of my glass, I nearly said my name was Hot Milk. Then, despite doing my best to avoid it, I couldn't resist saying I too was called Ghislaine.

I left the café at the right moment, dipping into Charonne métro just in time to see Eagleback approach with his face downcast. I crouched on the stairs until I was sure he had gone inside, making sure to return to Léon Frot by a route that avoided the café.

It was late when I got back and Elias was asleep in his chair. Same room—but a new silence. I slept restlessly on the bare floor, needless to say. I woke to see him gravely making coffee and accompanying it with a cough that lasted longer than a news bulletin. It was four in the morning and he was wearing winter socks that had successfully collected most of the dirt on his floor. It was intriguing to think what he had gathered there, and I found myself thinking of it for the first time—whether he was in his right mind at all. The way he looked at you like you had caused him an injury.

Over a breakfast of burned coffee and the previous day's bread, Elias explained himself—sitting at a certain angle so that I had a good view of his testicles sliding out of the bottom of his shorts. In a week he would be going to Tunisia to see his family by which time I would have to find alternative accommodation. Elias' reasons for going home were private, he said, drawing his finger across his neck for emphasis, the way you would when threatening murder.

Early the Following Morning

I positioned myself near the entrance to Eagleback's building—a neat perch on the kerb between a bin and the back of a van from where I could observe the morning exodus. There wasn't a second when I was off high alert.

I stared without wavering at the glass doors and saw every kind of whacked-out character—serious faces, sad faces, puzzled ones—but no one resembling Eagleback or even Ghislaine. I needed to be careful as far as she was concerned. Someone could hop in the van and drive away quickly and I would be exposed. Being found sitting on the street as Ghislaine left for work would not stand up to much questioning. I was ready to roll away onto my stomach and run for cover if the moment called for it.

There they were—it was difficult not to erupt to my feet and bow from the waist. But I had forgotten about their car so it was a shock when I saw Ghislaine crossing towards my side of the street, where it had been parked three or four spaces along. I bounced around on my haunches with my bum scraping the ground before taking off in the beginning of a clumsy sprint. To cross the road I had to risk being seen by Eagleback, who was taking his time following her. I moved so fast that I couldn't have been more than a pale blur.

I was now crouched on the apartment side of the street and they were opposite me, in a world of their own. Eagleback said something and whatever it was Ghislaine nodded and slipped into the car without a reply. Now he was alone on the street, his face creasing and straightening, creasing and straightening, as he fought tears. His eyes were as wild as you would see in a mug shot. Thus I found myself following him along the street to school.

Following someone—or following them undetected—is not a skill easily acquired. There Eagleback was and there was I ten feet behind.

I'd never seen Saint Maur so busy. The pavement was mercifully thick with children, even an old man with a cane offered cover. He slowed me down too much though, so jaywalking was called for—an arm aloft as I stepped into busy traffic. Eagleback accelerated. His outfit was easy to track and when I caught up I used another huddle of children as a shield. But they were dragging their feet and Eagleback was accelerating away. It would have been much easier if I had known where he was going. I could have drifted back a little, been less eager. As it was, I got close enough to synchronise footsteps.

The streets around the school were filthy with 4x4s depositing children. Toddlers emerged from moist goodbyes, the vibration of their high-pitched voices harmonising with idling engines. I milled around amongst the parents who had arrived on foot. I took my chances that Eagleback hadn't seen me. My outfit was the problem—I was the only one in kitchen clogs.

Eagleback had to be one of the youngest teachers and, from the amount of handshakes he fielded as he entered the playground, the most popular. My view was momentarily obscured by smoke from the exhaust of a motorbike, this one dropping off a child in soccer boots. The kid was standing apart from his friends—he might not have had any—and I used him as cover. I removed a week-old chouquette from my pocket and handed it to him. The kid regarded the morsel with suspicion and me with bafflement. Now I got on one knee to hide—as if I was making a proposal. Having regarded it with contempt, the kid was now eating the pastry.

Eagleback was buzzing around, rounding up the children while taking an interest in their playground game. He seemed to be enjoying himself as much as they were. This deepened my curiosity—there wasn't a trace of the distress he had shown on Léon Frot.

I was still kneeling, with the child in the soccer boots awaiting my next move. Only when I told him that there was no more food did I realise that my hand was clenched white around his.

The fading exhaust fumes could not have been mistaken for a parting mist but that's the way it appeared to happen. Eagleback was turning around to answer a child who was refusing to line up with the others. The young boy was exhausted from playing and he didn't want to go inside. The boy in the soccer boots ran inside and in the thronged street I stood—certain that Eagleback had seen me. The morning sun was warming the heavy white clouds cushioning the roofs of the school building. I took a moment to bathe in it, almost forgetting for a moment where I was and what I was intending to do.

The corridor as I crept along it seemed to go on forever. Everything was at a different height—the steps were shallower and the door handles were hung lower. Even the water fountain in the corridor was the height of a small chair. The classrooms were screened behind glass walls. Most of the children were still bubbling with the excitement of the playground and I passed unnoticed. The corridors were congested with tiny coats and I could smell wax from the crayon drawings on the walls. A little boy on miniature crutches was chatting with the school nurse.

—Vas y mon chou, she said, addressing the child as though they were lovers.

This was a happy little school—and Eagleback was waiting somewhere in it for me.

Another row of windows and a moment later I was standing at an open door as he led a class of six-year-olds in a song about the seasons. The time for sunshine and holidays and playtime was not far away. He was there before me, absorbed in the music and the important message he was communicating. Now he was becoming a tree, presumably to suggest the coming of autumn. What would I say? Probably I would fall dumb before him. What if he asked me who I was? He would know more than I did.

The children were imitating his movements with their hands above their heads. Eagleback paused the performance to explain the concept of tumbling leaves but the children seemed unhappy until the music resumed. Although he kept his eyes open as he was singing, he did not seem to notice me standing at the classroom door.

I was already halfway into the room by the time Eagleback looked over.

He cut the music and smiled and nodded, as if he had been expecting me. His raised hand silenced the children. He walked past me to the door at quite a slow pace whilst instructing the class to sit at their desks and await his return. The corridor was a better place to talk anyway.

In his hand he held—not a detonator—the remote control for the stereo.

—Do you think it's appropriate to just walk into a school? he said.

—Just wanted to say hello.

—This is a school. There are children.

—Sorry this is a little abrupt. Turning up out of the blue.

—You don't know me. You don't know me and I don't know you.

Some kind of force was inflating him so that he loomed over me. My mouth opened every time he stretched his neck and I let out a laugh.

—Would you prefer it if I called the police? he said. They will be here in two minutes. Unless you go now. Now.

—How about later? We can talk later?

My hand reached for his as he walked to the classroom door.

—Two minutes, they'll be here in two minutes, he said, staring past me before stepping inside and shutting the door. The singing resumed almost immediately.

Funny How Everyone, Even People with No Memory, Need a Break from Being Themselves

After a couple of days staying with Elias I met up with Ghislaine. Smoke was rising from somewhere further along the canal as we ran. There was a whiff of beef tea as I followed her along the towpath. We covered five miles in no time at all and soon we were sitting on a bench in the playground on Square Maurice Gardette. There was an old man with his feet wrapped up in plastic bags on the bench opposite. An unusually lovely melody, something I could tolerate, drifted from his old radio and our lovely evening was such that I wanted to open up to Ghislaine.

Our conversations had to count for something, even though most of it—from my side—was made up. For this purpose, I was recklessly prepared to invent a first love and a first heartbreak.

—I was in love once, I said. Love is great.

—What is so great?

—You know yourself.

—Who is your lover?

—Was, I said.

—Yes, she said. Is.

—Ah no, I said. You know yourself

This was my first time in one of these conversations and I was keeping track of who said what—a little of her and a little of me. Of course, her part involved talking about Eagleback. They had been going to her sister's house in Orléans for Easter and she asked him to buy an egg and—as I knew only too well—he bought an exorbitant chocolate orb and eggs and orbs are not the same thing, are they?

—From Bertrand Rose? she said. An Easter egg is design for children, their palates.

She rhymed palate with weight.

—And the thing he buy cost nearly a hundred euro, more. And it make their niece very bad herself. Another one arrive at the apartment after. And Jerome say he doesn't know anything about that. That is a novelty, no?

—That is, I said.

—Let me get this straightaway, she said. He is frantic and he buy the egg from Bertrand Rose. N'importe quoi. I throw him as far as I believe him. Chocolate orb is helping nobody. We dump it.

The phantom aroma of sweet dough and hot sugar rose from the bench underneath us. It wasn't that I had any pity for Bristles or her colleagues—Cheeks aside—but I had stolen from Ségo and then restlessly patrolled that corner of Paul Bert for days for the cake to end up in Ghislaine's garbage chute.

—This pours over me, she said.

—Do you never run with your husband? I said.

—Quoi?

When she said that, meaning what, I thought she was saying quack. Quack.

—Sorry for asking, I said.

—No, you can ask. But it's going to rain. Let's get ourselves around and around first. Before I am made of sugar.

Ghislaine insisted we stop on Voltaire in another of those movie set cafés. At least we were on the terrace and seated so that each of us could face the street. We were in an enclosure awash with posters for shows and blackboards featuring set menus that offered very little without a supplement, which seemed to defeat the purpose of a set menu.

On the street some woman was applying lipstick while walking and laughing on the phone. A cab driver slept standing up beside his car.

—I will invite you this evening, Ghislaine said.

She wanted a glass of rosé and a cigarette, which she cadged from the waiter. Ghislaine's way of sipping the wine slowly felt advisory, something I wished I had managed that night at Daniel's place. I requested a glass of cold milk, which the waiter wouldn't allow. I asked for Nutella without the crêpe but no to that, too. I took a cup of hot milk instead.

—Do you anyway had the bad problem with wine?

Ghislaine spoke quietly but directly. In this we were the same, she and I. We asked straight questions, because why not?

—Don't like the taste, I said.

—I am not nearly as massive in wine. But you ask me about my husband. Here is the history of him. He is dragging the enormous casserole behind him. Because he fuck people. This is for truth. He live the heterogeneous life. You can already imagine that this is a surprise for me. I am frozen now. And I kiss someone. An accidental guy in Pigalle. What do you think on that? I am wild awake thinking on it.

This brought forth an infinite number of questions—not about the man in Pigalle but about Eagleback. Chief among them was a certainty that I had been among his women. One of them.

I offered Ghislaine a multipurpose, —What happened?

—With my kiss? It happen. It is no good that Jerome is making winkings at me. It is over the balcony I will put him. I am enormous with sadness. And I am a fountain, always crying. I fear my lachrymal functions will be extinguished.

—What can you do?

—Change is an impossible dream. Geometry has always been an abysmal mystery. For example, one and one doesn't necessary equal two all the time. Not good because halfs are handicapped unity that depend on all other half to make one. You see when I meet Jerome at first it is a really good time. We are ideal pirates. But quite simple, he believe in facile money. What is the? I pay the boring things. Detergent and the ticket in particular for the métro. I do not deserve this picture. Now he has the supreme job in the school, they do him an assistant to the chef. This is very genial. Of course, he always occupies himself spending surprise money on the cake no one likes in all of the day. He is a child. It is the superb word to use.

—Was he having an affair?

—This is too much, I'm sorry. Your face, I can see. And you are thinking so much that I am hurt. Nothing he can do is hurt me. It pours over me. Okay, now I am stupid with wine and I want to run this away. Is that how you say it? Run it away?

Ghislaine left to pay with a faithful promise that we would run at full pace all the way back to Léon Frot. As I was beginning to lament another wasted run, I noticed something on the wall behind where Ghislaine had been sitting—a sign with my face on it.

I peeled the poster from the wall making sure to appear as serene as possible to anyone watching. I had not seen myself since those pictures taken by Ellen from Illinois and this one explained very little other than being as bleak a thing as I'd ever seen. It was a formal pose and the portrait was precisely framed—but I was huddled into myself, as soulful as a billygoat, and I wanted never to look like that again.

Under the picture were the words—Personne Disparue.

The poster said that I had last been seen at Gravy two days previously and that I was likely to appear disorientated or distressed. It explained that I spoke bad French and was more comfortable in English. My calm expression in the picture, staring ahead—some kind of visionary saint—seemed to foretell disaster.

When Ghislaine returned the poster was crumpled so tightly that I was able to enclose it within my fist.

Daniel #3

Eva missed work from time to time but never without letting anyone know. Daniel spent a day and a night investigating her world, or what he assumed was her world, the streets around Buttes Chaumont. There was no sign of her amid the sweaty walls of Rosa Bonheur although any one of the backpackers or junkie runaways had her look. No sign of her in any of the non-denominational phone shops on Rue de Crimée or in the nano-village around Avenue Secrétan. He thought he caught a glimpse of those chef's pants outside Bolivar métro but no.

Daniel had just gone to bed when his father sent word (via an assistant) that someone wanted to speak to him. No matter that it was five in the morning in France. Two minutes later, Eva's father was slowly panting on the line. He sounded subdued and annoyed that Daniel hadn't been relaying enough information.

Tony kept on saying, —How is she?

—I told you. She's well.

—Is she working?

Daniel had the previous weekend visited the Jeu de Paume so found himself saying, —She's actually working as a museum guide.

—What does Eva know about art?

—More than I do, I can barely keep up. She's in that whole gallery scene. Openings and whatnot. It's very, you know.

—No, I don't know. What does she say about us?

—What does she say? I don't think she really thinks about home too much, if you know what I mean. She's busy.

—Do we have to be worried?

—One thing you should not do is worry, Daniel said. She has a bunch of nice friends, she lives in an amazing place. It's not a million miles from the Père Lachaise cemetery, in case you're a Jim Morrison fan.

—I'm not.

—Look at it this way. You're a young woman, you're in Paris. Wouldn't you be having a ball?

—I suppose. But she's never been the type of girl to have a ball.

—A ball is what she's having. That's all you need to know. I'm seeing her later. Want me to say anything?

Tony hung up. The poor man was worried about his daughter and Daniel hadn't answered one of his questions truthfully. People liked to say you withheld information in order to protect someone; the truth was Daniel was keeping Eva for himself. He put up those posters for his own sake and no one else's.

Some years ago, on the morning of his thirteenth birthday, Daniel's father took him for a drive along Beachside Avenue in Westport. They'd come out before breakfast and, because his father was wearing Keds, Daniel thought they were going to play tennis. He wondered about the rackets. He was really starving, too, but the important part came when they passed through some unfinished gates into a dirty field. This was not the kind of place they ever went on a Sunday and, until his father urged him to follow him out of the car, Daniel was ready to stay where he was. His father had the delicate step of an indoor man. Yet that morning he was pacing, a boxer at the start of a bout. Daniel was familiar with his attitude to money; Pa was a generous man who gave people whatever they asked him for. Often it was less hassle than not giving, he said. Anyway, at the time when most of his friends were getting bar mitzvahs, this mulish teenager was about to receive an absurd parcel of land worth, in today's money, about fifteen million dollars.

Of course, Daniel's father slipped in the mud as he said this. Daniel helped him up, the first time he had ever done that.

Pa's usual propriety returned when he spoke, hands on hips and chin raised.

—Daniel, he said. Your brother is gone. Your sister is dead to the world. Odds are everything will be yours. My hope for you is that your path will always lead you back here. And when it does I hope you'll think of this morning.

Most of it was over Daniel's head. All he knew was he didn't deserve this gift and didn't really want it. He would have been more grateful for a hot dog from Blackie's. He studied the mud stains on the knees of his father's chinos. It became clear this was a smiling, expectant Oscar speech, exactly the kind of thing his father never did but was doing now.

This can't be mine, Daniel thought. This should belong to someone else.

—It's big, is all he said.

Daniel's father took some wet, sour-smelling leaves and soulfully pressed them into his son's pocket.

—This is a taste of what's to come.

This was not the only thing he said that day that Daniel didn't understand, but he was able to gather one thing: they barely knew each other, by a teenager's measurements anyway, but his father seemed to love him (deeply, by their family's standards) and he was determined that this would be a positive and momentous morning. And somehow that positivity and momentousness would colour Daniel's life. A few years later, around the time of the epiphany of the tasseled loafers, Daniel decided he'd had enough of the positive and momentous life. Never mind that his prized field in Connecticut had doubled in value or that the family's building in Manhattan was good enough for Ted Turner and Billy Joel. It was not the back story he wanted.

It wasn't exactly embedding with the troops, but Daniel was proving himself by bussing tables, slowly and poorly, at the Wiltshire Inn downtown. His job was to float trays from one end of the room to the other. He was twenty; too young to drink but old enough to smoke and some nights he would be so high that he would have to wear glasses to disguise his swirling eyes. Tracy, his manager, assumed he was a flamboyant young man, which wasn't the case.

The floor team were mostly Hispanic, and all of them surly, and he was truly grateful for the language barrier. The floor staff weren't required to speak, anyway, and they weren't supposed to. This is how Daniel's evenings passed, hazy and eventless, until one night his father walked in. It was unusual to see either of his parents anywhere below MSG. On top of that, his father had heart attacks like other people took vacations and Daniel hadn't seen him since the last episode. Nor had he told anyone where he was working. Nevertheless, his father was unaffectedly happy to see him, even though Daniel nearly ran him over with a full tray of water glasses.

His father was on the town with some men who resembled hotel concierges but were probably lawyers. He was watchfully sipping Vichy Catalan but his friends were irascibly ordering top-shelf cocktails and getting everything slightly wrong. Their fierce faces suggested a hearty and recent ingestion of cocaine. Pa, on the other hand, was calm. His gambler's eye absorbing the busy room, the door, and Daniel.

The Wiltshire had two sections: Saint Tropez, where his father and his friends were, and Siberia, the patio. Daniel thought it was a good idea to stick to the patio. But each time he looked at the floor to avoid his father's gaze, Tracy told him to concentrate on the room. When his father came to find him, Daniel tried to hide behind some greenery. He was so wasted that the plants were fizzing. He could hear air entering his lungs. His father said his name four or five times.

—Conrad? Is that lady your manager?

—Uh huh.

—It's just that she said she was going to get Daniel to refill our water and then you came over and you refilled the water. Is everything okay, Conrad? No, you're not okay. You're ripped, aren't you?

Out of ideas, Daniel stood to attention. His father's hands fell to his side as if to say, Come on, enough.

—No, Daniel said.

This wasn't his father's first humiliation. At seventeen, Daniel liked to say he was the only son of a widowed school janitor from Louisiana. At nineteen, he moved onto being an English 'scholar', with a vowel-driven accent to match.

—No? Do you not have anything else to say for yourself? I'm listening.

Daniel was kissing the air in front of him. Tracy tilted her head from the garden's entrance to say she had noticed. Daniel left a trail of sparks, and didn't stop moving all night. In lulls he took to sweeping the sidewalk, almost polishing it. Misting and polishing glasses behind the bar.

Pa kept looking his way. And what a look he was giving off, full of kindness and decency and confusion. Later, Tracy came over to tell Daniel that the quiet man in the booth with all the rich idiots had left a tip for the hardworking busboy.

—Do you know him?

Daniel shook his head, sucking in his breath.

—Doesn't matter, she said. You were exemplary. Stellar work.

Daniel thanked her with a tearful smile then went outside to look for his father, who was standing on Bank Street.

The friends had gone and alone under the streetlamp his father looked stooped and tired; someone who had just lost a very large bet. Daniel was still carrying an empty tray and he set it down to announce himself. He wanted to ask his father if he'd enjoyed his meal but Pa didn't turn around. Daniel cleared his throat, attempting to eke out the cough over a second or two. He took long breaths, faced the street but when the car came his father got in it without looking back. Stoned Conrad of the yeasty dreadlocks and accents had gone too far. They did talk after that and his family's fund continued to underwrite his existence, but over time his parents didn't want much to do with him.

Daniel was alone and apart from his family. He didn't believe that Eva should live alone and apart from hers.

The Picture in Saint Michel Métro

Exhausted but not from running, and energised but not from running, I made my excuses to Ghislaine with a promise that we would meet the next evening. It was raining warmly but I was for the first time too tired to walk home in it. I knew how to get into the métro without paying, that wasn't the problem. But any journey to the north east of the city would involve changing at Châtelet, something I wanted not to do.

In Saint Michel station, another poster—placed over Liam Neeson's face on a movie advertisement—made me shudder. I could see that someone had graffitied a tear rolling down my cheek. Passengers reached the bottom of the stairs and pushed past me. One strong shove, given my disrepair, would have sent me under a train.

The train arrived and I felt its roar.

Onboard there was no opportunity to recover from seeing my face on a poster. My sweaty hands kept slipping on the rail. Just as long as I could survive until Châtelet I could try walking again. Two stops, one more after this one. Whether it was the stale sweat or my stranglehold on the handrail or the forceful way in which

I stood my ground as passengers disembarked at Cité, the other people standing in the carriage gave me plenty of room. Some tourists headed for the airport struggled on with their bags—I gave them no leeway although I did wonder upon seeing them if there was a way out of this city. There had to be ways.

Almost dancing off the train when it arrived at Châtelet, I felt a familiar uneasiness. It sent me to a bench for respite as the other passengers made their way towards their connections and the exits. There was no noise from any trains, no noise at all in the station but the voices from the stairwell—the laughter fading to a surprisingly tuneful murmur.

I could hardly begin to get myself up the escalator to the exit, through the stench of human waste, the sickliness of the lighting, past shiny, sticky walls and the withdrawn faces of the passengers on their way to the trains, past the never-ending battle amongst the station's permanent residents for the best pitch to spend the night—and the sense that I had once been one of them.

Elias' door was locked when I returned and attached to it was one of the posters. I didn't take off, as earlier I might have done. My jaw was in my chest and I needed somewhere to sleep, even for an hour or two. The room housing the gardening equipment was locked and I did not want to insult Elias, who had been so kind, by drawing too much attention to myself.

My hair and skin were greasy from the run and the simmering threat of rain in the sky when I stepped onto Léon Frot came as a kind of relief. I stood under it and watched the water bounce off me.

I was haunting the street in search of a free doorway—a body was stirring at the entrance to the recruitment agency—when I saw the welcoming bundle outside the Monoprix. The cardboard was packed up so tightly that no matter how hard I pulled I was unable to release any. But I found that by pushing two bundles together I could construct a makeshift platform and, pleased by this, I settled down to rest.

I had been out for the count and was taking no notice of the person shoving me—until I was being rocked back and forth so violently that my forehead cracked against the supermarket's locked door. When I turned around, the young woman's eyes spoke before she did. I was in her spot and I was going to have to move.

She was expressionless and spoke neither French nor English—was there barbed-wire in her throat?—although there was nothing much to misinterpret.

I heard her shout, —Ti qij rrobt.

I'm still not sure what that means, but she might have been saying she would fuck everything I owned.

Now I was being dragged across a wet pavement by my hair. I tried to explain that I meant no harm, that I could be on my way, but I was silenced by the crack of a knee against my cheekbone. The dehydrating taste of blood, familiar from my leap from my apartment window, returned to my mouth. The girl feigned walking away then brought the sole of her dirty running shoe to within centimetres of my face, a neat trick. I had survived that at least. Then a good idea—I thought I could divert her by crossing the road but as soon as I moved the girl had me by the hair again and then I was on the ground where she kicked me, just once but very heavily into my chest.

This wasn't the end of it—each time I tried to get to my feet I received a blow, either to my ribs or my head. Columns of snot merged with the blood from my nose. The girl was shouting but after a point I couldn't hear a thing, which served to emphasize everything else. I thought I might be imagining the tearing sensation, as if she was pulling out some of my hair, but I didn't think to touch it to find out.

I tried to tell the girl I'd had enough long before the notion occurred to her. Again she said, —Ti qij rrobt.

She had an industrious way about her, frowning with concentration as she continued to kick me. I curled myself into the size of a pillow and for no good reason I yawned—because I felt this is not happening to me I could actually yawn, as though I had all the time in the world to reflect that I was incapable of making myself vanish, which was all I wanted to happen. I wasn't there. It felt like I wasn't there. Everything, even the creaking sky, became translucent and for a moment I just drifted off—which was some feat, considering what was going on.

The morning heat was making vague, nasty statements. I was sitting on the kerb outside Gravy—exhausted and feeling as old as coal—when Ségo arrived.

I had not gone up in the world since we had seen each other last. There was crusted blood around my mouth and on my cheeks. My hair—some of it had been torn out—was thick with dried puddle water. My hands and fingernails were blackened. I couldn't do anything about the flies circling my head.

Ségo saw fit to address me warmly. —Did you get in a fight?

—Someone got in a fight with me.

The naughty step.

—Arms up, Ségo said. Give me a cuddle.

We hugged without saying much more. My petulance was related to shame—that in running away from the restaurant when they needed me I had behaved terribly, that I had refused Ségo's kindness and I had collected everything she had done for me and thrown it in her face.

An extended silence as she took me in. My various farmyard aromas thickened the air. But the smell was the least of it.

116

—Did you know how worried you made us? And you look gross. You look like you have something. Have you washed since you left?

—What's that got to do with anything?

—You don't look good.

—Can we make this a little faster? There's some things I need to do.

—Like what. Do please tell me what it is exactly you need to do in a state like that.

—I could do with some money actually. Does the vegetable store need looking at? Bet Amadou has left it in a mess.

—I don't think we need to concern ourselves with that right now. We've been looking for you. Poor Daniel's been out of his mind.

—The posters? I said.

—You saw them?

—Here and there.

—Where here and there?

—Where have I been? Where am I living?

—You want to tell me that?

—No.

—Maybe you're happy living the way you're living.

—I am.

—But there are some things I think you should know.

—There's nothing I need to know.

—In that case, let me put it this way. There is some simple information I feel I should share with you and you are free disregard it if you wish. Do you know what you were wearing when I first met you? Do you know where you were? What you were doing? Can you remember anything?

—Not a thing.

—Okay, I believe you. I've asked you before and you said you didn't know. If you don't know you don't know. So, let's go to my place and get you cleaned up. Then we'll start with what I know.

Ségo's idea to go to her apartment was not phrased as a question. That we travelled there by taxi suggested some kind of emergency—how unusual and unpleasant to view the streets from that angle and at that speed.

She hung around in the bathroom until she was satisfied that I was going to wash instead of smashing the window and throwing myself out onto the street. Not having one of my own anymore, I had a fascination with other people's bathrooms. Of course, another flick through the notebook would be appropriate. I would read it in the bath—that's what people did, even though this was the first time I had taken one. Until now it had been the watering-can trickle of the shower in the apartment or nothing at all.

The rising steam freed me from having to look at myself in the mirror. The water pressure was so strong that the rapidly filling bath resembled a basin of milk. I knew I was in there somewhere. Dirty and naked but mostly obscured by steam like an anguished portraitist had changed his mind and was trying to paint over me at the last minute. My ribs were sending out the signals normally emitted by my forehead. I had to admire the girl who had given me the beating—she was thorough. And there was no way that was a fair fight. The bruises shone brighter than fresh liver and some part of my face was singed. Actually getting into the bath was another matter altogether. I heard myself protest as I dropped stiffly into the water—little expressions of shock, one after another, as if I was eavesdropping on a salacious conversation but was being simultaneously sworn to secrecy.

Unstory

December 6th 2011, La Pure Café. I've had a full bottle of
wine already. I should go home but it'll be cold there. Unless I've
left the heat on, then it'll be too hot. Anyway—things don't look
good. They're coming. It must be that Dad is dying and they're
coming to say goodbye. They're really coming. After Christmas,
'when the sales might be on.' As if they need to wait for the sales,
even though Mum'll come with ten empty suitcases. I remember
the first time we went away. This was before Dad made his money.
Malta, the three of us living out of a cheap suitcase in a destroyed
hotel—refugees waiting to be evacuated. I was nervous about
getting lost in the airport, clearing customs, whether there were
bandits in Malta. We played hangman and ate cheese sandwiches,
and I was scared Mum would drown in the sea or get bitten by a
scorpion or be burned through the enormous hole in the ozone
layer. I needn't have worried about any of that. Things aren't great
with Jerome but they're going to change. He's leaving her. From
the sounds of things she mightn't even notice. My place would
work for two. We're always there anyway. Don't even think he's

been in all the rooms. Have I? We've been talking about this. But I haven't told him what I really want. A little place in the country. It has a ring to it. Near Arles. Yes, there. If I'm organised I can do my work from there, too. Imagine that. That's always been my dream, a garden or, better still, a shining conservatory with old metal chairs like these ones. There'll be pots of sweet peas— juice-coloured and barely scented like skin. In the garden I'll have a bench where I can go to read and work if the mood takes me. My God, that's lovely. Better stop dreaming. Better get on with it. I put the rent on the credit card again.

December 18th 2011, La Pure Café. Some things that are guaranteed to happen on my parents' visit. Dad will drink the duty free in a oner and then it'll start. Dying and Tony Blair and St Kevin and all that. They'll go on about what I'm wearing. I'll buy a twin set. Some pearls would keep them quiet. They'll want to know why I don't cook at home. They'll want to know if I go to Mass. No churches in Paris, I'll say. They'll want to know why my mugs don't have handles. Because they're bowls. They'll ask me why I have wallpaper with sparrows on it. Because I do. They'll ask me if I'm on drugs. Course I'm not on drugs. I've run out. What'll they say when they see all the weight I've lost? Nothing, because they won't see it. I haven't kept it in the freezer or anything.

December 23rd 2011, Café la Perle. I could do with going home for Christmas. I could do with going somewhere for Christmas but no invitations as of yet. Jerome said we could spend at least some of Christmas Eve together. A few hours. An hour or two. An hour. Half an hour. Let's see how it goes. I should be spending it with my lover but Christmas dinner will probably consist of Picard chicken nuggets defrosted on the warm pillow. Jerome suggested we meet at BHV and do our Christmas shopping together. He expected me to take it seriously, too. What would have happened—would he have asked my opinion on a gift for his wife? And then he would tell me I was in a funny mood. I wouldn't have put it past him to ask me to hold up knickers in her size. And the thing is, I would have done it.

Shampooed and Scrubbed to Within an Inch of My Life, Listening Face On

The notebook was an SOS. Whoever she was, its author—me—was an expert in self-delusion and by the sounds of it very little else. To become that messed up, I guessed, had to involve some bad luck.

And I was barely able to walk after the bath. The water had been so hot and my bones were tired from all the running and walking and not eating and worrying and the sleeping on Elias' floor and the not sleeping at all. I didn't count on this being easy but climbing onto Ségo's sofa was a stay of execution. There was definitely something off-duty and intimate about it. I asked for a glass of water, in order to appear respectable and to buy some more time.

—You want me to get you water? she said. Shall we follow that with the moules marinière and a glass of Muscadet?

—Water please.

Ségo returned with the glass and some pastries in a grease-slicked bag. Not wanting to do anything out of line, I ate mine above a plate. The whole thing about comfort was beyond me—I had noticed that at the party. A mezzanine of poetry and a ladder to reach it, candles that smelled like cakes and plants that appeared to grow out of her floor, even some contraption—a sculpture on a plinth—that could have been a giant vagina.

Ségo's back was sore, so she wanted to lie on the ground.

—Does this feel strange, if I talk to you from down here?

—A little.

—Too bad. So do we have everything we need?

—For what?

—So we can begin. One day, not long before Christmas, I came to work to find someone had broken a window and had taken up residence in our kitchen, eating whatever she could get her hands on. I had set out an enormous leg of boiled beef the night before and she ate the entire thing. Not to mention downing a litre or two of soup. Not to mention throwing it all up over herself when she was done.

I listened as you would to a ghost story. I had wandered into their lives—no, broken in through a window—without a word on where I'd been. It didn't take me long to set up residence.

Ségo conceded that our set-up was a strange one, that anyone else would have carted me off to the gendarmes.

—You refused to leave the kitchen, she said. I don't know where you'd been but they'd been starving you. You were filthy, much worse than you were today, so I guessed you'd been on the streets for a while. You didn't know how long. I gave up asking questions after a while. Though the answers were funny. Whenever I asked you a question you answered with the object right in front of you. You said your first name was knife and you came from a place called fridge. You gave us a nice look at yourself too. One day you walked into the dining room as naked as a newborn.

There wasn't a word of this I recognized. Nor could I offer any argument. I had to sit back and admire the vagina sculpture and accept what I was being told.

—We got you cleaned up as best we could. You were pretty gamy. And the dirt under your nails. Way deep in there. We made you scrub yourself morning and night. Poor thing. It wasn't so easy to get you under control. You spat in Amadou's face whenever you saw him.

—No wonder he doesn't like me.

—He likes you. We all do. We just worry about you.

—And what happened then?

—You stayed and we never asked you to leave. It would have been a cinch to contact the police. Believe me, there were days when I just wanted to turn you over. But every day that passed you seemed calmer, and you were so comfortable in the kitchen. After a while you became useful. Are you okay with all this? Say stop anytime you like. We don't have to cover everything today.

But I was a natural, she said. Working so quietly and quickly they believed I was meditating. Ségo, who knew more than I did about myself, kept a close eye on me. She let me away with a lot. I was only occasionally moody and she put this down to the headaches.

—At the beginning. Every day the same conversation. It even became funny after a while.

—Why funny?

—Your hallucinations. You were walking a dog. Wherever you wanted to go the dog would follow and wherever the dog wanted to go was fine by you too. It was very sweet.

—What kind of dog was it?

—A bassett hound. I don't know what kind of dog it was!

—Just asking.

—It was a dog. And then you and the dog had to catch the train because you had to go to Paris to meet someone.

Some days it was Nicolas Sarkozy, other times it was Astérix. And this is perfectly normal by the way. Your brain was just scrambled. They ran so many tests. There were sedatives in your system and Hippolyte was considering prescribing you antipsychotic medicine but when your confusion faded he decided against it. He was confident it would correct itself in time. And it did. There were no more hallucinations. There had never been any paranoia, nothing like that. You were a little girl finding her way in the world. You were so worried about everything, getting the slightest thing wrong. Then you found a way to stop.

—How?

—This is going to sound weird, but I think it was because you stopped wondering. Some days I could actually see you not thinking and it made me smile. That's all I ever wanted for you. Whatever we threw at you you picked it up. Kitchen work is hard work. It's not for everyone. But you seemed so happy. You passed every test we set you. Until it changed. You changed.

I had enough of a grasp on reality to mark this change against the morning I had spotted Eagleback at Bertrand Rose. But I was stopped cold by what she said next.

—I'm just not sure what to do, she said. I don't know if I made the right decision to keep you to ourselves. The right decision for your sake. Daniel doesn't think so. Don't you wish you knew more?

Ségo's face was uncharacteristically solemn. I had no clue what she was thinking, whether or not I was about to be reported. Either she had that in mind or she had been in touch with the authorities, the embassy, say, already. My guess was that she would give me one more chance. Calling the authorities would have been cruel, and Ségo was anything but cruel.

She got up from the floor so that she was sitting cross-legged—this was better for her back, she said. She began stroking my hand and I asked her if she knew what had happened the night I got drunk in Daniel's apartment.

—He won't say what, she said.

—He won't say or you won't say?

—He said you kept on calling for Tony Blair.

She let this roll around her mouth, giving the vowels air.

—It's a dream. Or an old password or something, she said. Your mind hangs on to all sorts of dumb shit.

—I don't have any passwords.

—But you must have had, once upon a time. It's debris. It'll wash away.

—Ask a question, I said. When can I get a password?

—Is that what you want? Do you want to look after yourself? From the look of you this morning, you don't do too well for yourself on the streets.

Ségo was on the money there. We turned our attention to food—the brief burst of pleasure of a roast chicken with stale bread to soak up the meat juices.

I wanted to remember my favourite meal as a child. Was it chicken? Or something bad from a packet or good from a blackened pan? Trifle or an August tomato? Whatever it was, I'm sure I licked the spoon and ate with my hands, as I did now, and with my mouth open. I hoped that once upon a time I ate better than a child whose parents had gone away for the weekend. I wondered if my manners had been better than they were now. Did I burp into my hand or a napkin? Would I have folded the napkin across my lap or made it into the shape of a bird?

We ate the meal and I washed up, making a job of it because I wasn't sure what to do with myself now that we had finished talking. The dishes were shining and I made sure the kitchen was spotless from top to bottom. I got a kick from cleaning out her cupboards the way I did at the restaurant.

—Nobody can say you're not good, Ségo said. You clean like some people fuck.

She asked if I wanted to watch a movie—Daniel had told her I had so many still to see. It wasn't even six o'clock but I wanted to sleep for the night, and I dozed during something about a cartoon rat in a kitchen.

When I awoke Ségo asked me one question after another—plans, plans, plans, plans, plans, plans, plans, plans, plans, plans, plans. My refusal to answer any of them amounted to the same thing. I had been lying to her about Eagleback and I was going to continue. The door was open for my return to work, she said. She had all the power in the world over me but, when I said there was no way I could return to Gravy, she didn't pester me to change my mind. She simply gathered up some food and some old clothes for me then followed me to her door.

—One last question, she said. Since you're so keen on answering questions today. What did we do wrong?

I was beginning again, again—and the softness in Ségo's tone made me want to reconsider. Before that day I'd never said goodbye to anyone and now I did so with my eyes lowered. I walked out of her apartment quietly promising a swift return, to which there was no reply.

Cellar Smells

The problems started when I got to Elias' door. The poster with my face on it had been replaced by a handwritten note explaining his absence due to an urgence familiale. He would be gone for another week and, whether anyone liked it or not, all building maintenance would have to wait until then. He had a way with words did Elias.

His door was locked but I remembered him telling me that he had made soup in the basement. Behind an unused bicycle rack I found a distressed metal door. I pushed the door and was caught off guard when it opened. I slipped inside to find myself on a shaking metal ramp that led to a cellar housing the garbage chutes for Block D. I got used to the dry heaving surprisingly quickly, but it was the most violently epileptic barrage of smells I could ever recall. I didn't suppose it mattered what I did down there but I wanted the place tidy anyway. I busied myself with the bits and pieces Ségo had given me—a couple of chef's jackets and my first pair of jeans, some old Levis. A doorless fridge was the cleanest thing in the room and I used it to store the clothes.

I didn't go near the food she had stuffed into the cloth bag but I guessed at a few days' worth in the bags of nuts and sweets—I counted ten bars of cooking chocolate.

The exposed bulb cast an alarming shadow on the cellar wall when I moved so I stayed where I was—operating by match light—and took in the wall-mounted orgy of fuse boxes and ventilation shafts. The dark stains on the wall in the cellar could have been blood as much as oil. It should have been scary to sleep there, but I don't think that I was frightened because I was able to bear most things. I slept soundly amid the sound of snoring insects. But as soon as I was outside in the morning the sky felt buttery and the air—I still think about it now—was sweet.

Unstory

January 1st 2012, Rue de Bac. It'll take a while to get over this one. A woman crying alone in the rain on New Year's Eve. There's an image as big as the city, as old as my heart. I bought some Dior shoes (properly uncomfortable, impractical, black as oil) and since Jerome had told me he was out of town I wanted to take them out for the night. I don't know what the shoes looked like but it felt like I was walking along a set of sharp railings. Schiste had no free tables but it suited me to occupy a stool at the bar for an hour or two early on. There was a compulsory menu featuring some strange game bird which resembled a splatted seagull. I assured them I would drink enough expensive wine to justify not eating. Bafflement was expressed on their part, not a fuck was given on mine. There was the atmosphere of a family gathering. Some nervous characters at one table fingered their water glasses but most of the other customers had joined the waiters on the tiled floor, where they were dancing in formation to some Balkanish music. A man, the owner I think, did air-trombone. The restaurant cat hid in someone's handbag. There was all you would need for the kind of randomly joyful scene that was out of reach of most visitors to Paris. The champagne they gave me tasted like the water you'd used for boiling an egg, and I was brow-beaten into ordering a wooden board piled hugger-mugger with snouts and what have you. Nine o'clock already? No memory whatsoever of the past hour. The water-drinkers vacated their table and wished me a sheepish Bonne Année. I wanted myself gone, too, but moving was a challenge. Very potent, that flat champagne. I had a weird premonition, no, a vision. A prolonged second or two of confusion before I copped that it was real. I don't recall seeing him enter but there beside me, efficient as a mugger, was Jerome. Jerome, with whom I'd been expecting to spend the night. Jerome, for whom I had bought the shoes. We looked at each other—me pretending to be sober, him looking like he needed to run to the bathroom—and smoothly we went along with being strangers. Would he have disowned me if I had spoken? Would I have been able to speak at all? The wine had the better of me. I was groping the air to steady myself when I noticed the woman oozing all over the restaurant's owner. After a few moments of this, as soon as I realised who this person was, I confirmed that I had paid my bill and then I was out of the door and down the road to Belleville métro, the rain destroying my stupid shoes, the perfect end to New Year's Eve—the perfect thing to happen when you have just met your lover's wife.

Ghislaine Pronounced Leaving as Living

The courtyard was quiet. I watched Ghislaine pull the waistband of her leggings up to her midriff and tighten the laces of her running shoes several times before setting off from Léon Frot. I followed her on foot at first. Running did not come naturally to her, especially on her own. I predicted she would divert into Le Rouge Limé, either now or later.

An African family passed by, carrying bibles. Perhaps it was an appropriate day for simple truths. The little boy was getting uppity—his mother was telling him he was no genius and that she was going to kick his ass. It was difficult to keep on top of all the languages around here. But there was something about a Sunday morning that lent credibility to this visit to Eagleback's apartment. I imagined he would be more interested in me today, too, away from work and his sing-songs—then I pictured his face before he walked away from me in the school corridor. Never mind. I was outside Block D and in a minute or two I would be looking at the real thing.

I didn't have to wait too long for a young family to leave so that I could enter the lobby. I called the lift and pressed the button for his floor. The lift's interior was mirrored and the combined reflections were disconcerting. I couldn't help watching myself trying to avoid my reflection. Half-glimpses of several awkward angles. I looked nothing but startled and the more I swivelled to avoid my reflection the more the lip-licking seemed reptilian.

On the eighth floor I found a light switch and walked up and down reading the names on the doors.

Saillard, Buronfosse, Courault, Rietsch, Cooper.

His apartment was at the end of the corridor. I don't remember ringing the bell but the door opened and there he was—as soon as he saw me Eagleback closed his eyes and held his breath.

The thing to do would have been to say hello. His hand gripped the top of the door. I followed the path of his eyes. What I could see of the apartment over his shoulder was as slick as the hospital. A step up from what I was used to—Eagleback looked fine, too. But his hand was raw-looking and now I saw that the patches on his neck, which I had thought to be a skin condition, were in fact scars—an untidy assortment of gummy dents on his forehead and on his cheeks and all the way around his neck.

He stepped into the corridor, reluctant to conduct this conversation on his own territory.

—You know me, I said. You know me. Don't say you don't.

—You shouldn't have come here.

—Can we just have a conversation?

—I can't think what we would have to talk about.

Eagleback was supposed to ask me inside. He was supposed to be pleased to see me.

—You should go, he said. Do you need money? I'm kind of busy right now. But if you need money?

Was this normal? When the person who holds the key to your past tells you he has to go, because he is busy—no more information than that, just busy. And you know what he feels for you is pity, nothing but pity, something you wouldn't waste on an animal.

Eagleback slipped behind the door and was gone. It was another few moments before I could move my legs—one-two, one-two—to walk along his corridor and press the button for the lift.

What was I supposed to do now? Visit the Louvre?

I was, for the first time, stuck. I took a run up the hill to Belleville. Meekly I looked through the windows of Schiste. The doors were locked and, since the notebook had bestowed on the place a kind of immortality, I had to check I was looking at the right place. It was thirty degrees outside but it was winter in there, not that I could see much—the room had been leased by spiders. A perfectly good stockpot had been rolled away on its side. On the bar I spied an old reservations book with the petrified look of a forgotten bible. Where was the cat in the handbag? The owner's trombone? Ghislaine and Jerome on that New Year's Eve, those old songs?

He was my heart and my reason for living. I crowed this over and over.

Ghislaine stood and hugged me when I dropped into Le Rouge Limé as if by chance.

She spoke as though we were old friends.

—Care to sit together by me? Warmed milk, yes?

I was still worried the filth of the cellar had been baked into me. The sourness had to be obvious but she didn't seem to be bothered by it. It wasn't so much the dirt but my attitude to it, which was turning to indifference.

Ghislaine's good manners soon gave way to something more tentative. Her face, even the amazing structure of her nose, seemed over-ripe. When I mentioned that she looked tired, her sense of humour for once was a little off.

—Have you been espying on me? I have no sleep. Maybe tonight I try to count the muttons.

—Good idea.

—I have a portion of information for you, she said. I am going to be leaving Jerome. I am a pigeon that will not return.

—You're kidding, I said. What are you going to do?

—My parents at Grenoble. I cannot sleep in the same roof any more. And I have been a fountain all the day. I do not think Jerome is my teammate. This is for truth. I make it be loud and clear for him.

Even though we were opponents—that's how I viewed us—I regarded her with a sense of kinship. Eagleback half-existed in Ghislaine, in her descriptions of her life, which was partly his life and, I was hoping, partly my life. When I considered it, I half suspected him to walk in and join us.

—It's not like you can't come back, I said. When you've cleared your mind.

—Yes, my clear mind is my premium dream. We are having immortal discourse about this. He fail. He is a quiche.

—A quiche?

—Like that. He fail so many time. For many moments anyway he is seeing this woman. I am wild awake on this and Jerome is lost in a pretty dream of his. Overwhelm completely. He become irritating when I touch him, so many perfect signs. He answer the phone when there is no ringing. When it ring he disappear. This pours over me. He turn his innocent eyes to me but a fuck is a fuck, you know? I make the performance of it. And then the crash.

Crashing on Place de la République—the busiest square in the north of the city—would have been an act of great extravagance and designed for maximum impact. We must have been bulleting gaily along Boulevard Voltaire. To recreate the scene on the square—lights, confusion—would involve teams of trained professionals. Stuntmen up first. Traffic cops. Ambulancers.

I remembered my teeth slicing through my tongue, giving the sense that my mouth then my head then the whole car was filling with blood—then, strobing pain, and the feeling of wanting to undo my seat belt and escape and not being able to.

But did I remember being cut out of the car? Did I remember skateboarders using us as an impromptu ramp? The sirens resembling the finale of a rave?

No, I had no idea what had happened—no memory whatsoever of the crash or its aftermath. There would have been sirens, though—but all I had was Ghislaine's cool reportage.

—Catastrophe, she said. And they are in the car together. Voilà. That is why I am leaving. If you want a slice of my mind, I am obsess-freak over this.

I wanted to ask her more about the crash. But Ghislaine said something about another glass of wine then went to the bathroom.

Her phone was on the table. Jerome's name was beside a button and I pushed the button. I could have been calling for the waiter or a taxi but no. I was actually calling Jerome. On the screen there were more strange symbols—Jerome's photo and his details all laid out. You may have asked me to get blood from the phone as much as stop the call but I managed it without knowing how. Remembering aussieinparis@xmail.com was less of a challenge than stopping the call.

Ghislaine returned. She sat down with a smile, making no mention of the fact that she had removed the mascara from her eyes. You weren't supposed to exercise in make-up anyway.

She upended the last pale drops of wine into her mouth then suggested another drink—but I could not have stomached any more milk. Now from my old friend Ghislaine I wanted nothing but escape.

My First Letter to Eagleback

Chocolatebread@xmail.com: That was me at your door. That was me at the school. But things have changed. We have so much to talk about. Everything etc. I am not the woman I was. I don't remember a thing. I am alive but I don't know how. I talk strangely and I don't remember much but everything else is the same. I have a sweet tooth now. So be prepared for sweetness. I smell like a barn though, no matter what I do. But I am the same as before. I imagine our perfect day together. I wouldn't smell that bad, I'd make sure of that. I'd smell like fresh fruit. No, ripe fruit. How about that? Ripe fruit. I'll leave the rest up to you. I saw you and something changed. I knew you when I saw you. I know that I know you. We all want to find ourselves. We all want to find love. Don't you? This might mean nothing to you but it means a lot to me. Do you still believe in love? I believe in love. If you meet me you will know. You will understand like I understood as soon as I saw you. Yes, it is true that I haven't been well and that I am not well. But I will get better. I will wait here for you to reply. It doesn't matter how long it takes. I can wait.

Best regards.

Loose Change

I wanted to remember holidays I'd taken and the impressive places I'd been. The diary had said Malta and Arles. Arles? These were just names. I hoped that at least there'd been meadows and wild flowers—in summer sunshine of course. I did my best to conjure those moments from the never-nice eleventh. In some respects my life was a holiday anyway, in the same way that children are always on holiday but they don't know it. When was the first time I worked? Real work with meetings and bought coffees.

I couldn't remember anything, anywhere—not even Arles, certainly not Malta, but I was always inventing places I had to be. Apart from finding an internet café where I could write to Eagleback there was nowhere I had to be. On my second morning waking up in the cellar I did what you shouldn't do, although it didn't occur to me not to. I begged.

The competition to patrol the cashpoints on the best streets was immense—the ATM on the junction of Bretagne and Turenne in the Marais was the most sought-after. It was beginners luck when I found the patch unmanned. I spent seven straight hours cross-legged on the ground, going into a trance after the first hour.

More questions for Hippolyte & co. My toothbrush looks old, how old is good? What colour is good when I wipe? I saw a picture of myself and I wanted to stick pins in it. Does everyone do that? Can I ask something else? Paris is for lovers, but it's not even a nice place to live in. What is romance? Should I cry more? Should I clean the plughole? Tampons ruin the mood, don't they? Is it possible to have sex with someone you don't love? What if I don't want to have sex at all? Can I just say so?

It was a long day—I could have given birth in that time—and it took great effort to sit so still and consider the news about the crash. It felt better to have a specific cause for my memory loss. It could have been a number of things—better a crash than being bedridden after some unnamed trauma.

Customers from the bakery on Rue Debelleyme dropped off food—not only sandwiches but salads—without slowing down or speaking. I thanked them like mad although I don't know why they expected me to eat salad. I kept my eyes closed most of the time anyway and the coins piled up.

I was staring at a fixed point on the pavement when I heard a familiar voice.

—Beats working in a restaurant anyway.

Daniel was standing before me. Delighted with my profitable day's work—and dizzy with exhaustion—I waved him away. Such tenderness as remained between us was carried in his attempt to lift me off the ground. After a full day of sitting there, it was, I imagine, akin to hauling a corpse.

He was on his way to Le Baron Rouge to stock up on wine from the barrels.

—Wine doesn't agree with me, I said.

—I don't remember that.

Daniel, of course, was being deadpan. And I, of course, was incapable of being strategic.

Le Baron Rouge was wooden and listing and the barmen were leaning to compensate, as if they had just come ashore from a long time spent at sea. The bar wasn't busy—the street was full of people, passing through, yakking—so we sat inside. The change in my pocket was a nice reminder of my successful day. Daniel wanted to toast to that and to forgetting he was supposed to be upset with me after my behaviour at his apartment.

—What do you want to drink? I said.

—Ask the man, Daniel said. He'll tell you what's good.

Something was slamming itself against the middle of my forehead but I ignored it. I went up and asked for any old white, a litre of it.

There was a young woman sitting on a stool at the end of the bar. Her head was bowed—her bare arms reaching out from the fashionable coat she was sporting as a cape. There had to be a reason she was inside on such a golden evening. The glass she was drinking wasn't her first and from the way she was attacking it she was intent on another. I knew, though, that she was waiting for someone. She was watching the door.

The memories weren't unwelcome but they did arrive without warning—in the way of a sudden sore throat. It was so much more powerful than reading about yourself in a diary.

I remembered a visit to Aligre market just next door to Le Baron Rouge—we had been awake all night and we were the first people there, watching the traders set up in their sleep. I could see Eagleback clearly. His skin was not troubled in any way, not back then, the beard was lighter—he must have grown it since the crash—and the hair shorter and scratchier. His arms were around me and he was laughing at something I was saying.

I was wearing cat's eye sunglasses and orange suede ankle boots that I fussed over when the fishmongers began to sling their ice.

I knew it had been real, how we'd kissed until my chin bled, how we made no arrangements, there was never any talk of them, how it was acknowledged without saying a thing that we were hiding in plain sight at food trucks or in Le Baron Rouge. Every day somewhere new. It seemed to me now that we were surrounded by a beautiful bubble of love. But the memories began to fade at the exact moment Eagleback went to speak. In the clutter of it all, I could picture the damn cauliflower, I could hear the traders' calls, I could hear the ice skittering across the market floor. But, attempting to recall what was said—and what was heard—was as impossible as fixing a postage stamp to a broken heart.

Daniel did his best with the wine. He called for some cheese to help force it down. We were there so long so the rinds started to pespire in the heat.

—Hey, he said. Do you ever wonder where you came from?

—Do you?

—I know where I'm from. Never wonder about your family?

—Nope.

He spat out a cheese rind.

—It's not like I'm asking you to take part in a gangbang, he said. It's simple curiosity. What if they're wondering about you?

I laughed in Daniel's face—a laugh as withering as time-lapse photography. It had one effect, though. He changed the subject.

—It's so hot here, he said. Even the wine is sweating. What do you say we get out of town for the weekend?

—Arles, I said.

—Where it's even hotter than here? I was kind of thinking Ireland, but you'd need a passport. My folks have a house on Île de Ré. What if it's available?

—No, I said. Arles.

Unstory

June 15th 2011, Hotel du Nord-Pinus. Arles has everything, even a bull ring, Jerome said. Which may be filled with enormous pink rabbits for all we've seen of it. This weekend is what life is supposed to be like. Life without life. I wasn't feeling well, but being on a train together and checking in to a hotel was a dream. Cue an incident in the hotel room—some crying, a call to reception—and now Jerome is asleep and I'm writing this just to stay awake, just to be here. Tum-te-tum. Anyway, he'll wake up and then maybe we'll see the doctor and get some more sleep. No one will ever make the mistake of calling us a couple, yet look at us now and all you will see is two lovers—even for these two days, that's what we are. What can I do but hug my knees and wait for him to wake up?

June 16th 2011, Marseille-Paris TGV. It's something to see our names side by side on our seat reservations. I've taken a photograph—because I can't believe it—and I'm looking at it now, although our names are slightly blurred, as if we're travelling too fast through time. As we change at Marseille, Jerome, who hasn't spoken much since we checked out of the Nord–Pinus, says, What if we just stay here and don't go back to Paris? That fat guy wanted to sell us his restaurant. What if we take him up on his offer? We could live in that hotel, I say. I'd love to live in a hotel for a while. The penthouse. Great view of the rooftops. We did get to the bull ring in the end. We climbed to the top for the most succulent sunset ever—I thought it was digitally manipulated. Jerome was for once wearing the T-shirt I'd bought him. I suppose it's unfair to buy him things he can't wear except when we're together. He's sitting across from me now. I've never seen him so mellow, so wiped out. Me too. There is a lot to talk about but I won't alarm him with anything more taxing than penthouse talk. This means we are either revealing ourselves completely or tapering towards a last goodbye at the station. I don't know what's going to happen when we're back in Paris. It's not that I kid myself that what happened last night will make it any different. There isn't much to say that we haven't already discussed. Jerome will want to leave things as they are. We'll pull into Gare de Lyon, he'll hail a taxi and so will I.

Ms Of Course Not

There was the sense of having dug closer to the core of the planet. The light was denser in the south and the Hotel Nord-Pinus oozed the appropriate kind of mystery. The lobby was gauzy and smelling of the hereafter—although I'd never seen one there was an air of a monastery for people who cared about their sunglasses and their luggage. I was instructed by a departing German to take a good look at a glass case filled with pictures of Picasso and bullfighters and Warren Beatty and whatever. But the German was wide of the mark—walking and looking took so much effort in the heat.

I settled in an ailing armchair while Daniel checked us in, then went straight to the room to shower. The other guests checking in were either doing so reverently or in disappointment. One couple—vociferously South African—were mewling about the cost of parking.

—I'd like to check out right away, said the man.

—But you've just checked in, said the woman on reception. Her skin was astonishingly weathered—a riverbed at the bottom of a dry canyon—and it looked as if she spent a lot of money trying to combat this. Her hair had been braided loosely and very carefully.

—Let me speak to the owner.

—I am the owner, she said.

—I want to check out.

—You've just checked in.

—You can't detain us against our will.

—I don't wish to, said the owner. But you have just checked in.

A truce was called when the South Africans accepted the offer of a free cup of coffee on the terrace overlooking Place du Forum, where earlier we had passed a young guy dressed as a Roman centurion. Whatever he was doing in that outfit—a long shift of driving away barbarians—he was finished for the day. He was downing Fanta and his eyes were bloodshot from the incensey joint he was smoking. I was against the idea but Daniel mentioned my day begging on Rue de Bretagne and gave the guy some coins. The centurion swooned as he examined the donation, then laughed and spat at our feet. Even now, indoors, I could feel him staring at us.

I took my opportunity to speak with the owner as she made the coffee. I asked her if she remembered me. As if to preserve energy in the heat, she spoke absently and faintly.

—I see a lot of people. I am sorry.

—His name was Jerome. Cooper. That is his name. And he had a beard. He probably did. And I was me. We were here as a couple. Not as a couple, but as a couple.

—Like you are now? What would you like me to say?

—Did anything happen?

—We get a lot of marriage proposals here, if that's what you're asking.

—Did anything bad happen?

—Nothing bad happens here. Ms … ?

—Of course not, I said.

Daniel didn't like the bedroom.

—It's kind of chic, he said. But it's a little bare for what you pay. Why did you want to stay here again?

—Picasso stayed here.

—I bet Picasso liked a shower. Do you want to sit in a hot bath on a day like today?

Not a great deal was possible other than sex. Once we'd had cold baths and made love without disturbing the bedclothes, I went downstairs and tried one more time with the owner. Of course, if she knew me she would have said. But no. She adjusted her braids. This and the frown directed at the iced tea on the reception desk said my investigation was over. She would speak to me only of where to go for dinner.

—Maybe you like this place near the amphitheatre? Not Provençal so much, so you will like it. Your man will love it more than you maybe. But this is fine.

—Do you go there?

—I eat here.

—Should we eat here then?

—It's better if you go there, she said.

I knew where I was going or I thought I did. But it was hard to drop my pace to match Daniel's. He was softened by sex and he was trudging—but I had been spooked by the stoned centurion and wanted to keep moving. It took us ages and we were filthy with sweat before we found the restaurant.

La Boucherie was presided over by a prosperous dog and his happy owners, a couple from Lyon called Loïc and Fanny. On top of being too hot, Loïc was producing a powerful broth of meat sweats. He immediately said he remembered me but only after mistakenly welcoming Daniel back and asking him if he still wanted to buy the restaurant—Fanny still came as part of the deal. Daniel was, I could tell, playing along by considering the offer. Fanny was in her husband's opinion the best meat cook in all of Provence. As he took in the room—greasy tiles, vital organs on a marble slab—Daniel seemed to agree.

Loïc went behind the bar and bustled impressively for such a fat man, doling out raw beef heart and ghostly white cheese to anyone who crossed his path. It was manly, difficult stuff. I nearly asphyxiated myself on some of the challenging bread.

—Sure that guy doesn't know you? Daniel said. Maybe in one of your past lives you were a Camargue cowboy.

These flights of fancy appeared whenever Daniel felt like he was fading into the background.

Loïc was feeding the uneaten food to the dog, but it was nearly forty degrees and even the animal wasn't hungry. Daniel began making quick work of the next course—slyly he dropped a piece of braised chicken neck into my unwittingly upturned palm.

—Well, you can do better than bread, he said.

I dumped the meat—a greasy mess resembling chewing tobacco—in my mouth, where it sat until I spat it out a minute or two later. I knew in my heart that scenes like this one were associated somehow with Eagleback, and that I had been here before and, what's more, had left little trace.

I looked at Loïc's smiling face as he grappled with our next course and a fractious assortment of objects from my past began to appear. A waffled white dressing gown, a blood stain on a wall, another on marble, a full glass of water by an undressed bed. I couldn't explain it to Daniel and wouldn't have anyway, that the past—which had been light years away—was now forcing itself upon me and might at any moment arrive and physically haul me out of the restaurant.

I was starting to remember being here with Eagleback. I remembered Loïc's wheezing, his vapours, his morbid waddle.

I remembered the way he ogled his wife and his chubby hands on her colossal arse. I remembered the food and the way it kept on coming and coming until you begged for it to stop. I remembered enjoying, for once in my life, mouldy things and the sinister texture of the ligaments, ears and gizzards. I remembered the tumblers and the sour wine. I remembered we were pretty pleased with ourselves at first. It was early but we had by no means been the first to arrive and we squeezed into the last available table. I remembered snail shells and red wine in an ice bucket and I remembered crying. But I wasn't eating then either—not that I refused to eat but that I wasn't able. Eagleback seemed to be waiting in silence for someone else to arrive. I didn't remember leaving the restaurant although I knew that it was the end of so much—options, for one thing, whatever they were.

I think Daniel figured something was the matter but I managed, in my own way, to keep all this to myself.

In the Nord-Pinus' churchy bathroom that night, a tiny vein in my breast was jumping. It was a feeling that I hated but wanted to hoard. I had once driven something from me. What was it that came out? A calf? A bat? Torn water. Filthy, sweet water and something—my soul?—in the bath. Someone? Hardly someone. Besides. Whatever had left me took a good part of me with it. Picasso and bullfighters and Warren Beatty and whatever.

Daniel #4

A funny thing happened when he went to pay the bill that morning. Eva had made a bed for herself in the cool of the bath, so it was just Daniel and the hotel's owner, who didn't mind one way or another when he settled up.

—Now or later, she said.

—Let's take care of it now.

—Or later?

—Why not now?

—If you are sure.

Daniel knew the difference between friendly and not friendly and there was nothing to suggest that she made life easy for people. However, the early hour seemed to be working in his favour.

The owner surprised him with a warm, inquisitive look when Daniel gave her Conrad Weston's credit card.

—Mister Weston? Can I offer you a coffee?

It was still cool enough to sit on the terrace overlooking Place du Forum, but the terrace was not a good idea she said. There was something in particular that she wanted to discuss and she didn't want to be overheard. She suggested the hotel's bar, where she made a show of lighting the drowsy lamps and positioning Daniel at a tiny card table. The bar was stocked hopefully with rare vermouths and he surprised her by asking for a breakfast aperitif.

She found some Suze then topped it off with beer; a first.

—So you have enjoyed your trip? Of course, yes. Some people come here and they wonder what all the fuss is about but you understand us, I am sure of that.

—I would definitely like to return another time, he said.

—You will, I'm sure of it. And your friend, this is not her first time here.

—I'm gathering that.

—Did she enjoy her meal yesterday evening?

—No, not really. But I don't think either of us is responsible for that. I liked the place though. The owner guy, he's a real dude.

—A dude. Like that, exactly.

Daniel's interest in talking was dwindling. The dinner with Eva had not ended well and he didn't care to reminisce about it so soon. He and the owner made out there were other topics for discussion; they talked about the size of the portions at La Boucherie and agreed that they were too much, then they discussed French food, the difference between restaurant food and the meals you had at home, at which point the conversation started to fall in on itself. She must have known before he did that they were getting to something. She left Daniel alone in the bar and when she reappeared she absentmindedly took a sip from his drink. She presented him with a silver plate bearing a folded piece of paper which seemed to hover into his hands: a doctor's bill from Eva's previous visit.

Was there logic, maybe some kindness, to her presenting it to him on a plate? The bill was crammed with information that meant nothing to him. Daniel read it despairingly and without understanding. He knew the words but not what they amounted to. The owner took it for granted that he needed to know that the bill hadn't been paid.

—What is it for? he said.

She replied with a low wolf whistle.

—Talk with your friend? Now I will book your taxi for later.

Daniel used all his cash to pay the doctor's bill. They already had his card for the room. And he wasn't charged for the drink.

Eva hadn't spoken since they left La Boucherie the night before. She didn't speak in the cab to the station nor as the train pulled away from Arles. Not much, apart from pâté sweats, to show from their trip to Provence. It was even hotter than the day before but the carriage was air-conditioned and it was mostly empty. They sat with sticky forearms side by side. Her face flickered in and out of the light as she dabbed her sweaty forehead on the shoulder of Daniel's T-shirt.

Eva began to doze and he knew not to speak until they were approaching Paris. He woke her by resting a cool bottle of water on her cheek. He didn't have the strength to mention the doctor's bill.

—Hi, he said.

—Are you angry with me?

—Not really. Not at all. But that was a weird trip. I don't know what came over you last night. You were about ready to blow.

—It was the heat.

—The heat. And the fact that you need to start talking. I understand if you don't want to talk to me. But you should talk with someone. Have you spoken with the doctor? Have you seen Eagleback?

—Train is empty, she said. No one but you.

The carriages swayed as they entered the station and they fell into another silence. They trickled along the platform, with her holding back, as though she wanted Daniel to go on without her.

Having lost his nerve, he wanted to leave her alone, too. This trip was a mistake, from her point of view as well as his. If nothing else, it had confirmed the failure of Daniel's project and his failure as a friend, when a friend was all Eva needed. They shared another bottle of water on the station concourse.

—It's a losing battle, Daniel said. Me, the heat.

A wry look from Eva as he combed his fingers uselessly through her sweaty hair—and there would have been a time when he insisted they take refuge from the heat in Le Train Blue. There were very few problems that wouldn't dissolve before a sodden baba au rhum.

But Eva had read Daniel's mind.

—I don't want food, she said.

France was all well and good but was best put behind him. It was a harsh country, he didn't know another way of putting it. Everything Daniel had seen of Arles made him long for Connecticut. He longed for air-conditioning as standard and cheerfulness. His blood moved at the thought of processed food. AT&T. Pâté fucking depressed him. Loïc depressed him, and Fanny. Eva depressed him. He went through the motions of inviting her back to his place and when she wrinkled her face he found her a cab. She stooped, as though she was being forced into the car. Eva had this awful way of appearing vulnerable when she wasn't stretched to her full height. He pretended not to hear when she told the driver that she wanted to go to Ménilmontant.

Daniel paid the fare and the car pulled away into the vastness of the city. Then, deciding that the only people who could help Eva were the people who knew her best, he searched his phone for Tony's number.

The Universe Adjusting

Hippolyte was not surprised to see me—that there I was, ready to talk. It was nine in the evening but I presumed you could talk at any time. There was something specific I wanted to ask him. A circular kind of question that smothered everything else in my head whenever I considered it

First Hippolyte disappeared into a room next to the one where he saw patients. I heard him lose his temper on the phone and then he was back. The air conditioning was on full so he handed me a shawl the weight of a paper tissue. No jelly beans this time, as far as I could tell.

—So, he said. Here we are again.

So was such a short word that I felt immediately indecisive. It put me in mind of ordering in a restaurant, something I hated to do. It was a while before I was able to speak—to say that there was something I needed to share but I didn't know how to express it.

—I am starting to remember, I said.

Hippolyte smirked and at first I felt like he was making fun of me. Then I began to sense kindness in his impartiality, which was all I asked.

—As you know, my memory is inadequate.

—It's not inadequate, he said. It's incomplete. Everything is incomplete. Your situation is just more pronounced. Has your body sent you any information lately?

—Sorry?

—This is how you put it before, he said. Headaches and so on.

I was impressed that he was able to recall our previous conversations in such detail until I saw that he was referring to notes. I wondered if our conversation at Ségo's house had made it into his notebook and whether that kind of thing was allowed.

I told him that I was starting to remember things but their significance was unknown to me. I told him that I had been to Arles and I knew that something had happened there but I didn't know what. I told him I thought I'd been in a crash and this had to have something to do with my memory.

—That makes perfect sense, he said.

He could write notes and listen at the same time. I was feeling worn out already but I had not yet made myself clear.

—Let me give you an example, I said. I don't remember my parents. But I know that I have parents, somewhere. And I also know that I don't want to remember them. So that means I must remember something, if I know that I don't want to remember it? Understand?

Hippolyte understood.

—You know more than you think you do, he said. Your memory is a wild bird. It can never be tamed. Never.

I felt this not to be true but I didn't want to quarrel with him, so I said, —Wild bird.

—You understand what I mean?

—Well, no. But some things become enlarged. And other things reduce. Until they are insignificant.

I was referring to the diary, in which I was losing faith, whose contents had so infuriated me because they felt so distant—factual, yes, but no more than that. I told him what I had read—all the entries from Rose Bakery onwards—but nothing would please him. He seemed to want to focus on those areas, the point in the recollection where I became confused. He wanted me follow the lines of thought in which I had the least interest.

I almost had to shout to make myself clear.

—Don't you see? This is why I am here. This is exactly what I don't want to talk about.

—Talking is the only way we will get anywhere.

—You don't understand what I've been saying. Is there a way I can not know all this?

Hippolyte pouted, as if he had been insulted.

—I don't understand, he said.

—How can I choose what I remember?

—So you don't experience any bad memories?

—That kind of thing, yes. If I can't remember something it can't cause me any pain.

—Short answer?

—Yes please.

—You can't.

I felt more than ever that I had done something wrong.

—Is it a ridiculous idea?

—No, it's beautiful, but it's impossible. You can't choose.

All this time I was conscious of the fact that, apart from the crash, I hadn't mentioned Eagleback enough. And I thought I ought to. Out it all came.

—The man in the car, in the crash, he is called Jerome. I think we were lovers. I know we were, I just don't know when or anything. Or I do know when but not how.

I could see Hippolyte registering the name. He recognised it, I knew it, but he wouldn't say anything other than, —And?

—And what?

—Do you want to remember him? Or not?

—I want to remember some things and not others. I just feel I would be better off if I knew everything that happened between us. It feels like we were in love. It feels like I should know more about being in love.

—What if it was also something painful, are you prepared for that?

—No idea. But I would like to choose what I remember.

Hippolyte laughed, this time without any sarcasm.

—Something tells me you have this process all figured out. Have you made contact with this man?

—I know where he lives. I've made contact. A few times.

Hippolyte hesitated. Had he decided this was a risk but didn't want to say as much?

—In that case, you must be prepared for anything. Are you prepared?

The phone on his desk rang and he answered it, treating the call as an intrusion. Instead of massaging his fingers, as he usually did, now he was twiddling them. He hung up and apologised because he would have to deal with the person who had been on the phone.

I responded to his question anyway.

—You mean what if I find out what happened and it's a bad memory?

—Exactly. What if it's bad?

On the way back to Léon Frot, I stopped off at the tabac in Oberkampf to send more emails to Eagleback. It wasn't that I was trying to persuade him of anything—it was just a reminder. It didn't occur to me that he wouldn't reply immediately.

I stared at the screen, assuming there was something wrong. There was nothing except the reflection of my startled hair. With the next email, I mentioned that I had discovered some information from an 'old friend'. I didn't mention Ghislaine's name, not yet, nor did I say anything about Arles, either. In the next email—this was twenty of them so far—I used the heading Crash. In the next one I sent only three kisses xxx.

It was so hot at night. I was grateful for the algae-cool of the cellar. On the ceiling I saw nothing but glowing ice floes in the same frame as out-of-control refineries. Thunderstorms sending interrupted messages. Marauding tidal waves on their way to sweep me and Eagleback warmly away.

A dreamy, dreamy sky the next morning. It was 8 a.m. and I had returned to the tabac. I asked for some water and whether the shop had a bathroom. I asked the Algerian guy at the counter if I could open the front door for some air, and when he refused I took a few minutes to stand outside. When I came back I circled the computer, refusing to be overtaken by fear or excitement or anything else, all before opening the email.

Since I had met Eagleback—going to sleep every night, in the apartment, on Elias' floor and in the cellar—I had hoped for one thing, that when I awoke in the morning life would be different and a chance meeting with someone from my past would change the direction of my life.

Now he had replied, matter-of-factly, to one of my messages. For a second I thought he had used my name, but he was referring to the other Ghislaine. His wife, of course.

I read the mail again. His tone was this side of cold and I had to read it another few times before I took in what he was saying. Ghislaine would be away, he said. He was promising to meet me that night, if he could get away. At seven I would go to an Indian restaurant near Gare du Nord. It would be just the two of us.

I typed my reply carefully.

Okay, I wrote.

When I returned to Léon Frot, Elias was there in the courtyard, shirtlessly strimming weeds—the exertion looked as if it was about to trigger a heart-attack.

He tipped his head back and laughed when, just to keep things simple, I told him that I was back for good. I wasn't going to mention the poster if he wasn't. He embraced me—and, have mercy on us all, I felt his hairy, sticky skin on mine. I sat on the wall as he distributed weed killer all over the gardens without ever looking my way.

—Roohi, he was saying. Ya roohi.

I chatted as he shook out the can of poison before chopping all the shrubbery—deliberately—into blunt, ugly shapes. An unlit cigarette stayed in his mouth the entire time.

I was wearing my clean clothes but Levis and kitchen hand-me-downs weren't the right kind of look for my evening with Eagleback. I took off on a little shopping trip, just to see what I could find.

I stepped into the glare of American Apparel on Vieille du Temple and ran through it without breathing. The shop was so crowded and the changing rooms were too dark to see. Someone had smashed a mirror. As far as I could tell, the first outfit—something cropped and black—made me seem gaunt, or in grief. I wondered if my chef's whites would have to do after all. In the men's section I saw—it poured over me—a T-shirt with an eagle on it. I could have bought one to wear as a dress, but I stole something at random—shorts, and the green T-shirt with the black zig-zags which wasn't my style exactly—and I saw my evening coming together.

I Would Have Chosen Somewhere
Else To Meet

The men in Grandmère Indienne wondered what I was doing there. They had made the room more festive with a mural of a shining sun but the place felt like it had once been submerged and then excavated, like a pond or a pit. There were the smells of stale fat, tangy sweat and nicotine—reminders, I thought, of idleness and the pointlessness of male company.

The tables in the dining room were packed so tightly that I became acquainted with the shiny backsides of the men coming and going from the tables alongside mine. No doubting, though, why Eagleback had chosen this location. As soon as he got here I would suggest to him that we go someplace else.

The waiter kept on saying, —Krpaya aur bred deejie.

I think they wanted me to order something.

I stopped watching the door after a while and kept my hands under the table to avoid playing with them. When the waiter offered me some poppodums, I wanted to extend the conversation—soccer or hair gel or something. The chutney they offered me tasted strange. I savoured it slowly, since Eagleback was so late. Soon they began to treat me with devotion, as if they saw in my eyes that I was lonelier and more eager than the other diners. I was brought water, I got fresh ice without asking for it. I spent as long as possible with the menu, looking at the photographs and languidly turning the laminated pages. I even started on the wine list before pretending to be struck by the dried flowers. I needed the bathroom but I was scared to go in case Eagleback came and went in my absence.

An hour was long enough.

The strangest thing about realising Eagleback wasn't coming was that it allowed me, finally, to consider that I was hungry. If I was going to spend the last of my money on a lentil pancake then I was going to enjoy it. Everyone was eating them with their hands. I could have just slipped away, but that would have been accepting defeat. I asked for some more of the chutney and some rice. Funny how disappointment made you feel so light—the way you were supposed to feel when you were in love.

I got back to Léon Frot just in time to see an ambulance crew gingerly loading a zippered body bag onto a trolley. Many of the building's residents were there—more of them than I had ever seen before, tearfully standing shoulder to shoulder. I got snippets of their conversation, sniffing accompanying all the tears.

The trolley, wobbling under a dead weight, was unceremoniously dumped on board. The crew members walked to the front of the ambulance with lowered heads. I was expecting sirens but they pulled away quietly.

The door of Elias' room had been broken in and inside a conference of people in uniform was taking place. A young policeman was slowly going through the contents—everything seemed fascinating. The policeman was wearing gloves but he wasn't a neat worker. He was making notes in a notebook like the one in which I had written—you could tell from the way he was working, just glancing around, that he was just going through the motions. No one seemed to notice me either. Nor could they have made any connection between me and Elias anyway. My face was some kind of holy picture. All I could think was—what a life, and what a way for it to end.

Elias had been found dead on the grass beside an empty tub of weed killer. One of the women in rollers said half a wine glass would have been enough to kill him but she reckoned he drank a full litre. She kept on repeating the word litre. There was something admirable about that. Good old Elias. Ten times the recommended dose.

By now the women were saying he was a creep. I had gathered Elias wasn't the type to have friends but it was a shock to hear him described as a peeping tom. Someone said he used to camp out in vacated apartments to spy on the rooms opposite. Someone said there were claims of missing laundry, underwear, and that he was supposed to have left Tunisia because of a scandal involving young girls his daughter's age. Poor things—their families destroyed. On top of his shady past, someone said that Elias never did any any of the things they asked him to—the weeds, yes, but it was already high summer and that was too late. The only reason they had never reported him was because it would have been such a bother to hire someone new.

Those women didn't even know Elias. I wouldn't have called myself a good judge of character—but I knew more than they did, and that he took care of the apartment complex well enough.

Above Léon Frot the sky was bloated and the bushes and trees were dishevelled by wind. It was a war—the reverberations underneath me and faraway. When it began to pour all of Elias' friends and neighbours elbowed each other out of the way to get inside. I stood in the courtyard, expecting something—there was an elongated silence then nothing.

No, the storm wasn't supposed to mean anything.

I was standing on Rue de Charonne, soaking wet in my shorts. I was watching the rain rise as steam from the pavement and I was thinking about Elias and that I would need to spend the night somewhere. I was considering I might go back to the cellar when I saw Ghislaine approaching from the courtyard's side entrance. She was moving slowly, at the pace of someone walking an elderly pet. I had to suppose she was leaving—she was carrying a bag—because people returning from a trip usually looked more relieved to be home.

—Ghislaine?

—Oh yes, I said, barely remembering that was supposed to be my name, too.

Her eyes circled my new outfit.

—I believe to a certain extent you live the Pippi Longstocking life.

Ghislaine was wearing a very heavy quilted coat which was not right for these temperatures at all but must have been useful in the storm. Her curls had been twisted into an uncomfortably tight bun. Her complexion—and everything else about her, that coat especially—seemed dull. I noticed that her bag didn't seem to contain clothes but concealed the angular shape of a box or the base of a lamp.

She was definitely leaving. Living. Leaving.

I pivoted to allow her a clearer exit, if that's what she wanted. Ghislaine frowned, either at me or because she was registering something over my shoulder. A locksmith was patching up the door to Elias' room.

Every time I spoke it seemed that she was dreading what I might say.

—Going anywhere nice?

Her laugh drifted off into nothing.

—Away from here. It is the same history.

—I'm sorry, I said. You seem very unhappy.

—Don't be, Ghislaine said. You can't find happiness on every corner of the street.

—It's not a baguette, I said.

—No, she said, with a sudden smile. Happiness is not a baguette.

Maybe the reason why Ghislaine so absentmindedly hadn't mentioned Elias was that, like Ségo, she already knew the answers. She knew I had been staying in the cellar and that I had been due to meet her husband in an Indian restaurant that evening. Or maybe she was saying, in so many words, that she wanted to be on her way.

—My father is coming and we are making a journey by car to our castle. I guess I am still saying goodbye. You make an odyssey to Ireland, no?

Ghislaine didn't expect a reply. She hoisted the bag to her shoulder before facing me with a polite smile you would reserve for someone you were stepping over in a shop doorway.

This Is Fucked Up

At first I thought Eagleback wasn't there. There was no answer so I knocked again and then knocked again, thinking—what if he is there? If he didn't want to see me three hours ago why would he want to see me now? I blotted the moisture on my forehead with the short hairs on my forearm. The lingering rain was pronouncing my curry smell. I hadn't slept much and the next thing I knew it was catching up on me. I yawned and the first yawn led to another.

Eagleback answered the door just as I was in the middle of a silent roar. He seemed somehow to have gotten younger over the past few weeks. His skin was smoother, pearlescent and sumptuous—but I saw his eyes were even warier than before and, tremoring in their little pockets, I willed them to take me in.

Drawing a deep breath, I said, —Are you waiting for someone else?

—No.

I was a fool, a nervous fool in soaking wet shorts. I had a picture in my mind of the storm and what it would be like to be back in it. That's what I would remember about this, being so wet.

I looked past him. The light from where I was standing was as golden and moist as honey. It had taken me a month from the first morning at Bertrand Rose to get here.

—Ask a question? I said. Have I been here before?

—What do you mean?

—It's a valid question.

—Of course you've been here before.

I stepped inside, just like that. Thinking of it now, it seems strange that I was feeling so nervous or self-conscious.

I couldn't remember having been here—nor could I remember not having been here. There was a white laptop humming on a porridge-coloured couch. The drooping heads of the lamps echoed the posture of strolling dinosaurs. The organised shape of the dust on one of the side tables suggested the recent removal of an object—this had to be whatever Ghislaine had been carrying in her bag.

Someone—not Eagleback, I was sure of it—had arranged off-white roses in an old milk bottle and by the looks of it they had been there for a while. The roses were the colour of the wall which was the colour of the floor. There were a few experiments in colour—one of the dinosaur lamps was the colour of pomegranate seeds. Otherwise, the room overall was the colour of a dirty beach, and had been put together so as to say very little about its inhabitants.

Eagleback sat in a spindly dining chair whilst trying not to occupy it. When he invited me to sit on the sofa I attempted to mimic his posture and ended up holding myself in the way of a prim aunt.

—Nice T-shirt, he said. Very you.

I took a breath instead of replying as he expected me to.

A man was smoking on the balcony opposite. The thrown light from his TV making him seem casually demonic.

—Did you hear about the caretaker?

—Elias? I said.

—Was that his name?

—He died.

—He was a sex freak. Ghislaine just called. They went through his phone and all his stuff and there were pictures of young girls.

—Maybe they were his daughters? I said.

—Maybe they were his daughters or maybe they were the young girls he was fucking. Some young girl's underpants found in his room.

They were mine, I knew. I was quite skinny around the bottom.

—That's not fair, I said. Maybe he had a girlfriend?

—Maybe there were bodies under the floorboards?

This conversation had one purpose—it allowed me to study Eagleback. His eyes, for instance, were unlike Daniel's jewels. What they were were reflective surfaces for my confusion.

—There's some pizza in there if you want it. You look hungry.

—Had a curry earlier.

It was meant as a joke, I couldn't help it. We were in no way behaving like the lovers I assumed we'd been.

—What do I call you? I said.

Eagleback frowned again and paid close attention as I repeated the question.

—By my name.

—So I call you Jerome?

—What do you expect to call me?

Eagleback—I couldn't call him that any more. But Jerome did not stick to him at all. It implied an intimacy we had yet to earn. I had a name, too, everyone did—Bristles, Cheeks—and I didn't want to use his until I knew mine. The next question was obvious—who was I etc?—and the next, they were lining up. But I wasn't any good at following a straight line in my brain.

I should have asked him more questions but I fell back into silence before saying, —Ask a question? Did I like chocolate?

—Did you what?

—Did I like chocolate?

—This is fucked up.

—And you will have to tell me about yourself. I have no memory. I said so in the email.

He assumed the slow, annoying voice of a robot. —I'm Jerome. I'm from Australia.

—But what are you doing in Paris?

—C'mon, you don't have to ask these questions.

—I do. I really do.

He shook his head. —This is fucked up.

Neither of us spoke for a moment. You would have thought I could have come up with something, after all this time. But I had lost all sense of the outside world, the physical world.

I began carefully.

—There are some things you need to know. How should I put this? Something doesn't work in my brain any more and I don't know who I am. I wish I did but I don't.

—You're freaking me out.

Another sudden yawn—as if I was bored by all this or I didn't want to go any further with the conversation. It just remained for me to run off as I had done on Ségo and Daniel. But the yawn was so intense that my ears popped and thus the atmosphere changed.

That Would Be Me

Had I been searching for the wrong person? The first thing that occurred to me on hearing who I was—who I had been and what I used to do—was to be afraid of her.

Eva Hand—three syllables that were easy to say and wouldn't take long to type.

Once upon a time, she was born and raised in Dublin but had lived in Paris for more than five years, where, in an attempt to break into the walled world of music journalism, she wrote a blog called The Waves. The blog wasn't very good, apparently.

—Very shouty, Jerome said. But you were getting better.

There was no more trace of The Waves online but he insisted on showing me a screenshot on an old phone. There wasn't much to see in the photograph—most of it was hand and glass behind which was a bleary face barely recognisable as the person I was now. My face was the colour of steak and my hair, in wonky cornrows, had been dyed an avocado green. I looked distracted. I looked tired.

Jerome told me that we first met at a party in a beamed loft in the Marais owned by a famous English singer who spent five minutes scowling at everyone before leaving to buy drugs.

—Why were you there? I said.

—Good question, said Jerome. I had a friend who worked at La Perle. He got the interesting hook-ups.

I was, he said, wearing a long tweed coat that resembled a cassock. Under the coat I was wearing purple harem trousers and a neoprene top that Jerome said reminded him of the goofy T-shirt I was wearing now. You had these amazing nails. Painted black. Tapping off the screen of your phone.

—Not any more, I said.

He took a look at my filthy hands before sharing another detail. There was always blood on the toes of my ballet bumps.

—Didn't that put you off?

—The opposite.

I seemed happy on my own, Jerome said, happy to be drinking whatever was put in front of me while scrolling through my phone. It took a full hour to fend off his advances, which were as subtle as a falling piano. There was one bathroom at the party and we kept everyone waiting as we fucked standing up, over the sink. Apparently I said I wasn't afraid of him, I was afraid of not being with him.

—Pretty slick, I said. What does that even mean?

—It means we had to be together.

—There and then?

—We were a lethal combination. We could have gone somewhere else, I suppose, but it made sense to get on with it.

So it was that in the first weeks of our affair we were incapable of considering or even recognising the outside world. What we decided to do—what I decided to do—was check into Le Bourg Tibourg for weekends. So long as it was available on room service we didn't care if we lived on cornflakes. We may as well have been fugitives, at the very least teenagers—stirring ourselves only to leaf through menus and exchange trays with the night porter. There were anxieties of course—Ghislaine—but we fought them off with champagne.

Jerome all but gave up on work altogether. I took him to dungeons in So-Pi. Throbbing air. The darkness studded with dilating eyes. We'd hobble home fungal by the end of it—up for two days at a time, three. When I got a new apartment we started to meet there and to have sex in my hallway—faithfully and without variation—every day at the end of the school day. It was never that we were compatible in any way that wasn't physical. It was never that he was going to leave Ghislaine. It was never that I wanted him to.

He said.

Jerome was full of stories—listening to them it seemed as though I would have been out of it all the time, more out of it than some sad safari park lion. I had to take his word for it, even though I might not have remembered it anyway, given the state I was supposed to have been in. Hell bent on intoxication in the nought-to-sixty style—I would put away lethal substances like breakfast.

—Sometimes you wouldn't leave your apartment from one week to the next, he said.

I was, according to Jerome, a woman of means. Or that's what you would have thought if you had visited my apartment on Rue de Bac. Impressive, echoing hallways could not disguise that I was, to put it mildly, an odd case. But I had to be doing okay—why else would I have spent three thousand a month on a ground floor apartment in the seventh? Why else would it have had three bedrooms and two bathrooms when I lived there alone and, according to Jerome, rarely left my bedroom? The mirrored art-deco sideboard I bought from the famous antique shop next door got cracked within an hour of delivery.

—Do you remember the sideboard? he said.

I didn't remember the sideboard. No, I should say that I remembered the object but I didn't remember buying it or the saving up of the five thousand euro for it, if saving up is what I did.

It was hard to imagine why I would want such a thing. Jerome was, at first, very sparing when it came to the source of my income. It was just assumed that I was rolling in money until one day he saw me shoplifting. I lingered in jewellers but stole milk.

—You never cared about money, so I reckoned you must have had a lot of it.

That was one way of putting it. I had accumulated debts that, when he recounted the amount, made me wince. Fifty thousand. More. The figure loomed—a brick wall built inches from a window.

I used to make a big deal about flowers and would buy them only on Thursdays from Lachaume. A taxi would be required to go to the métro. I spent a shameless amount on a Royal-Pedic mattress and bought a rabbit fur coat and threw it away when I botched up the job of dying it blue. I bought velvet curtains for my bedroom but discarded them when I didn't like the dusty smell.

—Who paid for all this? I asked.

—You paid for everything with credit cards. Your parents paid the bill.

I could only crunch my eyes shut. My parents—who might have been Las Vegas entertainers for all I could remember—always appeared in my mind at the wrong moments, when I was lipsticking mirrors and flicking towels. Where were they when I over-tipped in restaurants, when I honoured the baby Jesus, when I picked up other people's litter?

—This isn't good, I said. What about Arles? Aligre. The good places.

—You don't remember Arles? he said.

—Enlighten me why don't you.

—You really don't remember?

—How many times do I have to say it?

My insides shrivelled—my heart the size of a dried pea—when Jerome told me that I had been pregnant.

This is how he remembered it. The sense of anticipation to the trip was similar to the eve of a birthday or the build-up to Christmas. True, we had not been getting on, but peace had been restored in expectation of a weekend of hotel tomfoolery. Jerome's words. Part of him—his words, again—was in love with me. On our day we were every inch the loving couple.

Then the story lunged forwards.

I became distressed in the Nord-Pinus. Jerome was confused but I knew what had gone wrong. Not until he started to freak out did I share what was the matter. Two weeks before we went Arles, I had found out I was going to be a mother, but the cramps I had been experiencing privately for days were worsening and I was bleeding so heavily that the blood ran all the way down my legs. With the bleeding came the possibility, finally, that something was the matter. It would have been better if I had gone to the bathroom sooner, he said. He said I came across as careless somehow.

I felt a roar in my head when Jerome said all this—a mesmeric roar that said I was to blame, as if all this had come about as punishment for a brief and dizzying cameo of happiness. Apparently I put up with the discomfort for a few more hours without saying anything to Jerome. Things grew cloudy and that evening I had to ask the owner of a local restaurant— Loïc presumably—to get me to a doctor where I was given the medication I needed. I then told Jerome the uneasiness that had been consuming my body had subsided. But I had been only five weeks pregnant and by his logic it did not matter that much—it was more a question of putting it behind us.

That was it, Jerome assumed. His delivery made it seem like he was hoping for nothing more than a clear conscience and the confirmation that I had been treated cordially. When we returned from Arles, we just got on with things. This is what you are supposed to do when one of you is married to someone else.

I asked Jerome for a few minutes to myself. I toured the apartment. Here and there I saw where Ghislaine's life had been carefully removed. In the kitchen I stood at the sink and filled a glass of water, grateful that it was water. All that talk of alcohol and being pregnant had made me feel anxious. Besides. I was suddenly starving, too. The butter was runny in its dish and behind some strange poultry there was a jar of Nutella which I knew I liked. I ate and ate. It didn't matter that I was using a licked spoon to eat from the jar—something Ségo wouldn't have tolerated—because I didn't intend to leave any behind.

Who remembers what they ate when they first went on a plane? The name of the boy christened next to you? Would I look back at my pregnancy and the end of it and think of Nutella?

When I had eaten all that I wanted to, an image—dark at the edges—came to mind. A bedroom in my old place on Rue de Bac. Between the heavy curtains and the dimmed lights I couldn't get a sense of the time of day. There was music playing and I could see myself in the bath. I could feel the rich steam and the water was creamy with my rinsed-off body lotion. In this scene, Eagleback was standing at the door. There was something else on his mind that we needed to discuss urgently.

Then Jerome entered his own kitchen with a bewildered look. I didn't say anything. It was easier to wait until he was able to speak, to tell me that Ghislaine was on her way upstairs.

Ghislaine flipped when she saw me in her kitchen. Three words were all it took to send her over the edge. You Need Nutella.

I wouldn't leave. There was an incident.

Dear You

Her cobbled street was still and eerie. Ségo acted as though it was such great news that I'd turned up at her door on the stroke of midnight. She stepped forward and wrapped me in her arms. Her smell was sweet onions and it was the best smell in the world.

—My God, she said. You're like the fucking rat from that movie.

The naughty step.

I tried to eat the supper she made for me but it wouldn't stay down. The water from the rice pot—whatever Ségo gave me I tried it. It was embarrassing at first but it felt better to have someone else there. Not until she began to clear up the rice did I begin to amble around after her. I hated secrets, the need for them—but this was my dilemma. My urge to share everything with Ségo—visiting Jerome, the baby, my fear that it concealed something else—and my instinct, due to her suspicious attitude, that I should keep it to myself.

I told her just a little about Jerome—that whenever I thought of him my heart surged, that when he had been telling me all that stuff about Eva Hand it was for my own good. That I needed to see him again—if only to hear why, since I had been such a mess, he had ever been with me. I didn't tell her how Jerome—not Eagleback—had gotten me pregnant and how it had ended somewhere in Provence. I glossed over Ghislaine and Elias, too, but I told Ségo about the crash and how that was it, it had to be. I was in a crash.

She took this in her stride, using the tone she reserved for menu meetings at the restaurant. Yes. And? Not sure. Okay. Next.

—But what do you think? I said.

—I think you should try to eat some more, she said. Then you should get some sleep. Focus on regaining your strength. Everything else we can figure out later.

I wanted to remember my fears, if I was ever scared of anything at all. Different things at different times—an earthquake or being left behind in the city after an evacuation. Or was it the first time an insect ran over my face? Or the first time I touched myself or the first time I drank the milk in someone else's house? I should have been scared of being a mother or not being a mother. Was I worried for my soul, that I allowed something to die inside me and therefore I didn't have a soul or I did have one but it resembled my indistinct speech—I spoke as though I never wanted to be heard. I spoke as though nothing I said was true anyway.

If I could have seen those MRI people again I would have had some more questions. Is there any of the child left inside me? How much would there have been? Armpits and nails and knees? Gums? Was there a single moment? Would it have known and would it have panicked—a kitten in a sack? Can I have a funeral? Are you absolutely sure there's none of it inside me? My breath tastes weird—it's a low, sour-smelling flame—is that why? Was there milk yet, my milk, enough to fill a bottle? Will there be any side effects? Am I allowed to say that I'm relieved? Am I supposed to keep it secret? Will I get in trouble if I don't? Am I in trouble now?

Before she went to work the next morning, I asked Ségo for a pencil and paper so I could write some letters. I didn't know the first thing say to a child—she would have been nearly two years old—until I sat in Ségo's amazing garden. I imagined chasing her around a sunlit yard until we were both breathless and thirsty for the lemonade that would be waiting in the kitchen. I didn't possess a good way of describing the miraculous way flowers come to life but I got my point across.

Writing about it only increased the longing. But the unusual thing about these daydreams is that what began as a lovely day always ended the same way—sometimes it was just all blue, the grass, the house and everything. I was the luckiest woman in the world to have access to such happy memories—of course, they were not memories but that is how I viewed them.

Dear You, I went to the zoo today so I could tell you about the animals. Your father was so bad-humoured that I went alone and then my heart sank because it was snowing and the monkeys were all shut away. There were two of them behind a door but I couldn't get a proper look. I bought some gummy bears at the kiosk and did not eat them because they were for you.

Dear You, You shouldn't bite your nails so much. There isn't anything else I can think of at the moment.

Dear You, I bought you a book today and I wrote your name inside it so you'll never lose it. I think you'll love it. In the book there's a girl just like you. But you'll see that when you read it, my darling.

Dear You, I stood in the garden today and waited for you. I was trying to make amends for not being there yesterday when it was so warm. I did not see you.

Dear You, What I look like, so you will know me when we see each other next. I look like you but you would not recognise me because I have gotten so old.

Unstory

January 7th 2012, Rue de Bac. I don't know how many times I've told her that Paris is colder than Dublin in winter but Mum has gotten herself tanned the colour of a house brick. Dad doesn't waste any time letting me know what he thinks of the fake tan. He can't bear it. His face can't bear it. He has his I've-got-cancer indigestion smile. It comes from his gut and it says 'this can all stop now'. It's raining cats and dogs when they get to my part of town. The scrum on the métro gets Dad all worked up. He can't believe there are no cabs. Dublin is ridden with them. He huffs and puffs and I think he is on the verge of passing out. I am sure something leaks out of me when I see where they are staying. They have ignored all my recommendations and have chosen their own accommodation, Le Meurice. Because the Ritz is closed for renovations. I'm in awe when I see it. We make plans. They want day trips. They've just arrived and they want to leave. They're worried that my Paris won't be for them. My life is full of things they don't understand and therefore mistrust. I never wear skirts but I have worn a pretty skirt and sandals so they don't think I've gone too rock & roll. They think writing about pop is a difficult phase for me. They have perfected a new look of disapproval, to which they give another outing when I show them my latest posting on The Waves.

January 8th 2012, Rue de Bac. Seeing the sights and so on. We are now intimate with all the sights.

January 9th 2012, Rue de Bac. I explain in advance that everyone has a way of expressing themselves and this apartment is mine. They don't like the things I like. Et cetera. How was I to know that they'd love it? Dad is agape at the ceilings, relieved that his daughter should live in a place with cornices. I am agape that he is agape. And relieved, so relieved. We have obviously reached an understanding, painstakingly avoiding the obvious. Was there a conversation behind the scenes? I bet there was. Let's all just have a nice trip, shall we? All they have to go on is what I tell them. So I don't tell them that I've run out of money and I can't afford the rent. That I stole the towels in my bathroom. That I haven't earned any money since I arrived here. To top it all off, Mum wants to cook a proper dinner on their last night. (Did someone say they were leaving? Hooray.)

January 10th 2012, Café Breizh. The conversation starts quite idly. We have gone for lunch (Dad insists on saying 'going for a massive crêpe') and my parents do what parents do and they have a word with me about boyfriends. Not that I have much say in the matter. They have someone perfect for me. He doesn't live in my kind of world. He doesn't do music or 'a blogging' but he does have a share in a thriving software business. I have to convince them that Jerome does exist. I want them to see me with him, I want them to see my nitwit grin. Well, I'd love to meet your boyfriends, says Mum. Boyfriend. If we can call him that? Yes, you can call him that. Why don't you invite him for dinner?

January 11th 2012, Café la Perle. I leave Mum to do the sales without telling her they haven't started yet. She'll be relieved to miss them anyway. I need to speak to Jerome about dinner. No way he'll agree to a dinner with my parents. The thing with Jerome is it has to be his idea. Take it or leave it. I usually take it.

January 12th 2012, Rue de Bac. We'll just buy an apple pie, says Mum. Do you think he'll mind that I've bought a shop pie? I don't think he'll mind. A pie is a pie. Does he like cream or ice cream? Straight pie, I say. Oh, she says. There has to be something we can do that's better than dinner on our laps in my apartment. What about a stroll in the Tuileries or a boat trip on the Seine or the café where Dad saw the steaks the size of a tea towel? Then I have to explain to Mum that my kitchen isn't exactly geared up for banquets and she says we'll make do. My kitchen equipment amounts to some napkins stolen from their hotel and a pitch-black dinner set that cost more than my rent. I think I was drunk when I bought the plates at the marché aux puces because I paid more than twice what were asking. I hope I was drunk. That's a lot of money for plates. I give thanks and praise when I find a colander (no idea how that got there) and pray that whatever Mum makes will involve straining pasta. I meet Jerome for a coffee after school. It's silly and I know it but I want him to meet Mum and Dad. I want them to see me with him. To see how far I've come. It doesn't have to be mystical, or wonderful. It just has to happen. But Jerome has his head in his hands about coming for dinner. Whatever is wrong with him, it's nobody's fault, or I don't care whose fault it is. He says very little, preferring to drink his coffee. Of course, one of us has to say something. Otherwise we're just sitting there, but not Jerome, who is cold on the terrace, who has had no lunch. Not Jerome, who prefers to drink his coffee. Not Jerome, who stuffs both the little biscuits into his mouth without so much as a what-have-you, who, when I mention that I would have liked a biscuit, too, orders one for me then leaves me to eat it alone.

Daniel #5

Maybe he was tired from the early flight but Dublin was not much to get excited about. The famous beer Daniel had at the airport tasted like doo-doo water. The cab was rife with an old tractor smell and from its window Eva's hometown seemed warped and listless compared to Chicago or London or somewhere with a decent skyline.

—Let me guess, the driver said. You've come to find your ancestors.

—Nope. Mine go back to the Mayflower.

—More time to tear into the the pints then.

—I just had one.

—One pint? the driver said. An accusation.

Daniel wasn't so much tired as under a cloud. The night before he'd had dinner with Hippolyte. Daniel knew Eva had been to see him (she went straight there when they got back from Arles) so he dropped a line explaining himself. Hippolyte was childishly keen to talk. He came back straightaway to suggest Bones in the eleventh, so it would be by no means a straightforward dinner. But Daniel intended to get his money's worth.

Hippolyte was already a little drunk when he arrived, dispensing bisous to everyone in his path, even people he didn't know. In Daniel's kind of mood, a libidinous drunk was perfect dinner company. Unless you reminded yourself that he was a psychiatrist you would have thought Hippolyte had come out to drink and gossip. Daniel made attempts to be subtle (his worries about La Plongeuse, a little about her and Jerome) but Hippolyte was quick to go into details. Their sessions hadn't been frequent but they were always cordial, without being too revealing. Recently she was more concerned with putting things out of her mind.

—It is too easy to remember things poorly, he said. So she doesn't want to remember at all. This is not very typical, but you should know that she has no interest in herself. She is always moving.

—What about Jerome? Is she staying away from him? She mentioned Eagleback, right?

Some food came and Hippolyte rummaged around in his offal without consuming any of it.

—She mention him, yes.

—Is she seeing him?

—She can see him, she has seen him, but I don't know if she is seeing him. If she does not offer the information I do not torture her for it. So she has seen him but I do not know if she is seeing him.

Daniel made his question clearer.

—Is she fucking him?

—She could be fucking him right now, Hippolyte said. And I know Jerome, a little bit. I would not be surprised if he walked in here and started to fuck this carafe. He is bizarre like that, I think. Look under the table. Do you see the little crack in the floorboard? He would fuck that, too. The plate, if there is a crack in the plate. He is on it.

—Did she mention her family? Her parents. Her home life.

—Yes, said Hippolyte, who had taken to a simultaneous conversation with the waitress. He was asking to read her palm and she was telling him to eat his dinner.

—Is there anything I should know? Daniel said.

Hippolyte said he was going outside to smoke and that he would use the time to consider the question carefully. There was a Japanese girl standing on Godefroy Cavaignac and Daniel could see Hippolyte telling her a story wherein his two fingers were pointed under her chin in imitation of a revolver. Hippolyte mimed the recoil from the shot in slow motion. Now he was flapping his arms, also in slow motion. A drunken idiot, certainly, but it did seem like he was telling the truth about Eva. Then again it must have seemed as though Daniel was telling the truth too.

—Well, Hippolyte said upon his return. I think this girl has put up with a lot of difficult things in her life.

—I assume you discussed these difficult things. Isn't that why she went to see you? Or, you think she's suppressing something?

—I am a psychiatrist not a gypsy, Hippolyte said. But I think something happened with her parents and she does not want to acknowledge it.

—Do you think she is telling the truth?

—She believes she is. It's not my fault that she doesn't talk about the things she wants to forget. It could be that she remembers something in particular and she just won't say. Then why would she ask me to talk and then not talk? I don't know. Anyway, why do you want to know all this? She is here, she has no memory. Voilà.

Daniel was very quick to inform Hippolyte that fate worked both ways.

—Did you come here by cab or métro?

—Walked, Hipployte said.

—I came by métro. And you don't hear the gypsy walking up and down the carriage with the shoebox say 'this is my destiny'.

So why should she take it for granted that she washed dishes, for minimum wage? But take it for granted she does. Unless she faces her past she is destined to be enslaved to it. Her life is just another form of confinement.

He was just getting warmed up but Hippolyte peered at him, more sober than Daniel had first thought.

—Unless you are going to help this girl, you should leave her alone.

The sense of gloom remained as the cab pulled up at Eva's parents' house. Daniel couldn't fail to admire its imposing slate roof, the educated curve of the shingle, whereas the property itself was as straightforward and imposing as a small hospital.

He interrupted the Hands in the middle of an ongoing conversation.

—She's wondering if we'll want to eat later, Tony said.

—We're having a special lunch, Maeve said. So we mightn't want a big performance tonight.

—This woman has known for thirty years that there will have to be complications on the scale of nuclear war to prevent me from eating dinner in the evening.

It looked as though Eva's parents did all their clothes-shopping at airports. Maeve was, if not healthy, then not as overstuffed as Tony, whose skin resembled varnished teak. When he got off his stool to make cocktails (pints of them) it looked like either one of his knees might explode. They soon got down to the business of discussing Daniel's parents which, blessedly, brought out his creative streak. He described their most recent skiing trip in voluptuous detail (in Gstaad they lived near Valentino, whose pugs were a menace) and by the end of the story Daniel started to believe it had actually taken place.

No tour of the house was offered but Daniel could see from the kitchen window that the garden ran all the way to the sea, separated only by some small but possibly treacherous rocks. The bay was about as clear as Chinese soup. Maeve, meanwhile, was busying herself as if she was expecting royalty. Within minutes they were magnificently presiding over a lunch of freezing gin and caviar. Daniel thought: they are showing off, sending confirmation to his parents that, yes, the Hands were thoroughly schooled aficionados of the luxurious life. He wasn't going to argue. The fish eggs were coming out by the shiny shovelful and without too many qualms they abandoned themselves to the merriment of a good lunch. Tony made no secret that he intended to run the gamut of the offerings, and Maeve went about things with the regulated watchfulness of a senior surgeon. A black speck dropped on Tony's lap and it received her curious stare before removal with small tongs. It didn't take long to realise that Maeve's dedication was a spin-off of her nervousness.

She wanted some music to accompany lunch: La Captive by Berlioz.

—It was Eva's favourite piece.

—Not yet, Tony said.

He was eating as though something needed to be chewed back to life. Between mouthfuls Daniel listened to more of Eva's story.

—Let me tell you something that probably won't surprise you. Eva was a nervous child. What do you call it, but she had the shivers. The yips. Bats in the belfry. You'd find her dawdling on the shoreline, staring at the sea all day.

—She was thoughtful, Maeve said.

—Very thoughtful. And, in all her fits and starts, happy as much as unhappy. We have nothing to answer for, you know.

Tony flicked his wrist and the promised Berlioz eked from some hidden speakers. The sound washed over everyone (rich, forceful, although it failed to awake anything in Daniel) and it bowled him over how exuberant Maeve became. From her eager expression Daniel was expected to be awestruck but he wasn't awestruck. The music seemed musty and gave him a melancholy feeling he couldn't account for.

Tony said, —Eva could play Bach's Cello Suite by the age of five.

—With her nose, Maeve added.

Eva was always a good little girl—as conscientious as a security guard, they said. She was six, perhaps a little older, when one afternoon she came home from school and Tony was waiting at the gate. It was the softer side to her father that few apart from Eva and her mother ever got to see. He drove them all out to Greystones where there was a man with instruments of all sizes in so many states of repair. Eva sat on a low stool as her dad told her the luthier had been building this instrument for a very talented musician, a little girl.

She didn't go back to school that morning but sat in their living room with a newly restored child's cello. All week Tony led her through her scales, ensuring that she completed the painful and boring hand exercises. Needless to say, she didn't play again for another ten years, when she set her mind on a standard of excellence she was not destined for and didn't achieve. When she picked up the cello once more, she was in her father's view a prodigy, which Tony, over his muesli and quite casually, announced as fact to Eva and her mother. After she had been talked down from applying to Juilliard and the Royal College in London, Eva practiced ten, twelve hours a day for her pre-screening audition for the Conservatoire de Paris. Tony planned to spend the summer beforehand as her tutor, when in fact he didn't know the first thing about the intricacies of teaching music to a family member. Within a week they were communicating by slamming doors. Professional tuition had to be sought and paid for. Masterclasses. Eva's repertoire expanded and her hopes grew.

—An entire summer trying to understand the composers' souls, Tony said.

Then a difficulty following an ear infection left Eva incapacitated before her audition for the convervatoire. She failed at the first attempt and again the following year.

This was all well and good. Daniel was enjoying being Conrad for a day and they were, he thought, having a lovely afternoon. But there were some things he thought Tony and Maeve needed to know.

He flashed his best American smile and said what he had to say in a single, hoarse breath.

—Don't worry, she's healthy, she's happy, she's fine, she has friends, people who care for her, but Eva has problems with her memory and she's got some work to do to catch up.

Tony's response was unexpected: a hot groan, the kind of exhortation Daniel imagined was used in the bookmakers when a prized horse, anointed with a thousand or two and all Tony's accumulated optimism for the world, changed its mind and sat down before the last fence.

Tony slapped Daniel on the shoulder and said, —Take your drink with you.

The house was more or less on the beach but the view from Tony's study was obscured by smoke-caked blinds. There was a cigar-burned paisley scarf, some balled socks. A fountain pen had burst and grown into the carpet, but there were signs of hope, too: a full, yellow wall of *National Geographics* spanning many decades, newspapers from June, May, April, going all the way back.

Daniel was waiting for Tony to speak, but the silence suggested they were about to pray. Soon he had almost forgotten why they were there. He sensed Tony weighing things out. In that way Daniel was reminded of his father. There was always something calming about the talkings-to. Daniel could only ever identify them by the careful way the vowels in his name would be elongated

They remained silent until Daniel let it squirt out.

—We've kind of been dating, he said.

—As long as she's happy, Tony said with a doctorly lack of warmth. But we did tell you our daughter had a vivid imagination. So what you're saying about her memory, or whatever it is, it doesn't surprise us. She's always been a very creative girl.

Daniel inexpertly swirled the ice in the gin.

—She has a charming way of looking at the world.

—Not even that, Tony said. You should know that it is always easier to embrace something you can see in its entirety. That's why, with all respect, when it comes to my daughter, I can see what you can't.

Daniel listened, as well as he could, to the deft description of Eva's mental health problems.

—She was a worrier, he said. I lost track of the number of times I was supposed to have gone bankrupt. I mean, I have had ups and downs, but not the way Eva imagined. She got so excited about everything. Having cancer was too much for her bear.

By the time her father had transformed Eva's teenage sectioning, and eventual sedation, into an inappropriately bland narrative, Daniel was unable to make any kind of sane analysis, he just couldn't manage it anymore. He considered himself to have two options: either to tell Tony he could look after himself for the rest of the day, or to disappear altogether, not in any dramatic way but quietly and quickly.

Tony's face was visibly paling. Daniel was steeling himself for more but, without any preamble, Tony clapped his hands and announced they were going for a swim.

—We haven't had too much to drink yet, more's the pity. What say we clear our heads?

The famous swimming place near the house was nothing but a dim and muddy puddle. As far as Daniel had seen, the Irish were soggy people living on a barren rock, however much they liked to flog it to all the world as an island paradise.

Daniel was impressed by the matter-of-factness of Tony's size; although the tiny white Speedos he must have meant as a joke. He was tanned as a hazelnut, too. Daniel watched Tony slip into the water on tip-toes, as if it was his first swim in some time, then minced after him in his shorts. The water was cold but no colder than the air. It seemed strange that nobody seemed to be actually swimming as much as bobbing about; but as soon as he went to stretch out and attack the water he found that the swell was too strong.

Tony waited until Daniel was acclimatised before he began.

—If you really believe Eva has lost her memory, he said, you've been taken in. She is one hundred percent making this up.

This portion of the story was over almost instantaneously. The music of the sea rushed into his head and Daniel was puzzled as to why Tony chose to have this conversation here, as though they were in some spy movie; the kind of location you chose when you wanted to confess a murder or commit one.

As soon as they were out of the water, Tony insisted that Daniel take a nip from his hip flask. Daniel tasted cigars around the mouth of the flask, then something just as unpleasant: smokey whiskey.

The changing room was nothing but a concrete bunker. Tony took his towel and held it at the ends, seesawing it between his testicles and his groin while growling. Daniel tried to look away, but there seemed to be balls everywhere. He wasn't squeamish, he had been in Russian saunas with his father, so these old men's bodies shouldn't have bothered him; but they did. Tony was drying his hair then his back, vigorously but without reaching most of it. Daniel held his breath until most of the men had found their underwear.

—Her mother was telling you about music school and all of that, Tony said. You interrupted at just the right time. We were about to get to the unpleasant part.

Tony's voice quavered but he hadn't lowered it. His eyes were raw and his cheeks were burning up as he worked his gaze around the changing area. He seemed proud to be talking within earshot of the other swimmers.

—Maybe we asked for this, he said. Or I did, for pushing her so hard. But was it so bad that she had to run away from us?

—And she stayed in Paris?

—More or less. Home for a while after the audition, about which the less said the better. Bed for a month or two. A few dead-ends then gone again. And I'll tell you why. They went in after Tony Blair and they got him. The tumour was no bigger than one of these fish eggs. Big man, small tumour, but it spread and they couldn't go after it. They had to fucking blast it out of me. No harm in a bit of aggression. Frightened the shite out of me. But I'm still here.

Everything else Tony was saying, in his wooing and serious tone, could be summarised as: do you know Eva? Are you sure? Daniel had heard quite enough already, he could bet on that. And here were Tony's ground rules: no lover can compete with the love of a parent. And it's your word against mine.

Tony stepped into his shorts then hitched his trousers over his belly. He took a draw from the flask and Daniel was sure he saw the dismal sea water shine, just for a moment. It may have been the tingling after effects of the swim but Eva's father was certainly making a very good job of appearing hospitable, possibly in seeking to manipulate him. And Daniel didn't know why anyone would do that. He knew the effort of lying. He knew the reach of a good story and how much they could hurt.

Tony offered another hit from the flask.

—Don't take any notice of that girl, he said. She knows exactly who she is.

Daniel knew he was supposed to feel differently about Eva now but he didn't and he wouldn't. He took a sip from the flask then bolted upright. The sky was suddenly bubbling.

—Gimme a minute, he said.

It might have seemed as though he was snarling but Daniel was actually retching. Tony's whiskey and all the swallowed sea water and morning gin and the fair-to-middling airport Guinness and the previous night's wine with Hippolyte were slowly drawing themselves out of his stomach. He moved sharply away from the changing area before scattering the waves with gaunt vomit. What was it Walt used to say? Daniel was good at making too much of nothing.

Unstory

January 20th 2012, Rue de Bac. I haven't written for a while.

February 3rd 2012, Rue de Bac. Dinner was fine. Mum was fine. Dad was fine. Jerome turned up, eventually. He was fine, too, after a fashion. Mum's shepherd's pie was yuck but no one said anything. There was lots of it, so there you go. She didn't know the French for mince and she bought the wrong cut of meat and tried to chop it all up herself. So the food was a disaster but, again, no one said anything. That's the thing. No one said anything. I didn't know why nobody was talking. It doesn't make sense, Mum and Dad were always talking. I could have suggested some topics: the meat was surprisingly tough, given how much it cost; the doors on the métro are a little stiff; people aren't as friendly as back home. Acceptable topics all. It was as silent as if we were all doing the crossword. Then Dad came out with it: What does your wife do, Jerome? Where did he get that from? Well, I know where it came from, but why did it come out? There were other approved topics, as I said. Meat. The métro doors. Jerome, in fairness to him, dealt with the question quite well. By ignoring it.

Mum, in fairness to her, chastised herself once more for getting the wrong cut of meat. Me, in fairness to me, I was the most captive audience you could have imagined. Dad? Well, Dad saved the best for last. I was this vaguely delightful … thing. He spoke about me as if I was—what?—a delicious chocolate dessert, a bunch of flowers. It was hard to say why he took such a shine to Jerome, and why he said, Can I rely on you to look after my sweet little girl? Was he going to offer two camels in return for my hand?

Rue De Bac

The entries in the notebook stopped soon after that, at the end of February 2012. Does that mean I stopped then too?

One day it was so hot that I found it impossible to settle, even with the windows open to Ségo's garden. I went for a walk for the first time in days. It was so strange to be on the streets again that I barely noticed the heat at first.

I wanted to learn about pregnancy so I went to Galignani to read a book. The shopgirl I recognised from Gravy—she would come in with her friends from Portland and drink the cheapest wine and share food and guffaw and smoke too near the kitchen window. She was on my side, I could tell, but Galignani specialised in fanciness and there was nothing she could do to help. Instead, she recommended a book on Cézanne.

—His stuff is so monumental, she said.

I lost my bearings immediately—where Ségo lived and where I was.

—What I'm looking for, I said to anyone who would listen, is Rue de Bac. Can you please tell me the way to Rue de Bac?

On Boulevard Saint Germain, in the baked blue of the afternoon, I was sure I saw a mirage. The afternoon was as dead as a distant planet. The heat was impure, electrical. My saliva was too bitter to swallow and periodically I spat what I could get out of my mouth onto the microwaved pavement. It was so hot that my chef's trousers chafed as I covered so much ground so quickly. Once I started to remember where I was my heart started to pound. I was used to feelings of inadequacy. Everyone in Paris has those, Ségo used to say. But here, passing café terraces full of Sheikhs with their own private table fans—Arabian film stars for all I knew—I could feel them slipping away.

My old stretch of Rue de Bac felt vacant, looted, unParisian. Café Répulsion was definitely gone. I walked up and down in a daze before I recognised the antique shop. I could not—not even in my most misguided fantasies—have imagined spending that kind of money on a mirrored sideboard. I was savouring the shadow and flinching at the prices on display, when out of the corner of my eye I spied a couple exiting the building next door. They were suitably startled when I leapt out of the shadow to stop the door from closing.

—Pardon me, I said.

Green and black tiles on the stairwell—I was interested only in the door on the ground floor. It was nothing special, a white door, but it was a wondrous thing to me, anyway. There was no name plate but I rang the bell, savouring its low note. I was standing by at the door with my hands in my pockets and a smile on my face—a smile because I was itching to share with someone that in there I had fallen in love and in there someone had fallen out of love with me.

It was the night of my mother's shepherd's pie, although Mum and Dad had gone by now. I was in the bath and Jerome was talking to me from the doorway. It was so good to feel clean—a cleanliness that came from not being dirty in the first place. I might have been drinking something, too. Now that I remembered it, I usually drank rosé in the bath. I was about to speak—to invite him to join me—when Jerome beat me to it. His voice was soft and suggestive and I didn't take it in at first.

—It's too bad things didn't work out between us, he said.

—What?

—Sometimes it just stops.

Jerome wasn't finishing things with me. He had already finished with me.

—You just met my parents, I said.

He snorted. Blow your nose on me all you want, I thought. I'm in the bath, I don't care.

Forgetting that he had just dumped me, and that he was the one who was supposed to be sorry, Jerome gritted his teeth and shouted, —I am not your boyfriend.

I yawned, as if to say he could shout all he wanted. There was a pain in my ear. I supposed that he must have hit me—because he had me by the throat. I couldn't breathe but most of all I was confused. Jerome gritted his teeth and squeezed harder. I felt useless, sick. His hands machinery around my throat.

—Can I go to bed now? I said.

He let out a roar and hit me again and again and again. I must have been bleeding heavily from my mouth, and I didn't notice the blood in my ears at first. Nor did my voice reach past my throat. What I wanted to say was, I wish we could go far away from here.

He was gone and I tried to sleep there in the bathwater—in its cold, dark soup—but there was glossy blood running from my ears. I rubbed it in my eyes and I lay there, waiting for him to come back. And it got through to me, all the way to the middle, and I was a dumb creature. Not a king of the jungle or your bird of prey or your teatime PG Tips monkey but your old baboon, the kind the other baboons pick on.

It was a fiasco, my life after that. Everything else was admin. Besides.

I felt no one in the world that night could have made such a mistake. Some of us have seen the thing break, faked our surprise, we have turned on ourselves. But did we feel ourselves disappearing under the water? Did we see the blow coming?

Candlelight was all I could bear.

Daniel #6

Daniel disembarked the plane at Charles de Gaulle in Paris to a fresh archive of cheery messages. Eva's father was extremely conscientious about keeping in touch; and there were all the emojis you could ever wish for, Tony was really spraying them around.

Don't mind all that shite at the end of lunch, was one message. And we didn't do enough damage to that gin. Not nearly enough of it.

Daniel had to mute the alerts on his phone when he found himself caught up in Tony's next batch of cocktails.

They say two isn't enough but three is too much. Where do they get that shite from? Have you tried gin and milk? Can you imagine? I wouldn't advise it old son.

Never tried gin and milk, Daniel replied. But the texts just kept on coming.

I bet I can drink more gin than you, Tony texted.

That wouldn't be a good bet, Daniel texted.

Further enquiries after his parents. How are they doing, anyway? Are they well? I bet they are, he texted. I bet they are. And here we are back at the gin.

Daniel visited Eva as soon as he could. Ségo had warned him that something had happened with Jerome and that Eva had been in the garden for so long that it was becoming her job. Ségo would set her up with things to do before she left for work in the morning.

The garden was drenched and Eva was drinking from the running hose. He walked over to the wall to turn it off.

—I was using that, she said.

—You shouldn't run the tap willy-nilly.

—Willy-nilly.

—I think we're done with the watering for now.

He mentioned the garden at the family's summer house on Île de Ré. He made a big deal of the hollyhocks, their candy colours and odd posture. His phone was stuffed full of desirable pictures of the island. Eva looked at them meekly as he described the endless days to be spent squinting at the flabbergasting sea. The island was made for old-fashioned French vacations, the green glow on the water, girls on bicycles. Girls on bicycles were the best he could come up with on the spot.

—Ségo is closing up soon. I'm going out there for a little vacation. You should come. Believe me, no one should live more than an hour from the coast.

He got this from his father. In anything he said, especially when he was trying to persuade you of something, Daniel had the conviction of someone running for election. As with all skilled politicans, there were omissions. He made no mention of that morning's weak moment in which he had invited Tony and Maeve to stay, too. Tony had responded (by text, excitably) and plans were already being made. Daniel really didn't know what they were going to do beyond seafood and swimming, but he would ensure Eva had her perfect sunset moment with her parents; and she would notice his hand in it and would love him for it.

—I can't swim, Eva said.

—You paddle. There's a gate that goes straight from the garden to the sea.

—What if I get out of my depth?

—You won't, don't be crazy.

The concrete of the patio was gradually drying.

—I've never been in the sea.

—Exactly why you should come. Just think, nothing to worry about but oysters and ice cream. Oysters. Ice cream.

—Together? Eva said. Yuck.

Never Not Amazing

I wished I could remember the first time I cried. Was it the first time I felt embarrassed? Was it at the end of *E.T.*, or when I was born—did I cry then? Was it when I was beaten up by Jerome? Did I cry then? Let's say I didn't. Being innocent in the circumstances—or assuming innocence for myself and why not?—was in itself a weak defence, since the circumstances involved a man who seemed glad of the opportunity to punch the fuck out of someone physically weaker than him and who was careful not to waste that opportunity.

There wasn't too long before Gravy closed for the summer holiday but Ségo thought it was best that I stay busy.
   —Looking for a job? she said.
   —I have a job.
   —Had a job. You walked out, remember?
   Back in my whites, it would be just the same as before. And it was. But nothing tasted right—not even sugar which was bitter, water was sweet, meat felt like cheese and so did fruit. I was doing a bad impression of the woman who had worked there only a

week or two previously. It was a struggle to catch up—it took me an hour to peel a single kilo of tomatoes, another ten minutes to stare at them until I remembered where I was.

Daniel exited the store with an armful of tins. He was stocking up for our trip to the island and jawing on about the colours in the August skies and other things he couldn't describe effectively.

—He thinks we've never seen a sunset, Ségo said. Au bord de la merde.

—You can almost smell the light, he said.

—If you've had enough to smoke, she said, back to work, Daniel. Let's eat.

For the staff meal I had braised some mince, which I took to be veal before realising it was pork only to be told it was chicken. Ségo gave me the look—the look that said this most annoying and common-sensical thing. Count to ten. Then she wanted to tell me about her idea for a summer soup. The vegetable store needed cleaning out in time for the holiday. The implication was that the stores had become a mess in my absence.

—We don't believe in waste, I said.

—No we don't, Ségo said, before we were interrupted by the ringing phone.

There had been a series of phone calls to the restaurant and Ségo didn't know what to do since the number was blocked and the caller, whoever it was, never said a thing. But I knew it was Jerome because he had been emailing too—Can I come see you? Now? If not now when?—and I knew he was waiting for me just once to answer the phone.

It was the same this time. No one on the line.

—Not even any heavy breathing? Ségo said. That's disappointing.

The calls continued over the next few days, usually first thing in the morning when there was a stronger chance that I would be there alone. Sometimes the phone rang and she would stomp towards it in a temper and I would imagine another braver me answering it instead of Ségo.

All we need is a period of adjustment, Eagleback, I thought. We can still see this through. Sparks could still fly.

Jerome seemed startled to see me even though he had been the one doing the loitering, on Voltaire by the métro. He was wearing the Eagleback T-shirt—finally!—and his face had been coloured by the sun since I had seen him last.

We found some shade under the canopy of a cordonnerie. I felt a small ache when he told me that every afternoon he had been waiting to see if I would be there. He didn't want to embarrass me at work—that was why he was waiting there in the hope that I would pass by. I was a little surprised to see him but not that much. I told myself his presence was a mystery. But that would be to ignore his continuing calls to the restaurant and his many emails.

—Dinner, he said. On me.

Jerome smiled as though he assumed he was irresistible to me, which maybe he was. I should have known better than to agree. It didn't feel right to be so chipper either. Not with these things we had to speak about—these gruesome things I had remembered which would be in no way reviving or good for the appetite. Instead of saying anything to that effect I told him I couldn't wait to eat.

Jerome insisted on taking me shopping on Charonne for something to wear that evening. He had selected an outfit for me, something he thought I would love, that he wanted me to try.

He tried to describe it to me then he said, —I think you should just see it.

—No one's ever done this before.

—What?

—Bought me a gift. Bought me something to wear.

—Yes they have. I have.

The saleswomen were dressed like astronauts—their eyes glassy but also on high alert for any nonsense. Of course, no price tags on the angular tunics and shoes made from tires. After a little cajoling I tried on the dress Jerome had been considering— an extraordinary silver shower curtain—and I was reminded of the young Japanese people who had started to come to Gravy since word had gotten out of A__ B__'s visit. The dress was made from the same kind of fabrics they wore—seemingly designed to withstand toxic spillages.

All I could say was, —Oh.

The dress was heavier than a sodden blanket but that didn't matter. One of the astronauts stood by as I swayed before the mirror, popping my shoulders and waggling my wrists.

Jerome stood close to me and whispered, —You should get it.

—Don't think so, I said.

—How do you feel?

—Dunno. Pretty?

—Why so uncertain?

—Don't know.

—You look amazing. When was the last time you felt pretty?

—Don't know.

I asked Jerome if I should change into the dress straightaway but he started unbuttoning my chef's jacket without taking his eyes off mine, without acknowledging that my last visit to his apartment had ended with his wife pulling me out of there by my hair.

—This is nice, he said.

—Do you think so?

It was the nearest thing to no I could think of. But I wanted him to guzzle my lips, and to pry me open and scoop me out. He started to kiss me and something was weighing against me. A galaxy. I was angry with Jerome—after all I had read and all I had remembered. I was angry at myself, for allowing him to kiss me and that I hadn't enjoyed a first kiss. I was angry that kisses were irreversible.

Where do you start with making love when you are feeling like that? My rash—hitherto limited to my groin—had spread rampantly. The bruises from my beating on Léon Frot still sparkled. The veins in my biceps were leaping. I watched him, he watched me—the air fragrant with wariness and impatience. How could two naked people manage to stare at each other without any true curiosity? My thighs felt about as sensual as chair legs. I made myself feel better with my hand, as though to ask him to do it would have been an imposition.

A quick tussle. A bubble of hot breath. I coaxed him inside me. Inhaling, exhaling, spookily. Pushing onto me, Jerome went over on his ankle, calling out in pain, but carried on—his eyes containing fury. I reached out and placed my palms against the wall. I had my eyes on him and was communicating my terror wordlessly. Thoughts of him beating me and then drowning and being burned alive flew past—the carriages of an express train. Which isn't to say I wasn't turned on.

We made fast work of each other in the end. I think I preferred sex when I was in a bad mood anyway. Two angry people licking the same ice cream. It was like you weren't alive at all.

Just Because I Worked In A Restaurant Didn't Mean I Liked Eating In Them

Jerome was pleased that we had gotten into the hard-to-get-into Renouveau, on Charonne, with its famous chipboard finish and ceiling covered with warped glass. At least it wasn't Schiste. He had left his Eagleback T-shirt on the bedroom floor in favour of a striped shirt that transformed him into a handsome deckchair. In the new dress I might just have stepped off a condemned farm.

I wanted to eat quickly but when I saw the ever-increasing subdivisions of waiters gathering at our table the promise of a quick dinner seemed unlikely. They had already swept in with vegetables arranged to imitate an urban skyline and, when I had eaten them, all I felt was ill on vegetables. The waiters kept on appearing just at the moment I was about to speak. There was no way to avoid their confidential whispers about the delicacies before us, that we could see for ourselves.

Jerome saw me looking around.

—What do you think? he said.

—A lot of rigmarole, I said. One of Ségo's words. I figured that once whoever decorated this place had an idea they just couldn't stop.

—Isn't it beautiful? he said

If beauty means throwing gold leaf at the ceiling, I thought, then yes.

I saw a rosy-cheeked young waiter pick his nose and flick it away. I exhaled involuntarily and he looked my way. Oh I saw you, said my eyes.

Every time I spoke, Nose winced as if he had been electrocuted—but when Jerome addressed him he was as unresponsive as someone under interrogation. Nonetheless, I thanked Nose when he arrived with the bread, once I had selected the bread I wanted, once he had placed it on my plate, and again as he left.

—That's four times you said thank you to that guy.

—And?

—You're supposed to be having a good time.

I became concerned with the back of a spoon for a while. Then we were both staring at a pale gob of purée and I was letting the mush fall from my spoon. It smelled of my groin after exertion. I returned it to Nose with a shake of my head. I was stuck on one thing—did Jerome hit his wife too? I never did ask him why he hit me. And I never did ask him what was so wrong with everyone else in the first place that he chose me. And what made us different now?

I couldn't resist asking him about his life with Ghislaine. Shyly he spoke of their marriage without noticing that I was holding soup in my mouth without eating it, any more than he noticed I was there at all. He recited the story of their fall. Comfort leading to over-familiarity—closeness to remoteness and so on through perfection and time and boredom.

I studied Jerome—his hands were clasped and awkward, dead as pastry. He was twice as forthcoming as anyone needed to be, on the basis, it seemed to me, of a failing marriage and his part in its failure, which he sought to correct by more affairs—affairs with me and whoever.

Nose grandly presented us with some precious little dumplings—filled with something-something—and it was tough luck that the first thing I did was drop one from a height into the transluscent dipping sauce. I was worried that I had ruined the dress and worried that I would cry out loud about ruining it so I ran to the bathroom—pursued by Nose & co—to examine the stain more closely. The fabric squeaked when I moistened it and it pained my heart to see a cosmos of brown dots. But I wouldn't allow myself to cry today, not over a dress.

Warnings. That's what the dots were—a warning. If Jerome hit me before he'd hit me again. If he was a monster once he'd be a monster twice. The reasoning would become more obscure. You Were Asking For It begets Just In Case which begets I Felt Like It.

Jerome was on his phone when I returned. I recognised his expression and tried to ignore it. He wore such a pitying look that I had to assume he was communicating with Ghislaine.

—What are you doing?

—I just need to do this, he said.

We were making strange progress—our eyes, our mouths showed it.

—I just need to know something, I said.

—Need to know what?

—Why you dumped me? Why you hit me?

Jerome peered at me and folded his arms. He was useless at being aloof, even now with something afoot—except now he looked not only uneasy but pained, as though he had been made a fool of.

—This is important, too, I said. I was in that car.

He was colourless, his discomfort as palpable as weather.

—You weren't there.

—I had to be.

—We had finished long before that. God, this is fucked up. I don't know how you lost your mind, your memory. But you weren't in that car.

—Who else was in the car?

Nose delivered some raw fish plated in an uptight arrangement and Jerome ate his in a single mouthful, angrily.

—It's not important.

—Then I'd like to know.

—The person I just texted actually.

—She was in the car and I wasn't?

—No you weren't.

—Another girlfriend?

This was standard stuff and at first I thought—with his expertly kind, solemn expression—Jerome was going through the motions. No wonder people fell for it. This poor girl on the phone, whoever she was. Me. Besides.

I squeezed the fish between my forefinger and thumb but didn't eat any. There was a herb sauce brushed alongside it so that the plate looked patterned. Very clever, I thought. Very confusing. The neck of the dress was bunching around my ears. Jerome sat upright before leaning forward, as you would do in a negotiation.

This was not our perfect day. I wasn't fussy but this wasn't it.

I had my face in my hands—either I was there for some time or Jerome was particularly impatient. I could hear him asking me to stop and I could feel my breath misting in my palms. My head didn't feel right. I hoped it wasn't what I thought it was. To offset the headache I imagined I was one of those divers breathing through an aqualung in an old marine conservation film. I imagined my skull caving in—that's what I presumed would happen if I ran out of oxygen.

I sniffed at my next plate—lamb blah-blah—and pushed it away. When Nose came to remove it Jerome made a point of reassuring him that everything was all right.

Then, to no one, he said, —This is kind of a weird one.

I didn't notice the shift in tone but there must have been one. Jerome was on the verge of saying something else. Gradually I began to feel starved of air, looking around the stupid room and suddenly feeling so desperately uncomfortable in that dress. I tried to imagine a victorious feeling of pulling it on for the first time. I tried to imagine knowing only victory. Not quite—and not quite extended all the way to not at all, not ever.

—You need to tell me who it was, I said.

—It's better if I don't.

—Who was it? I said.

Then it struck me that my inability to hear what Jerome said wasn't the same as him not saying it. Nose had been and gone without us noticing and I was devouring the petits fours—my face dirty with cocoa dust—when he repeated it.

—Ségo, he said.

Present Tense

I run barefoot from Renouveau. I boot down Charonne
and right along Faubourg Saint Antoine and scythe around
Place de la Bastille and head north towards the Canal Saint
Martin, my chest blazing. I can see the streetlights flickering
on, the city alight with a thousand lamps. I can see the giant
containers unloading at the back of the Monoprix—as if
someone is stocking up for a big party—and that gives me a
boost of energy. I fly past the silent canal, past the trembling
arms of a blind beggar, past groaning crowds, cornucopias,
whole worlds. My chest is blazing, my senses are tapering
into nothing, but I keep on along the quai feeling strangely
consoled—my soul winning its war with pain. I have crossed
a bridge from the beating by Jerome, and betrayal by Ségo,
towards the illusion—it is really nothing else—that I can
make a better future alone. As if I have solved another difficult
sum, I decide I can learn to live without either of them.
Joyless liaisons are behind me. Showy sex of the kind I shared
with Jerome in bathrooms, sex that shamed its participants
and increased the aggregate desire.

Daniel's place is not a visit I have planned to make but my feet are ravaged from running and I—maybe I don't need a reason. I have not seen him in a couple of days but the moment I get in the door he resumes the conversation about the vacation. The sunsets on Île De Ré are unlike anything I've ever seen or ever will see.

—I am going to lie out until I'm a rotten apricot. The beaches'll blow your mind.

When Daniel laughs his eyes shine—new coins—and, agog, it occurs to me finally that he might be in love with me.

—Can't wait, I say.

—You should see them.

—I intend to.

—Once in a lifetime, he says, to square that part of it away.

The amber light in his bedroom gives his skin a coppery tone that reminds me of Eagleback's on that first morning at Bertrand Rose. He has noticed the dress and the bare feet. I expect him to say something and he doesn't. But I know how I look and I know what he must be thinking. He sees that I am bamboozled by myself in the bedroom mirror. My hair is matted with sweat—as if oil has gotten into some bird's feathers—and when I pull at it I make it worse.

I step out of the dress and hand it to him.

Daniel dumps the dress in his laundry basket without paying it any more attention. The basket is nearly empty because he has been preparing for the trip. The little person inside me rejoices at the ship-shape columns of underwear. His hospital corners.

I perch on the edge of Daniel's bed. The sight of my skin— rosy in the mirror—gives me a little shock. I ask him for a T-shirt and he mistakes this for you know what. He runs a finger lightly along my arm but I am scared to kiss anyone now. Nor have I brushed my teeth since I left Ségo's place this morning—there has been no opportunity—and, even though it isn't the case, I know I will come across as careless somehow.

I inform Daniel that I want the T-shirt to sleep in and he fetches one. The cotton smells powdery. My bare skin smells of Fairy liquid and Jerome. Of course, I know the difference between lust and love and the difference between hate and love. I do—they're different.

Daniel gets into the beautiful bed and I follow. The headboard is carved and wooden. Here and there are flowers, small wooden roses painted in wedding-cake white. The pillows are larger than I'm used to and more comfortable, white too—the cases starched so they are cool against your face.

—Ask a question, I say. Did you know Ségo had a boyfriend?

—We've talked about it but it doesn't feel like her favourite subject.

Daniel asks me if I am okay with Ségo accompanying us to the island. As of this evening—as of an hour ago, unbeknown to him—I have resolved to put her out of my mind, so I say, —You know that guy I chased after outside Bertrand Rose, Eagleback?

I break off because I don't know what else to say. I have successfully herded a motorway full of speeding traffic. Besides. What was it Ghislaine said? Happiness is not a baguette.

He leans in and whispers, —I am here.

—I know.

The spectacle of Daniel's perfect dreads against the pillow case is too much. I have to cover my face with my hands because I have begun to cry—hollering with eyes tightly closed, even though I don't care that Daniel sees me or what he thinks. It isn't until I am crying—over Jerome, over Ségo, over nothing—that I understand that relief can be found everywhere. The act of crying itself is relief, in the way my face spontaneously vibrates and the tears spring out of me without me knowing how, feeling them roll down my face and into my mouth, their strange taste and the way they make me feel weightless and slightly drowsy and how they stop as soon as I am feeling better.

Daniel #8

Eva wakes up wired and muttering as if drugged. Daniel doesn't know why she wants to visit Buttes Chaumont before they leave for the island.

—I want to smell the forest air, she says. Before we head to the sea.

She wants something sweet for breakfast. Bertrand Rose is out of their way so Daniel finds a boulangerie near Canal Saint Martin. They are not the only ones up and at it: American kids with jet-black clothes and his same throaty Eastern accent are buying escargot pastries just to use as props in their photos. Everyone is so skilled at framing and composition but no one eats anything. There is enough discarded pastry to dam the canal.

Eva wants an ordinary bar of chocolate and Daniel gets her the next best thing: a pain au chocolat. He used to be able to track her by her sweet tooth. Once she had the palate of a baby, now she has no time for such dainty things. Now it's outrageously dark chocolate, the more punishing the better.

A dog follows her along Rue de Marseille as she rescues the chocolate and dumps the rest on the sidewalk. This isn't what

Daniel would do but he doesn't mind. Eva raucously applauds when the dog eats the dough and afterwards licks the cement clean. The dog comes and goes so smoothly that he must have known where she'd be and what she'd do. It's eminently believable to Daniel that Eva and this wily dog are known to each other; one wild animal to another.

When they get to the park it seems important to Eva that they lay together on the grass in something vaguely like a date. Daniel gets ice creams for a second breakfast and they eat them lying on the ground, their eyes tilted towards heaven.

Eva's breathing is as heavy as a rising tide.

—Since we're lying here, let's do some yoga.

—You know yoga?

—No, he says. But how difficult can it be?

She laughs. Daniel laughs, too, because Eva is eating her ice cream end first. It makes more sense, as long as she doesn't drop it on the grass, to leave the ice cream for last. It gets so he's eating his ice cream that way too. Impossible to deny there is something sexual in that. When Eva turns onto her back Daniel wants to yoga himself onto her and for them to kiss but she is apprehensive and so is he. There are so many people around, in the park, in his mind, maybe in her mind.

Official palpitations started two minutes ago.

Today it's starting: a family reunion on a sunny island, or, he guesses you could say, an outright ambush. Tony has been texting, practically bloodthirsty for the seafood, but the bed and breakfast Daniel recommended in Ars-en-Ré didn't grab him one bit. Tony was antsy about the partial sea view they were promised.

So long as it is near water I will eat cold Chinese out of a dirty shoe, he texted.

Daniel doesn't want to consider what all this means for Eva. Conversation isn't so easy today, knowing what he knows. It's a better idea to sit on the grass and watch the stoned Frisbee-throwers operating in exaggerated slo-mo. Somebody gets a beach ball in the face and Eva seems overwhelmed by something like nostalgia, although it can't be that. They whittle away at a few more subjects until she begins picking grass and throwing strands in the air.

The sun is already high and the sky has become white adobe. Her eyes shrink as she tries to describe her old life.

—Before Eva Hand or after her I was something else.

—Someone else.

—When everything fell apart with Jerome I think I lived here. I lived all over the city but mostly here. I slept on benches, under bushes. When I needed food I stole it from the bins of Rosa Bonheur.

Eva promises Daniel that she remembers sleeping outdoors as a feast of light.

—Too poetic, he says, even though her words today seem to glitter in the sun.

She snaps at him. —Were you there?

—No starlight in the city.

—There was.

—Too much glow, he says. The street lamps.

Daniel takes Eva's hand but she works it free. If this was a dream he'd be unable to wake her. She is fighting tears, and he doesn't know how to respond except to say they need to get on the road. He stands up and stretches his legs, scattering the torn grass. Now he has the urge to tell her that the plans have changed. Why don't we all just stay here? The city is so quiet in August. If we want we can have Paris all to ourselves.

As they descend the hill and exit the park, Eva looks at the lake and at the cedar trees and she tells him she believes there is no such thing as lost time.

—It's not a mystery, she says. It can't be solved. Once there was Jerome and after him there was nothing. I was caught up in a world that was too much for me.

—But now you are coming out of it?

—It's that simple.

Young Girl, Go Slowly

What if once upon a time I read a book that said, 'You must know that you have not done anything wrong. Your sin in your parents' eyes was to fall for a married man. A man who desired you, who considered you beautiful and kind. Your sin, your weakness was for a man with—you assumed—a tender heart. Your sin was to seek the life unknown. The dark waters. Your sin was to have nowhere else to go. Your sin, I suppose, was to not know your body. Your sin was confusion. Your sin was to part your lips in anticipation, in expectation, in having expectations at all. Your sin was to lay open your palms, outstretch your arms. Your sin was to wonder. To clarify—nothing you did, apart from not paying your bills, was a sin. I left you for dead. But I don't want you to forgive me. I'm asking you to forget me.'

Follow the A10 from Paris
to the D735

Daniel insists on doing all the driving as well as all the talking on the way to La Rochelle and the island. His topics include oysters and oysters—but, they're out of season, Ségo says—and the beach house which will be our new home for the next however many days.

Ségo is in the passenger seat and I am in the back. She is wearing sunglasses, which makes it easier to drift away in my mind. She is tapping out an imaginary piano routine, a kind of jive, on the dashboard. She looks for me in the mirror—her face says she saw all this coming. But one of us didn't see this coming. One of us has a broken heart. One of us wonders how long they are supposed to feel this way. Perhaps I am, after all, just a bad judge of character. But the real questions have only begun— always about love, my problems with love. Problems I will solve by never considering again.

She is watching me from behind those glasses, I can tell.

—I found out, I say.

—I figured. Jerome called me. He said you'd had dinner.

—Ask a question? I say. Why you and not me?

—There is no answer to that, she says. Are you angry?

I want Ségo to know what I mean without knowing what I am feeling, so I nod my head even though she is looking at the road and doesn't see me.

—Want me to tell you a story? she says.

—Is there a happy ending? Daniel says.

—No offence, Daniel, Ségo says. But I need you to be quiet for the next for few minutes. Eva? You want to hear what I have to say? You want to know what happened?

Hearing about Ségo and Jerome—from Jerome—has already been more news than I'm able for.

She continues. —Jerome was cheating on Ghislaine with you but then he decided he wanted to cheat on Ghislaine with me. Sounds nice and neat, doesn't it? His perfect conscience just wouldn't allow him to sleep with more than two women at a time.

—News to me, Daniel says.

—Please, this isn't for your benefit. First of all, Eva, you should know that I was reluctant to get serious with a married man. But Jerome did such a good job of talking me round. This was about three years ago, long before I met you. He was just back from a trip to Arles and I told him of my time there in some bullfighters' hotel. He knew the place, he said. The next day he turned up at Gravy with a bottle of champagne. It was supermarket champagne but I was overwhelmed anyway. Whatever, fuck it. I don't know how to put this, but I was just lonely and easily impressed by shit like champagne. He wrote poetry that didn't rhyme, you know what I mean? For the first few months we lolled around—fucking honeymooners at a resort. Such pert little things. Jerome seemed to be able to get away whenever he pleased. It was bliss, I'll grant you that. It was fine, for a while. It was a fucking lie, but I loved it at the time. I was so caught up in him that I didn't see what was happening. Before you say anything, I don't need any reminding that he was not the man for me. We spoke of Ghislaine from time to time, but more often than not we spoke of his friend Eva. The Irish girl with the attitude. That's who you were. We returned to the topic of you so often that my suspicions flourished. It took Jerome a while to admit that you guys were dating too. He didn't seem to understand fully what this meant to me, his girlfriend. I knew he had a wife but not that he had another girlfriend. Then Jerome finished with you. For good, he said. Not efficiently, exactly, but properly. I asked him where you had gone. We assumed you had blown off or gone back to Ireland to do whatever it is you did, or to London. Somewhere. You had been gone, for good, out of the scene for more than a year. Then we discovered you were back.

Does Ségo know where I spent my missing year? That I had a sleeping bag hidden in the alley behind Bertrand Rose? I remember a young baker giving me a just-baked and freshly filled Paris–Brest and that the hazelnut cream made me sick. I wonder what became of the sleeping bag—at least I had one, not every homeless person has a sleeping bag. I remember thinking I could get clean by jumping into the lake at Buttes Chaumont. Not so. I spent a year or more measuring my worth by how clean I could get myself. I remember walking into BVH, unimpeded all the way up to the fragrance counter. The way the Chanel No. 5 fought with my rot and the power I felt with a bottle in my hand as the security guard approached. The scent bloomed on me as I was led outside. I did this in department stores and pharmacies all over the city. I never went long without some Chanel. My picture of myself is of someone physically very alive and attuned to survival. Every time I was led to the pavement, I was afraid I would be met by the police—but I wasn't worth their while. Being more or less negligible to other human beings made the humiliation more bearable.

Does Ségo need to know any of this? Does she need to know that for protection I made myself into an animal? That was how I survived in my mind, as a beast alive in the city. A monstrous, faithful animal with nothing to fear except other animals like me; no use to anyone—dirty, tired and in the way. I told myself that I was more alive and that I was seeing the world through new eyes. But being ignored as you huddle in a doorway is not being alive, not when it's your day-to-day. You spend the days looking sideways for a kick of dust, a sudden dart. It is never more than waiting—and waiting for nothing. The best you can hope for is to let time pass.

—You wanna know what happened next? Ségo says.
—Does she? Daniel says.
—Button it, please. This ain't easy. Eva, you were in a crash?
—It makes sense, I say. Doesn't it?
—It makes perfect sense. But no. The morning we heard you were back, we had been about to disappear ourselves, to Normandy. Just for a weekend of nothing much except not-Paris, like we're all doing now. We used to get away once a month but Ghislaine had been making life difficult for Jerome and the trips were becoming a case of waiting out weekends in some hotel within driving distance from the city. We would fucking disagree on the hotels, the amount of money we should spend. We disagreed on the length of a weekend, whether it should be two days, three or four. We disagreed on these conversations, too. I said they were fights, but Jerome didn't think so. Without question, that morning's conversation was a fight. The mere mention of your name was an affront to him. It sounds weird, but I became the one to say you needed help. Jerome was aghast that I would be your advocate. We drove off from Gravy in a kind of

223

muggy silence. The argument began on the approach to Place de la République. She's been fucking dealt with, Jerome said. End of. You can imagine that in his accent. End of. We were entering the square from Voltaire and were cut off by a van, the kind of manoeuvre that would spike Jerome's aggression. He tried to overtake the van, as if we were fleeing a goddamn heist, and the car swung onto the kerb before totalling a fucking phalanx of Vélibs, maybe ten in all. Unfortunately, Jerome's concrete head survived the clash with the windshield, but I lay there in the upturned car. We were creaking. Apart from that it was surprising how quiet everything was. The traffic lights going through their cycle, over and over. Shattered glass on my forehead, and I was watching the upside-down carousel on the square, and all I could think about was you.

—Can I interrupt? I say. Were you okay?

—I'm still here, so yes. My back is gone. It hurts to sit. It hurts now. But it gets better when I exercise. Maybe I'll have a swim when we get there.

—You will, Daniel says. I hate to interrupt, I do, but we're crossing the bridge to the island.

The beautiful bridge to the island is bowed and it feels as though the car is flying over the water. It has really taken off. How can this be the first time I have seen the sea? I want to lick the blue water and through the window I try to. I open my hand and place it against the window. The moisture of my palm on the glass shimmers before it evaporates and for an instant the entire ocean is sucked into the car and we are—all three of us—completely submerged.

An Evening of Hardly Any
Weather at All

The house on the island—tucked away near Ars-en-Ré—has not been well looked after but I know instinctively that the journey has been worth it. It is, I can tell, the holiday house of a wealthy person who has asked someone else to choose the decor. The kitchen invites a second look. It says we live well but simply, just the way you're supposed to. If I had come to my senses here—instead of in Gravy—I might have thought I was raised by a family of tasteful smugglers. Woven sacks hang in frames and some piratey insignia on the mirrors to confirm that we are, indeed, by the sea. On the tea towels there are poems about boats and one in French about a drowning.

Ségo disappears to her room while Daniel flutters around photographing the broken shutters in order to blame the summer tenants.

—The letting agency should have a proper vetting service. Have you seen what those people did to the towels?

I ignore his suggestion that we skip up to his nominated beach—Conche des Baleines—where he wants to light a fire, sit in a circle and scoot through all the new music on his phone. I can feel water somewhere. I explore the garden and open the gate that takes me directly to the shoreline. All I want to do is be alone, if I'm lucky, on the beach right in front of the house.

The afternoon has been hazy but the haze has disappeared so I can tell we are facing the rest of France. A single gull lazes on the water. Another one patrols the beach. The patterns on the lacquered surface of the water start to move and the smell reminds me amazingly of Elias' basement. The beach is just as quiet.

Ségo comes out of the gate. She is wearing the bottoms of a striped swimsuit that matches the apple green of the shutters and she has nothing on top. Her creamy boobs wobble enthusiastically.

There is silence—but there is no comfort in it and it is harder to bear than the silence in the car. She is half in and half out of the water and she suggests I strip off and swim with her.

Only when I start to move away does she speak again.

—Everything I told you all happened, she says.

—Just not in the way you told me?

—I'm sorry it happened. Believe me, I'm sorry for Ghislaine and I'm sorry for you. For me. I was there, in the car. I'm sorry for us all. But it happened and here we are. Now I'm going to say the rest very bluntly and you're going to listen. The crash was the crash but that story I told you about arriving at Gravy the first time, it wasn't the whole story. Consider this a P.S. to a letter.

—What letter?

—Shush, she says. No letter, just what I said in the car. But, last November I saw someone familiar on the news. This was on the morning of the crash, by the way. So you can connect it all up. A young woman had tried to throw herself under a train at Châtelet and they wanted to know about her identity. It was you. That's why we were fighting as we were driving out of town. Jerome wanted me to leave you be. But you should have seen the picture. In a goddamn neck brace. I asked Jerome some questions. 'How do you think I survived in Paris at first? Do you think I just walked into a busy restaurant one day? I can't remember the names of the people who helped me. But they did. Don't you see?' I called the number on the website anyway. They put me through to the hospital and the nurse said you were at the wrong end of the platform. The far end. And the driver had been warned about a woman at Châtelet so he slowed the train enough to save your life.

Pallor in the sky. The beach is dust. A minute later I have yet to speak. Then I cry out as if something has collapsed inside of me. I can't hear any more—it is as though Ségo is pouring seawater into my mouth, only so much will go in.

I calm myself with some exceptionally shallow breaths, as if preserving air.

—I was lucky not to go under the wheels?

—They cut the power to the tracks. The train wasn't even delayed for that long. Kudos to you for making shit of trying to kill yourself.

—Why didn't you tell me all this straight out?

—I just thought, what if she doesn't have to know? She could just live in the here and now.

Seeing my widening eyes, Ségo invites me to question her. My expression must be an accumulation of the day's strange discoveries. She puts her hands on my shoulders to say that I need to count to ten.

—What kind of person throws themself under a train? I say. Maybe I was texting and I slipped.

—Yes, maybe you were texting. And you slipped. Or?

—It could have been wet.

—Indoors? Do you remember anything about the train?

—Nope.

—After?

—No.

—Before?

—Noooo.

—I think it's good that you don't remember, Ségo says. A bang on the head off a train will be sure to do something to your memory.

To Be the Woman Who Stopped
All the Trains

I can't bear to tell Ségo that I do remember. Clear glimpses, not from meeting her at Saint Louis nor from arriving at Gravy—I have to take her word on all that—but from a few weeks prior. One night I had found a phone card on the terrace outside Rosa Bonheur and tried to sell it, but I couldn't, so I used it to call the only number I knew.

Mum sounded stressed to hear from me. I don't remember what she said or when she went to get Dad. Nor does anything come to mind about my conversation with him—other than he mentioned St Vincent's Hospital and that Tony Blair was the size of a truffle. This he dismissed with a suppressed burp.

—He's not staying, he said. He's not invited.

A number of things were supposed to happen next. I was supposed to offer to come home, this was after asking for help in getting home. But I don't remember doing this. I don't remember saying goodbye. I know I walked out of the gates of Buttes Chaumont and headed all the way downhill to the busiest métro station in Paris. If you can't imagine what was going through my mind then neither can I.

Châtelet métro was a dying body, the tunnels that ran from platform to platform the poisoned veins. The tunnels were occupied by sleeping figures, the people who lived in the station. I was one of them. Every time I went down there to sleep—when it was too cold to sleep in the park—I had the sense of being in an evacuation. When Jerome beat me and left me—well, it was impossible to believe that life had passed through my hands. I had been pushed out of life and was no longer alive anyway, not really. Throwing myself under a train was the best idea I ever had. The last moments of my life, as I foresaw them, would be filled with certainty and ecstasy. I couldn't wait for the emptiness, of course—spotless and endless—but more than anything I was simply seeking humiliation. To be the woman that made everyone late.

I wasn't crying on the platform. I wasn't even speaking—there was no one to speak to. All I did was sit on a bench and watch carriage after carriage pass before choosing one. If anyone was calling me back I didn't hear them.

Now I wish for a moment that I was back there—so I could go all the way under that train, take its full force, spraying myself all over the tiles of Châtelet station, if only to silence my memory—because now I do what I have not done before, what I should have done before, what I couldn't do before. I see myself. And don't believe anyone who tells you that life doesn't flash before your eyes. I see myself stepping out from a little orange paddling pool—happy by the looks of it—to be wrapped up in a towel. A perfect little sausage roll.

Then, notions.

Then, Paris, and, for a while, fulfilment. Cauliflowers. Then, I was hearing my father talk about his Tony Blair. And just as I imagined Jerome's hands closing around my throat I looked up and saw the windows of the train shimmer.

Is this 25 percent, Hippolyte? Is this 50 percent? No percent?

One day Daniel buys sixty out-of-season oysters and Ségo tries to sell Gravy to a woman she meets while having a massage in Ars-en-Ré. She doesn't make the sale but she does post an announcement on Gravy's Facebook page to say that the restaurant will be closed for another week. It is understood that she is in touch with Jerome although he is never mentioned by name. Did Jerome hit Ségo? Did he beat her bloody and bandaged, too? But all that matters is that he has gone and I am safe with my friends. Still afraid—but not afraid in any of the ways that I have expected.

That night we have dinner around the bonfire on the beach. Daniel asks me to describe Eagleback—but I can't describe him because I can't see him anymore. It's then that I pull the diary from my pocket. I inspect the pages one more time, not to resuscitate old feelings—just a last blast before the book goes on the fire. Goodbye to my rambling and to the commotion of Eva Hand's bleary mind. It was crowded with too much—too much ink wasted on too much that was becoming more and more remote. The man smoking at the China Star? Did he keep a diary or did he know to leave well enough alone?

I don't have any of Daniel's special oysters but I do have a flavour of ice cream that I didn't think I'd like but is now my favourite. It's made with rum and golden raisins.

—Malaga, Ségo calls it.

—Why Malaga?

—It's sweet wine from Spain.

—Not rum then?

There they lie, the raisins resembling damp, well-fed babes. Beached in the sweet cream they taste concentratedly of happiness, even though I can't say I have just experienced it—happiness that is—only relief. To me they are the same feeling. I never know when I pass from one to the other. Happiness might be the simple feeling of relief magnified by a thousand million. Ghislaine was wrong—happiness is a baguette. It's rum and raisin.

Daniel #8

When he opens his eyes the blue sky is silent and he can feel the weight of another brilliant morning. They are walking along the empty beach and have stopped to watch birds dropping from the sky to fish for breakfast before they flitter away. He stares at the sky as though it contains the roll call of a recent air disaster, a feeling of dread that is not at all unusual but unwelcome and, this time, all his own making. Tony and Maeve, who don't belong here, are here anyway. They will have had breakfast by now and, thanks to clucky Daniel, are expecting to have lunch with their daughter at a restaurant by the water in Saint Martin.

Sometimes it gives Daniel a strange little thrill. Other times he wishes he'd left the fuck alone. But someone had to intervene. Someone had to make the necessary arrangements. It just happened to be him. Now he wants to tell Eva to run, to flee the scene once more.

She is transfixed by the birds. Not only that, it's first thing in the morning so she has some difficulty understanding Daniel when he says it.

—What would you say if your parents were to drop by?

—Do they have a boat?

Normally he approves of her jokes.

—I don't know how to answer that, he says.

—Are they fishermen?

He can smell the sand, the warming shells, and Daniel is as jaunty and confused as any man in his position has the right to be. He has brought a towel in case he might take a swim, as if this is all a lark, but the waves sound about as comforting as an iron lung.

—What would you say if you were to meet them?

—I don't think I would say anything.

The dunes loom and they are buffeted by a vaguely sweet wind. He says, —What would you say if you were to meet them today?

Not only is she unable to imagine meeting her parents, today or any other day, Eva is not prepared to discuss it. But she doesn't have to fear what's coming, does she? She'll be the same Eva when she knows, won't she? But it is Daniel who has changed. It is Daniel (who was only helping everyone out) who is not who he was. He takes her hands, and he whispers, and he tells her about himself, about filthy rich Conrad and his project.

They are entering a new territory of silence.

He could say something else, but he doesn't dare. Eva steps back and looks askance at him, as he supposes she should, as if he could go to hell, as if she wants no more from him than he might right this minute begin the long, lonely swim to La Rochelle and leave her to the beach and this bullshit surprise. She tells him to fuck off. Very slowly she tells him to fucking fuck fucking off. And Eva's face says this: the whole thing has to be a hoax, an ingenious one, a total shake-down to which she is incapable of resistance.

—So long as you're okay with it, he says.

It was never going to be the day for a swim. Some good ideas don't turn out to be bad ideas, they are bad ideas in the first place and can't be explained.

At the house they are beset by Ségo almost leaping over the gate.

—What took you so long?

—The beach is a certain length, Eva says. And we walked at a certain pace.

Daniel interrupts. —She's in that kind of mood.

—Please don't be, Ségo says.

He wipes his brow, ignoring Ségo's jousting gaze. She has a vicious and most profound opposition to this reunion; it is as invasive to her principles as it is (now) incidental to his. Eva has to be from somewhere, he has told her. And Ségo, who agreed with this and nothing else, guffawed this morning when she heard that Tony and Maeve were already on the island.

Daniel decides Eva is ready for the news.

—Your parents are waiting to meet you.

The words seem to roll around her head. A marble in search of a hole. She thinks this makes no sense. No one knows where they are. What they look like even. No, she says, her parents are a mystery and they should stay that way.

—They're waiting at Quai 53 for you right now, he says.

—How did you find them?

—They found me. Then I found you.

Ségo is all the while sizing Daniel up as if they are going to fight. She directs a mocking smile towards him before addressing Eva.

—They don't trust you to make it on your own.

Daniel interrupts, at the risk of running out of power mid-sentence.

—They care about you, he says. They care enough to ask me to help.

He tells Eva to expect a couple dressed as a pair of milky teas.

—But you can make your own mind up, he says. They're waiting for you right now.

Daniel takes Eva in his arms but she is as unresponsive as a roll of carpet. He kisses her and she bites his lip. It seems to him that she is getting worse as a kisser.

Prawns

From the bath I can hear Ségo and Daniel arguing—him for this reunion, her against. There has been a battle and he has had his way. At the mention of my parents, I try to drop below the waterline and out of view.

When I am finished, I parcel myself up in a towel as if a fire alarm has just been sounded—quickly and carefully, afraid of being fully naked for more than a second or two. I wonder for a moment if I should dress up—I don't know Quai 53—but I decide the bikini lying on the bathroom floor will do perfectly well. I dry my hair and leave the house to do what has to be done.

I dawdle so it's nearly two o'clock by the time I get to Quai 53. From where I am standing, behind a telecom van, I see the couple—whom I don't recognise—Daniel said would be dressed as milky teas. They are facing without any sense of anticipation a metal tray piled with prawns and melting ice. I have seen cheerier soup queues.

I go up to them and we make conversation as best we can—thoughts coming and going, coming and going. The sky is sugary and bright and Mum notices the restaurant has fairy lights dangling and they are burning in the daytime. We all nod in agreement. What a waste. Her eyes are loitering on the slender part at the top of my arms. I can tell very little from the way the tip of her tongue traces her top lip—I suppose there some bruises left over from my beating on Léon Frot. I suppose it has something to do with the weight I have lost. I really should have wrapped up.

—What kind of emergency is this at all? Dad says. Swimming togs. And prawns.

He is eating them daintily, solemnly. It is not his way, from what I've read. Already there is mayonnaise on him and he has made a pile of prawn shells resembling babies' toenails.

Dad talks, he is everywhere—the menu, the prawns, his business interests. The way he seems to assume I am interested in the millions he's made from part-baked bread. How he tries to explain that to me—he does his best anyway. It's already difficult to imagine him without money, since he seems built for it—equipped for a life where you pick up the phone and within minutes are the owner of a wind farm or, for half an hour, absurd amounts of Yen. From what I can understand he has on the day before he came here just made another million in burger buns.

He speaks to me conspiratorially about the quality of the fish here—the Atlantic water, he says—when it is likely the prawns come from Bangladesh or Mauritius, like the waiters.

—You can have all the prawns you want, Mum says.

This is forgotten when Mum seeks butter for Dad's bread—not that he should be allowed butter, she says. The waiter is confused and brings melted butter to go with the prawns, which are cold. Dad orders more prawns and the waiter tolerates his determination to speak in French.

The platter arrives suspiciously quickly and Dad pushes it towards me before changing his mind. He wants to peel one of the prawns for me.

—Allow me, he says.

I can't resist. —Allow you what?

I watch his gnarled hands do an absolute job on the first couple of prawns. The shells are geting the better of him and he squirts innards onto his shirt to go with the mayonnaise stains. Mum is willing him on but he must be nervous and under the table his shoes accidentally hoof against my bare toes.

—Give her the bloody thing, Tony. She doesn't want to be eating shells.

Dad picks one clean and hands it to me. He seems proud of himself and I enjoy the mauled prawn warm from his palm.

—Let's get you something to wear, Mum says. One of those stripey yokes. Your father could do with a clean shirt after this performance.

—We'll all get them, Dad says. Would you say there's any ice cream for sale in this town?

We find ice creams easily enough but when we set off to find T-shirts I realise that I don't know my way around. Dad looks cheated when I take a shortcut without knowing where I'm going. We end up in someone's back garden in the syrupy afternoon heat. There are some chickens strutting around and some butterscotch-coloured bed sheets drooping on a line. I act as if we were supposed to turn up here, but I'm unable to fool them for very long.

Mum's eyes have the intensity of someone who has for years been lost in the Amazon.

—It's alright, she says. We'll find our way. You haven't done anything wrong.

We make our way out of the garden and eventually find a street displaying shrink-wrapped espadrilles and billowing beach towels. At least being lost has brought Dad to his point.

—You're not doing this for fun are you?

—Just tell us you're all right, Mum says.

—I can't tell you that Mum. I wasn't doing well, but I am getting better. I've ended up being a dishwasher.

—You don't have to wash dishes any more, Dad says.

I can tell he means it. But I don't know what to say, since I like washing dishes. All that matters to me is to be by Ségo's side—a chalkboard of jobs to be completed to her satisfaction then ticked off. That is all I want to do. Cooking with my friends and earning their respect. How exhilarated I become, how satisfying to hear good words coming back from the dining room. The scabs on my arms and the cracked fingernails matter most of all. It is about no more than having worked and the good feeling of having implemented my system.

Mum gives me the rest of her cone to finish. I eat it so quickly and it's so cold that I sneeze and get vanilla ice cream all over Dad's shirt—that and the mayonnaise and prawn juice make him seem exhausted.

—At least the stains are in the right order, he says. Fish then dessert. Talking of which, you've gone very skinny. We might have to put you on the ice cream diet.

—I scream?

—You scream.

When Dad laughs his whole body moves like the man in the China Star. But he is handsome when he laughs, which—now that I remember it—used to be his favourite thing to do. I know he has been sick but I don't know if he is sick now. I decide he is and that he has been sick all along. It doesn't matter if the cancer is the size of a prized truffle or one of these prawns, it has been travelling quietly in him—all morning, all through lunch, and into the night it will do its work, which is to move. I need to see this and, as though the information can be found in a screen in the back of an aeroplane seat, I need to know how many miles there are until it reaches its destination.

—How's your ice cream? he says.

—It's nice.

—Mine's nicer. It's good but it's not as good as Teddy's.

—Who's Teddy?

—It was your favourite ice cream.

—I'd like to try it.

—Does that mean you'll come home then?

—Go on then, I say.

Peter Piper picked a peck of pickled peppers.

By the time we get back to the house—tired, but in matching Breton T-shirts—it is time to eat again. Daniel has been preparing a barbecue but a storm sets in and we are forced inside to eat. There are more prawns—he wasn't to know—as well as champagne, nothing else is acceptable. He begins jamming it down everyone's throats. He even hands me a glass I don't want.

Ségo is behaving as an anxious parent supervising a first date. She wants to talk to me so badly that she follows me to the bathroom. In case I need reassuring, she says. She doesn't want to admit that I have had a good time today.

—It could have been worse, is all I will say.

—Let me ask you something. Have you thought about what you're doing?

—Going to the toilet?

—That's not a good answer.

—What's a good answer?

—There's a life for you in Paris.

I want to reassure her so I go to pains to explain the things I plan to do when I get to Dublin—a real passport, the recovery of my official identity, possibly a visit to the bank to discuss all the money they are owed. A visit to the social welfare office just in case anyone wants to give me some. Mum and Dad have said they'll look after things but Ségo's not sure that's a good idea.

I'm not sure what I want to say in reply, so she says, —It's okay, you can just come back here to me.

I am to take this to heart, I think. And so—me first—we kiss. What else is there for us to do? It is not like other kisses I have known. At first, in the intolerable moment in which I know I'm off-tasting, I feel we are doing it separately.

—Give it a minute, she says. See if we like it.

I catch my breath and go back in. Ségo tastes of very little—not even champagne—and yet I feel a kind of greed, my kisses pouring out of me and ending in brushstrokes along her neck. She hasn't imposed herself on me but, like most things I know to be true, this has been her idea all along.

Ségo wants to do certain things and I want to do certain things but dinner is waiting. In something of a hurry to return to the world so I can discern how it has changed, I depart the bathroom in the knowledge that whatever we have just done—a mushroom cloud and lightning strike all in one—has made us both feel better. How could it not? Good kisses never leave the kisser.

It'sokayIt'sokayIt'sokayIt'sokayIt'sokayIt'sokayIt'sokayIt'sokay
It'sokayIt'sokayIt'sokayIt'sokayIt'sokayIt'sokayIt'sokayIt'sokay
It'sokayIt'sokayIt'sokayIt'sokayIt'sokayIt'sokayIt'sokayIt'sokay
It'sokayIt'sokayIt'sokayIt'sokayIt'sokayIt'sokayIt'sokayIt'sokay
It'sokayIt'sokayIt'sokayIt'sokayIt'sokayIt'sokayIt'sokayIt'sokay
It'sokayIt'sokayIt'sokay.It'sokayIt'sokayIt'sokayIt'sokayIt'sokay
It'sokayIt'sokayIt'sokayIt'sokayIt'sokayIt'sokayIt'sokayIt'sokay
It'sokayIt'sokayIt'sokayIt'sokayIt'sokayIt'sokayIt'sokayIt'sokay
It'sokayIt'sokayIt'sokayIt'sokayIt'sokayIt'sokayIt'sokayIt'sokay
It'sokayIt'sokayIt'sokayIt'sokayIt'sokayIt'sokayIt'sokayIt'sokay
It'sokayIt'sokayIt'sokayIt'sokayIt'sokayIt'sokay.It'sokayIt'sokay

It'sokayIt'sokayIt'sokayIt'sokayIt'sokayIt'sokayIt'sokayIt'sokay
It'sokayIt'sokayIt'sokayIt'sokayIt'sokayIt'sokayIt'sokayIt'sokay
It'sokayIt'sokayIt'sokayIt'sokayIt'sokayIt'sokayIt'sokayIt'sokay
It'sokayIt'sokayIt'sokayIt'sokayIt'sokayIt'sokayIt'sokayIt'sokay
It'sokayIt'sokayIt'sokayIt'sokayIt'sokayIt'sokayIt'sokayIt'sokay
It'sokay.It'sokayIt'sokayIt'sokayIt'sokayIt'sokayIt'sokayIt'sokay
It'sokayIt'sokayIt'sokayIt'sokayIt'sokayIt'sokayIt'sokayIt'sokay
It'sokayIt'sokayIt'sokayIt'sokayIt'sokayIt'sokayIt'sokayIt'sokay
It'sokayIt'sokayIt'sokayIt'sokayIt'sokayIt'sokayIt'sokayIt'sokay
It'sokayIt'sokayIt'sokayIt'sokayIt'sokayIt'sokayIt'sokayIt'sokay
It'sokayIt'sokayIt'sokayIt'sokay.It'sokayIt'sokayIt'sokayIt'sokay
It'sokayIt'sokayIt'sokayIt'sokayIt'sokayIt'sokayIt'sokayIt'sokay
It'sokayIt'sokayIt'sokayIt'sokayIt'sokayIt'sokayIt'sokayIt'sokay
It'sokayIt'sokayIt'sokayIt'sokayIt'sokayIt'sokayIt'sokayIt'sokay
It'sokayIt'sokayIt'sokayIt'sokayIt'sokayIt'sokayIt'sokayIt'sokay
It'sokayIt'sokayIt'sokayIt'sokayIt'sokayIt'sokayIt'sokayIt'sokay
It'sokayIt'sokayIt'sokayIt'sokayIt'sokayIt'sokayIt'sokayIt'sokay
It'sokayIt'sokayIt'sokayIt'sokayIt'sokayIt'sokayIt'sokayIt'sokay
It'sokayIt'sokayIt'sokayIt'sokayIt'sokayIt'sokayIt'sokayIt'sokay
It'sokayIt'sokayIt'sokayIt'sokayIt'sokayIt'sokayIt'sokayIt'sokay
It'sokayIt'sokayIt'sokayIt'sokayIt'sokayIt'sokayIt'sokayIt'sokay
It'sokayIt'sokay.It'sokayIt'sokayIt'sokayIt'sokayIt'sokayIt'sokay
It'sokayIt'sokayIt'sokayIt'sokayIt'sokayIt'sokayIt'sokayIt'sokay
It'sokayIt'sokayIt'sokayIt'sokayIt'sokayIt'sokayIt'sokayIt'sokay
It'sokayIt'sokayIt'sokayIt'sokayIt'sokayIt'sokayIt'sokayIt'sokay
It'sokayIt'sokayIt'sokayIt'sokayIt'sokayIt'sokayIt'sokayIt'sokay
It'sokayIt'sokayIt'sokayIt'sokayIt'sokay.It'sokayIt'sokayIt'sokay
It'sokayIt'sokayIt'sokayIt'sokayIt'sokayIt'sokayIt'sokayIt'sokay
It'sokayIt'sokayIt'sokayIt'sokayIt'sokayIt'sokayIt'sokayIt'sokay
It'sokayIt'sokayIt'sokayIt'sokayIt'sokayIt'sokayIt'sokayIt'sokay
It'sokayIt'sokayIt'sokayIt'sokayIt'sokayIt'sokayIt'sokayIt'sokay
It'sokayIt'sokayIt'sokayIt'sokayIt'sokayIt'sokayIt'sokayIt'sokay.
It'sokayIt'sokayIt'sokayIt'sokayIt'sokayIt'sokayIt'sokayIt'sokay

It'sokayIt'sokayIt'sokayIt'sokayIt'sokayIt'sokayIt'sokayIt'sokay
It'sokayIt'sokayIt'sokayIt'sokayIt'sokayIt'sokayIt'sokayIt'sokay
It'sokayIt'sokayIt'sokayIt'sokayIt'sokayIt'sokayIt'sokayIt'sokay
It'sokayIt'sokayIt'sokayIt'sokayIt'sokayIt'sokayIt'sokayIt'sokay
It'sokayIt'sokayIt'sokay.It'sokayIt'sokayIt'sokayIt'sokayIt'sokay
It'sokayIt'sokayIt'sokayIt'sokayIt'sokayIt'sokayIt'sokayIt'sokay
It'sokayIt'sokayIt'sokayIt'sokayIt'sokayIt'sokayIt'sokayIt'sokay
It'sokayIt'sokay.

Dad is accepting everything Daniel offers him and very soon
he is drunk—Mum, too. They ask Ségo for music and she plays
along as if they are boisterous regulars at the restaurant. It might
be the champagne but my mother wants everyone to know about
my childhood. It still doesn't seem to dawn on her that it is news
to me as much as anyone else. The way I am representing myself
has led everyone to think that I recognise what she's saying.

—I can't get over how little you eat. One or two tiny little
prawns.

Mum takes us all back. I was a greedy girl. Whatever anyone
else was having, that's what I wanted. Is that yours? No, it's mine.

Daniel asks, —What was her favourite?

—Pavlova, Mum says quickly.

—A demon for them, Dad says.

They go on to describe every variety of meringue there is.
Mum remembers my ninth birthday party—and the glorious
afternoon when I took a sponge cake into my bedroom, dropping
my face into it to prevent it being taken from me.

I am about to speak when Dad shushes Mum and puts a
finger to my lips. He invites me to join him on the rug before the
glinting light of the candles. He asks Ségo for music and we waltz
slowly and awkwardly to a song I don't know and don't care for.

My father dancing—I have no idea if this is out of character,
but he moves his feet with a certain grace, heedless of the wolf

whistles from Daniel. I am thinking Dad is well. I am thinking that people who have Tony Blairs don't drink and they don't dance. Or, maybe he is sick and this is his favourite song—he has many, it seems—and he simply wants to dance. I have to give him credit for wanting to dance and that his feet are working as they should. Dad coos the song's melody into my ear while drumming its tune on my back with his thick fingertips. There is very little chance of knowing if we have done this before.

I place my chin on Dad's shoulder to suggest that we should slow down to match the music—at which his feet become less nimble before catching on the rug. Perhaps to compensate for this he leans backwards and sways this way and that, blurring his face in the process so that he is little more than a shape—a recognisable warmth. Inclining his head towards mine, he dignifies the next few moments with the longest unbroken silence of the day. His eyelids are closing. Is he drowsy after the champagne? No, he is just closing his eyes and in doing so he is halting time forever. The dance continues. I am looking over Dad's shoulder—at my dipped head reflected in the windows and the night, and it seems as though he is already dancing away from me.

Touché

I do dream about bassett hounds in the end, as well various horny dealings with Nicolas Sarkozy. Sometimes we are in a hurry to Montparnasse to make the TGV from Paris to La Rochelle—Nicolas has free train travel because he was once president—and we make it just in time even though the poor dog is exhausted. Then one thing leads to another. Oh Nicolas.

Ségo has helped my parents secure an emergency passport for me but she isn't happy about it. On the day we are due to leave she is ostentatiously sombre, not only around Mum and Dad but me, too.

Daniel, meanwhile, seems heartbroken. All morning he has been huddled on the beach, his head cocked in thought. His eyes are swollen with hay fever, he says. But his nerves not only seem tight but torn altogether. I wonder about him—whether he needs help—but there's nothing I can do now. If ever there was a moment I would choose to forget, yesterday would be it. In some sarong he must have been wearing for a joke, he suggested we go for a walk while Ségo took care of dinner. One barbecue was

246

blending into another but there was no point in anything other than forbearance, not when my folks were in the mood for an occasion. There was something not quite right about it in the first place—I needed no reminding that this was my last night.

The more Daniel tried to reassure me that I had very little—even nothing—to worry about, the more I worried.

—It's funny how you don't see things coming, he said.

—Storms? I said. Being too literal is still my way of dealing with his oversupply of enthusiasm.

Above us there was nothing to see except unmoving purple and brown clouds. The waves were rasping at our cold feet as Daniel headed into the dunes with a whoop—another off-kilter gesture. We followed a path up through the dunes to a rough clearing. His expression softened to show that we should stop to admire something—it was quite an ordinary view, a tatty picnic area was about it. There were the blackened remnants of several bonfires and some teenagers were playing guitars further into the dunes. I couldn't see but could feel the sweet smoke from our barbecue at home.

Then, in what was a frantic moment for him, Daniel said he wanted to talk about something—it was nothing to worry about, he said. He didn't think so, he was sure of it.

He told me that my mother and father were indifferent to my stories. And, because life in Paris had become a story—not an *E. T.* story but a real story—they didn't believe my memory loss was genuine. Just too much, they told him. Daniel was short of breath and mumbling so I had to ask him to repeat it—whether he would go their way or mine should it ever come to that.

I held my breath and my temper then out it came—one for every miraculous, pathetic punch.

—No, no, no.

Daniel's cheeks are soft but his skull isn't and my hand really hurt. Also, he barely put up a fight. His beautiful face full of sadness and worry as he thudded into an accommodating dune. The commotion brought about the attention of a passing collie, which sniffed us up and down, perhaps wondering, as I was, when Daniel was going to get up. The dog took his time walking away, implying disapproval.

In an hour I will meet my parents at Quai 53 and a car will drive us all the way to Charles de Gaulle. For now, I am in an antiques shop on the harbour in Saint Martin—it's nearly empty in a very expensive way—and Ségo is waiting while the antiques man checks on the availability of some bistro chairs she wants to buy for Gravy.

It is thirty-five degrees outside but Antiques is wearing a black polo neck under a burgundy V-neck under a grey cardigan under a blue woollen jacket. He smells discreetly of furniture polish and I am scratching my collar just looking at him. While Antiques makes his call, he offers us a seat on the display versions of the chairs.

The metal is cool against my thighs. —Nice, I say.

Ségo looks rested after her week in the sun but far from relaxed. I've become fascinated by her skin, expensive and childlike. It is, as I have come to expect, as smooth and tight as a porpoise's. Whenever she hugs me—good night and good morning and times in-between—I can smell it, I can take her all the way into my nostrils.

My voice rises sharply when I say, —I'm excited about Dublin.

—You sound it.

—You don't have to be so mean about it.

I stand up quickly but the chair has stuck to my leg and skin departs metal with a fart noise that we ignore.

—They're my parents, I say.

—That doesn't mean that they value your happiness. It just means they're good at appearances.

Antiques finishes his call and addresses Ségo in an amorous tone. He tells her that some chairs have mysteriously appeared and they can be delivered to Paris whenever she wants. Assuming he has secured the sale, he lays it on thick.

Ségo turns to me and says, —What's wrong with the chairs I have?

We make our escape from the shop and outside I wonder if convention dictates that I should storm off. Start crying while I'm at it. Jump off the pier.

It's Ségo so I don't want to do any of that—but I feel there are some things she needs to know.

—Ask a question, I say. Can I say something about me and Jerome?

—You just gonna say mean things to get back at me?

—There is some simple information I feel I should share with you and you are free disregard it if you wish.

—Touché, she says.

—Touché.

—Touché.

—Touché.

—Touché.

—Touché.

—Touché.

—Eva, what is it you want to say to me?

I approach the stone steps leading down to the jetties and all the boats. There is a walkway that takes you over to the Quai 53 side of the harbour without having to walk on the street. The steps are in the shade and the stone is wet and cool, if a little narrow to accommodate two people sitting side by side.

—Are you alright? she says.

But it seems to me that Ségo wants me to keep quiet, and take whatever it is I have to say about Jerome to the airport and back to Ireland.

—Am I in trouble if you don't like what I say?

—Where do you get these things from? In trouble? No.

Ségo makes her way after me, coming to rest a couple of steps above where I'm sitting. Her knees are resting against my shoulders and she begins to give me a massage. I flinch at her touch at first but she settles into a rhythm where she is moving slowly along my spine as if pulling the meat away from the bone. She seems to want to push me as far as she can, waiting for a response—my sigh—before pausing and asking for my hands.

At one point she is waggling my wrists and pulling my fingers so that the sound of my popping joints resembles radio static.

Then she says, —Is this what I think it is?

I know I can nod my head and that this time Ségo will see me. Otherwise, with both of us on the steps and facing the same way, it's a phone call where nobody can hang up.

Ségo sounds embarrassed.

—He hit you, didn't he?

She is rubbing my shoulders and she adjusts the strap of my swimsuit. It is just as well that I can't see her face when I say, —Of course, this was after I had been pregnant with his baby.

—I knew, she says.

—Because he hit you too?

—Because he told me.

—Has he hit you?

—No.

—Not yet, I say.

Ségo is right to play it down. Although sometimes I wonder what would have happened if I'd had a baby. What if I had tried to test Jerome's love for me? As if there wasn't a finite amount of it. Now I will never know. And what my child has never known—how could it?—is that it would have affected every part of my life, those other areas—my feeling of aimlessness in particular—that did not turn out so well when it was left to me. As decisions go, losing a child may not have been the worst one I have made. But I did not make this decision.

—Are you going to see him again? I say.

—I doubt it.

I'm past worrying about Jerome now, I am—but I can remember Arles—and what went wrong in my body. Before that there was a beautiful hotel room with tiles and a terrace. We brought our own music and our own gin and made ourselves right at home. When we finished the bottle we called down and asked for more, but they said they couldn't give us gin—they could give us wine. The man who delivered it to the room took to us and said the wine was lovers' wine. And then, of course, something in me burst and there was all that fuss.

Ségo has her ears pricked but I don't share any of this.

Across the harbour, through the masts and sails, I can see my parents leaving Quai 53. Ségo's phone rings—it's my father calling, he's waving to us from outside the restaurant. I could be about to walk out of her life forever and it is the hardest thing I've ever had to do. Losing her is as feasible as persuading a drip back up a tap. Besides. Can I even begin to say what she has done for me? I won't even try.

يحور اي

I would rather be looking at the planes but Charles de Gaulle is full of shops which demand our attention.

—Let me see you properly, Mum says.

This is how she speaks to me now. The judge in a pet show.

I pull faces in the shop's mirror. A feather could be tickling my nose. Oh my heart, the scarf is the kind of thing worn by the Queen. Mum chatters to keep me interested in buying it—in her buying it—but the scarf does nothing a scarf is supposed to do and it costs all that money. Next door, in an undertaking as impressive and solemn as the signing of an international treaty, she buys me pearls. But I'm having a lovely time and when I'm having a lovely time I tend to imagine it can only get lovelier. And if it's what Mum wants, I am content to wear the tasteless scarves and pointless but correct pearls.

It is probably too much and certainly too soon but, before we have even left Paris, she says she wants to return to France. There's a place she wants to visit in Avignon—it's expensive, she says, but you get what you pay for these days. We'll go next spring, once I'm more settled. We'll drink the appropriate aperitifs under the perfect blossoms. Meanwhile, they are about to spend six thousand euros on a weekend touching their toes and cleansing themselves with raw fennel—although it occurs to me that vulnerable people, the category to which I've decided my father belongs, have come to expect too much from fruit and veg.

I feel embarrassed that my parents spend most of their time on holiday—but you would need to be a skilful orator to convince anyone that theirs is a life that needs adjustment. They are just rich and the vast world is very available to them.

And to me, Mum says.

We drive from the airport in Dad's enormous custard-coloured car. We reach Dun Laoghaire, passing by a beautiful pier that for the life of me I can't remember—I feel stupid for not recognising it. There is nonetheless a pleasant, savoury smell to the sea.

Mum shares her thoughts so far—that this will be the perfect place in which to resume my old life.

—I'm picturing walks along the pier, she says.

—Watercolour-worthy sunsets, Dad says.

They point out the landmarks—as though they have taken in an exchange student for the summer—but they only begin to understand my confusion, made worse by carsickness, when I fail to recognise the Martello Tower across the bay. They mean well and I know that—but my parents have to be told in a number of ways that I don't remember.

—There's our house! Mum says.

The bay before it is attempting to sparkle into life. The tired sea is one thing but there, Mum says, is the bandstand blown up by the Provos and new library that cost all that money. Teddy's—that's where we'll go for ice cream. A quick spin through Glasthule and St Joseph's Church is pointed out, briefly, as if I am expected to sculpt a baptism, first communion, and confirmation—an entire childhood—from some passing remarks.

We pass the beach in Sandycove where a pair of old men are returning from an evening swim in matching dressing gowns—an act, to my mind, of good old quiet defiance.

I ask Dad if he swims.

—I bet you look funny in your togs.

—He looks like a big fat candle, Mum says.

Dad slows at the gate to afford me a widescreen view of the house. Compared to what I know—Paris, dishes, dirty mattresses—it's the home of a lottery winner. Viewed from the garden, the large windows that brood upon the bay speak of a discreetly satisfying life within.

Dad has some work calls to make and Mum stage manages my entrance to the house, so I am left alone to explore. I spot interesting nooks everywhere—and there is so much hallway, far too much of it. The manicured parquet floorboards are different from the thick carpets I have envisaged, but so are the great piles of neatly stacked birch in the porch and by the fireplace in the first living room I come to.

The living room has the look of a sacristy—lace curtains the colour of a roast potato, from Dad's cigars—but the rowdy gathering of plants and vines in the conservatory is overwhelming. It may be the end of summer but the light is wintry. I let the vine tickle my forehead. I dig my face deep into the canopy of leaves and to my surprise discover that it is real—a harsh, stalky smell and a fist of grapes falling gently against my nose. They are dusty but underneath the dust the grapes are a livid purple. There is so much to see—plants, their names beyond me. I guess at orchids and I am sure I see geraniums. I congratulate myself for knowing the name by popping a grape into my mouth.

I am spitting the grape into my hand and wiping my hand under my armpit when Mum appears with tea—fetching hot drinks seems to be what she does. But she doesn't have the hang of my memory at all. I have to ask her explain things. Dad's routine—that, when he isn't in here, he is in his study drinking coffee, drinking wine, smoking, writing letters to papers, reading books on treason, betrayal and arson. Sometimes he just sits in the dark with his music but she says I am not to worry and his moods pass eventually.

—Why moods?

—It's your father.

—Is the cancer back?

—Is it back? It's been gone for, I don't know, almost as long as you.

—He looks like he has something.

—That's your father.

—Should he be smoking?

—He can smoke all he wants.

—But it'll come back.

The silence that follows is much gloomier than I expect. Mum pirouettes away, which says that I am to follow her.

—Leave the cup, she says.

I stand at the sea wall. I look up and see the mirroring effect the dusk has on the upstairs windows. What any of this signifies I can't be certain—but I understand something is afoot when Mum blunders towards the garage waving her arms as if shooing pigeons.

—When was the last time you played the cello?

Music seems to be an acceptable topic but I am learning to tune Mum out when she speaks. Or I am still listening but in a distracted way, the way you do when you're washing dishes—because by now I have adjusted to the fact that they have a surprise for me. It was only a matter of time before someone mentioned that word.

In the drab light my father does not look well—he is already sitting on an upturned wine crate, looking as disillusioned as a fisherman expecting bad weather before an important day at sea. He has rolled up his trousers and is putting on a pair of old combat boots which have been rotting by the garage door.

—There are jobs to do, he says. If you want to occupy yourself in the next few days, I'll be needing a right-hand man. Unless you have music to play.

It seems that once upon a time I wanted to be a professional musician.

—Missed the conservatoire by a whisker, says Dad.

I say, —What's the conservatoire?

—You auditioned, Mum says. Twice.

—I don't remember.

—You do remember, Dad says. You said music was your life.

Let's not pretend that I can remember—but I'm queasy and this comes on suddenly. My queasiness is seasoned with panic because I don't know why they look so worried.

Mum takes a while to unlock the garage door. She steps back so I am more or less standing there alone.

—Have a look around, she says. See if there's anything you can find.

The interior of the garage resembles the scene of an interrupted burglary. There is a box containing some tulip bulbs and when I lift it as instructed Mum asks if I see what is underneath—the leather handle of an instrument case. I remove the cello from the case, holding the instrument as though it has never been out of my hands. The point of this, apparently, is that it should seem like a happy memory. Dad is now standing at the door of the garage. Mum joins him, miming fascination at the scene. God knows how I try to return their anxious smiles.

On the stairs there is a framed photograph a child being rolled through snow. I turn the picture to the wall—just in case she is who I think she is.

My bedroom is vast and clean and half-painted. The floorboards go on forever and I decide I will wear them out with focused pacing. Mum has explained that they wanted to get the room ready for me but they couldn't decide on a colour for the walls—I suppose I could make too much of that, if I chose to. She also said we could pick out some furniture but the room is so big that it would worry me to fill it and I think I like it as it is—although I can't make out much of anything belonging to me.

I get into bed and out of bed. Maybe I won't spend any time in here. Maybe I will spend all my time in here. The sheets and pillowcases are new and very nice—the brand name would probably be big news for anyone into sheets and pillowcases but I don't want to know. I am not going in the direction of branded sheets. The wardrobes—for perhaps an hour I stand in front of them, attempting to answer the question of to whom those old jeans now belong and what purpose they serve.

It was a Saturday morning in Paris. Apocryphal. Much like the first day I saw Eagleback. I had wanted to travel alone to Paris but Mum and Dad wouldn't hear of it. Paris was to be shared, they said. The city photographs well but in three dimensions you have to contend with homeless people like I would become; scaffolding over the cathedral; forgetting your favourite route to that café and getting there to find it shuttered. Many such things about the meeting with the music teacher occur to me—she was going to help us with the pre-screening for the conservatoire and I was expected to walk into her home and confidently play Dvorak's Concerto from start to finish. Her living room floor was bare and scuffed and I was alone on it with absolutely no idea of what to do with this cello I had brought with me on the plane.

The bow was too light in my hand. The cello strings were made of toxic material and I was scared to touch them. A heavy sigh came from the teacher—a skinny woman in an oversized man's shirt. It was not what I would have worn to welcome strangers to my home.

Being out of your depth—in the sea, in space or, in this case, sitting before Shirt in her living room—involves fighting for air. I don't know what anyone else heard but the sound I made was of some burly men moving furniture. And this was attended by a moment of recognition. No, I could not deliver a convincing performance but my failure had been prepared for, long in advance of Paris, in my apathy to the one thing held precious by my father and mother. Music was something into which they poured meaning. This concerto—Dvorak in particular had been Dad's suggestion— was for them a deeply dependable structure which provided moments of discovery and release that, even when I could recognise them, I could be counted on not to see meaning in and not to deliver.

There was the scrape of a chair as Shirt left the room—the world was moving on—and I decided to follow, handing the bow to Mum on my way out. Later my parents had the cello shipped home, and here it is now. I pluck at it. At least I can say now that I never had the anti-climax of living my dream and being disappointed by it. Had I studied music with real intent—had that even been viable—would I have made it my life? To say that abandoning my dreams was out of character would be to assume that I was then, a girl of eighteen, the careful, supposedly obedient woman I am now.

It can't be 5 a.m. but Dad is sitting on the bed. On a tray is a teapot and two cups.

—You for or against tea, Evie? he says, using my name for the first time since Quai 53.

Tea must be a sign that we have weathered the storm.

—For, I think.

He looks at me and smiles. I don't expect him to appear decorative, but the damning evidence has added up—the sadness of those straining pyjama buttons and, on top of the cigar stench, the persistent strains of yesterday's gin. The worried look on his face as he deals with his trembling hand suggest problems of his own but Dad, I can tell, is trying very hard to keep his end of the conversation upbeat. I have not been there to witness the vitality leaving my father's body, though it is not hard to imagine—he is leaden-eyed and wheezing.

—We didn't know where you were. Thank God for your American friend.

—He's a good friend.

—Have you thought about what you might like to do?

—That depends on what I used to do.

—What do you mean? Dad says.

The voice is his but I barely recognise it.

—I might need a few prompts, I say.

Dad summarises—I was a fair and pliable student, my teenage years a relay of pseudo-survival and incompleteness, my career a dead-end narrative of small humiliations. Fired without hesitation from Superquinn, Tesco, Dunnes Stores, and, completing the grand-slam, Marks and Spencer.

—There any supermarkets left?

—Don't worry, he says. I'll buy one if I have to.

Dad is drinking from my cup now, as casually as someone who has just bumped into an old acquaintance in an unusual location—the context emphasising the fact that times change but people don't.

He asks, —Was life so bad that you had to start making things up?

The tea is cold in the cup, just how I like it. But I'm not sure I want anything he has made for me. He stretches out his hand but I don't take it.

—What was I making up?

I calm myself with some more shallow breaths. At the merest glimpse of Dad's face I glance downwards. He is already acting as if whatever was the matter between us has been resolved. And then it occurs to me, something I have not expected and cannot deal with—Dad reminds me of Jerome. In his way of being awkward in his own house, in his discomfort with other people's anxieties as much his own, in his—I don't want to think of it.

Jerome hit me only once but this will be all I remember. Dad has never raised a finger to me, and never would, but I think of him after the audition in Paris and his insistence that we go somewhere expensive for lunch and the way my morning was already attaining the status of anecdote. We sat on the terrace of Les Deux Magots, as I recall, and I watched them horse into the rosé and—because this was Paris—pretend that nothing bad had happened. Although it wouldn't be on my behalf, we had to celebrate something. It turned into quite the session—I watched a waiter approaching our table with an ice bucket share a look with one of his colleagues. No one ever ordered more than one drink at Les Deux Magots.

—Just tell me you're okay, Dad says. You'll stay this time.

Now I can name the thought I have had a dozen times— instead of making my way to Ireland and instead of subjecting myself to this, I should have stayed on the island. I should have stayed with Ségo. But I tell Dad I'll stay. I say I'll be glad of the break from Paris when, of course, there is actually little to be taking a break from. If I am taking a break from anything, it is the feeling that I will always be my parents' biggest worry and their only failure—parents rarely get the children they want.

—Your mother has breakfast planned, he says. I have to go into Vincent's to see the consultant. Just a formality, don't worry. He won't need to see me again after today. You and Mum can eat together when she gets up. I'll be back around lunch.

I manage to sleep but I am woken by the shock of another balloon inflating inside my skull. It is times like this when I wish I could disappear, fall back into whatever black hole from which I have sprung. I picture a cool, black pillow smothering my face. I try to move, to roll away—my muscles are bawling at me to—and, after another hour or more of trying to move, I wet myself on the new sheets, the steam rising from me as though I am a hot dinner. Soon I am cold, thrashing around in imitation of someone who has been electrocuted. But even within its fullest grip—a burning comet is on a tour of my brain—the headache cheers me, or insulates me, somehow. Then my eyes shut of their own accord and I become inert, counting myself lucky to have survived the worst of it. As long as that has been the worst of it, I can never be sure.

I am about to go back to sleep when there is a knock on the door. Mum has a basin of bone-coloured paint and a roller. She has all sorts of ideas for my bedroom and she decides there is time to paint one of the walls before breakfast. It's not something to which I've given much thought but she seems to want to get on with things and we agree that it's good to get as much done as we can.

Mum is a quick worker. She can climb and then descend a ladder in the time it takes me to dip a roller into a basin of paint and give the wall a good staring at. I can hear her even breathing—she is still fit at whatever age she is and her arms are even thinner than mine. We work in continuing silence until she decides it is time.

—I'd say we're all caught up on things by now, she says. I presume we're going to put all this behind us.

Another me would stand up for herself. Instead, I say, —I think so.

Mum is already standing back with her arms folded, the roller aloft so that it resembles a microphone.

—What do you think? she says. Is that a wall or is that a wall?

—Definitely a wall.

—Not sure you'll be able to sleep in here straightaway. The fumes will do for you. We'll make up one of the other rooms for tonight.

We take a moment to inspect the wall and immediately I see that on her side there are several spots where my brushstrokes failed to overlap, mistakes Mum is already rectifying. I move closer—as if I can finish the wall by looking at it—as she assuredly dabs at the gaps with her brush. We are allowing another few minutes to pass before admitting that decorating my room so soon has been a mistake.

There are three oranges in the fridge's fruit drawer but Mum says that's not enough to juice for all of us. As I wait for her to return from the shops, I get dressed in a pair of my old jeans. I feel nothing but strange in my old clothes—they are massive and could be anyone's—but obsessing over everything that has changed will mean I will never make it out of here.

Feeling my way quietly, I creep down the staircase that leads to the dining room and then to the kitchen and the narrow pantry where, surrounded by egg boxes arranged in impressive terraces, I decide to get started on breakfast.

I don't live here—and I'm certainly not a guest—so the only thing I can do is behave like an employee. There are no dishes to wash—but later I will implement my system, even though it will be impossible to go about things the way I do at Gravy. I will have to be careful with the plates.

I turn an egg over in my hand, top to bottom, top to bottom, like a life. Should I stay here—should that be viable—I will be facing more unhappiness, a great store of it. Not that I would seek out unhappiness, not now, I merely understand its value. It soothes me to see it in this way. And it's not that I wonder either—because not knowing is different from forgetting. I can make my own truth. I crack the egg in one decisive movement— Peter Piper picked a peck of pickled peppers—and I think what a foolish thing to do, to give Dad false hope. Isn't that normal? People do this kind of thing all the time. He must know in his heart that I am long gone. If he doesn't he will soon enough. I whisk the egg gently before adding another. Two is plenty. I finger around in the bowl, attempting to round up the bits of shell.

On the plane I order a little bottle of red and I pose with it. I can drink as long as I don't lose the run of myself—but I don't see that happening now. It doesn't have to begin today but I want to be an expert in something for a living. Daniel did say at the time that I had a real nose for wine.

The woman in the seat next to me cheers me as I take my first sip.

—Hate them, she says.

There is no point in asking what she hates.

—Me too, I say.

—I don't know why I have to drink out of plastic. I can taste it in the wine. Not that it's good wine, I'm not a complete fool, I don't go around expecting good stuff on planes, but it still makes a difference. How do you find it?

—It's very expressive, I say. One of Daniel's words.

—That's not how I'd describe it.

The woman says she works in analytics.

—Me too, I say.

I don't respond when she asks me where I work and for whom. À l'attention de Ségolène Carena. La Plongeuse Irlandaise.

From the window the world is white and soft. I smile at Analytics and sip my unexpressive wine in its wrong cup. Then I press the button in the ceiling and I ask for a gin and tonic instead, as Dad would.

Ya rouhi means you are my soul.

I can remember the first time I fell in love with something so beautiful that I prayed for it to be gone. The first time I fell in love, among a scatter of loose onions—well, I wasn't able to make it out. I used to sleep in the vegetable store at Gravy. It was a sickbed among the pumpkins and onion skins and I awoke one morning—or afternoon or night—to find someone tucking me in and stroking my hair. She then began her work, the cleaning and sorting and picking that would later become my work. Ségo was a busy woman but caring and showing it—without saying anything or having to—was her main occupation. The serious business of her mushroomy breath alive on my skin, even her being anywhere near me, became the kind of feeling you attempt to ignore but actually live for. I know from Daniel that some people fall in love as easily as stepping into a pair of clogs. Now I am one of them—love has grown in me somehow and is alive in me now. I am love-swept, love-bucketed, love-sucked, love-sickened, love-saddened, love-maddened, love-damaged, love-blackened, love-beaten, love-resistant.

I have walked all the way from the bus stop in Ars-en-Ré and now I am alone in the kitchen in the dark. There are dinner plates in the sink. Daniel and Ségo must have gone to the beach for a moonlight swim. I want something to eat, too—although they can't have been to the market in the last couple of days and there isn't much to work with. Some more of Daniel's oysters—that's what I feel like now.

There are some peaches, which I can grill and I'll eat them with tomatoes—there's been a glut because of the August heat. The knives are so blunt and I try my best to slice the peaches but they are over-ripe and one after another they turn to juice in my hands. Perhaps I won't grill them.

I know what I'll do—I'll go and see where everyone is.

At first, she doesn't notice me standing on the beach.

Then, —At last, she says.

She is floating and staring upwards, where the moon is at full volume—she sees me and lures me towards her with a warning about dangerous insects in the sand. I undress slowly. I have the shivers because I have not been into the sea yet, not even in the daytime—there was never the right moment. She offers to take my hand as inch by inch I creep into the gently fizzing water. Perhaps I sound exasperated but the opposite is the case. It is so hallucinatory that I do not expect to get wet.

—Count to ten, she says.

How I make it into the water I don't know but soon I am up to my waist in black sea and my throat is in shock and contracting at the very moment I need to breathe. I am too scared to attempt it of my own accord and I feel myself float just as I catch Ségo's smile. I feel the sky tilt and I become aware that I can move around in the water. It is no more intimidating than slipping from a stool.

A stinging wind takes over. It's impossible to escape, even in the water—but it isn't the sudden drop in temperature nor is it the goosebumps on my sunburned shoulders. It's something else, the knowledge I am being spared so much by being here with her. As my feet waggle for the mossy stones on the seabed I understand how a dead soul must feel when it leaves the body—a file being erased after so long in storage.

Ségo swims over to see that I'm okay, before inspecting the skin on my shoulder.

—You've blistered since the other day.

I dunk my face in the water and, getting a harsh mouthful, regret it immediately. Saltwater is spluttering out of my nose.

—Should I go back inside?

—I'll keep an eye on you, she says. There's going to be a storm. I'd hate you to miss that.

—Where's Daniel? I say.

—Went back to Paris, she says. He'll be there when we get back.

Sure enough, there is more friction in the air—it has been another hot day—and it starts to thunder and then it pours rain. I am snug where I am, watching the drops needle the water. My moonlit toes are so far away, the rest is private and beautiful. Of course, I worry that it is impossible to float with your eyes closed, just as it is impossible to imagine forgetting—but floating is just something you do. A little piece of mind, everyone deserves that much.

Acknowledgements

I am grateful for the existence of the following journals: *The Stinging Fly*; *The Moth*; *The South Circular*; *The Bohemyth*; *Banshee*; *Long Story*, *Short*; and *Winter Papers*. Much respect to the editors. Running literary journals, and reading them; it's what we all should be doing. Finally, I'm very grateful to these two allies: Dan Bolger of New Island; and Marianne Gunn O'Connor.